# The Strange Case
of the Dutch Painter

# The Strange Case
# of the Dutch Painter

Timothy Miller

SEVENTH
STREET
BOOKS®

Inquiries should be addressed to
Start Science Fiction
221 River Street
9th Floor
Jersey City, New Jersey 07030
PHONE: 212-431-5454
WWW.SEVENTHSTREETBOOKS.COM

10 9 8 7 6 5 4 3 2 1

978-1-64506-042-0 (paperback)
978-1-64506-043-7 (Ebook)

*For my sisters, Beverly and Nancy,*
*with love.*

# Prologue
## John H. Watson, M.D.

S herlock Holmes is dead. That news is news to no one by now, of course. The headlines have shouted it in every paper from San Francisco to Shanghai. It was blared endlessly on the wireless. Messenger boys went to sea for sailors rather than shoulder those bags of telegrams heavier than the burden of Atlas. The Esquimaux on his ice floe and the Bushman on the veldt heard the news within twenty-four hours of his passing, and mourned him each according to their peculiar rites. If I repeat it now, it is not because the world needs my confirmation. It's only because I have yet to convince myself of this: Sherlock Holmes is dead.

I confess I was surprised by the public outpouring of grief. Thousands attended his memorial, marred though it was by his spiritualist associates, who did their utmost to turn the ceremony into some kind of mass séance. My friend's career as a consulting detective had effectively ended with his retirement, over a quarter century ago. In latter years his name rarely made the papers, even here in London. A generation had come of age in ignorance of Sherlock Holmes. Or so I had thought.

Although I was grateful to see him lionized in the press, I was dismayed at the many inaccuracies (in some instances outright fictions) attached to my friend's reputation by the ignorance or indolence of the sensational press. No, *Westminster Gazette*, he was not connected to the royal family by blood. He never wed once, much less twice, much less in secret to the Divine Sarah; nor was he among Lillie Langtry's paramours. He did not serve on the front lines in the Great War, *Daily Mail*; General Von Stettin was alluding to an entirely different and more personal conflict. Some of the more responsible journalists camped out upon my doorstep, and I did my best to educate them. Yet there was one question they posed over and over, and for that I could supply no satisfactory answer: who was Sherlock Holmes?

Oh, I enumerated his habits, repeated his aphorisms, clothed him in his past glories. It was meat and drink enough for the gentlemen of the press. Barring his late brother, Mycroft, a man who kept his secrets closer than the Sphinx, no man knew Sherlock Holmes better than I. Even the rift that opened between us in his final years, brought on by his perverse fascination with spiritualism, was not enough to sunder our bond. I have painted his portrait in scores of accounts. But none of them ever scratched the surface: the inner man was a locked-room mystery. I was forced to admit to myself that I, who knew him better than any man living, barely knew him at all.

But Sherlock Holmes, reaching from beyond the grave, has granted me one last opportunity to peel away the mask. He has made me his heir. Not to the villa in Sussex, of course, nor to his bank account at Lloyds. Those assets, which hold no interest for me, have fluttered away to some distant relation in France whose name escapes me. What he has left me is the bulk of his private papers, a treasure trove of buckram-bound volumes and despatch boxes that makes the halls of Croesus look like a shepherd's cot. Since the day they arrived on my doorstep I've been working my way through them, ferreting out case files that might be shared with his public, but also hoping to unearth nuggets of a more confidential nature that might discover the inner man to me.

Accompanying his papers Holmes left an odd assortment of

miscellany, perhaps more properly called exhibits, that seem to be related to his cases. They range from the mundane—a set of brass waistcoat buttons, a spool of silk thread—to the deadly—knives, guns, cudgels, and a few crusted vials which I suspect may contain deadly poisons. Among the most unusual is a painting of a young woman playing the piano. It appears to be the work of an amateur, an amateur who harbors a grudge against paint and canvas. Even for a man with Sherlock Holmes's abominable taste in art, it is appalling. The signature scrawled across the bottom of the canvas is a single name:

"Vincent."

A few of my readers, versed in the kaleidoscopic fashions of the art world, may already have a nodding acquaintance with the name of the Dutch painter, Vincent van Gogh, who died some forty years ago in France. For those less conversant with that milieu, recent months have thrust his name into the headlines due to the so-called Wacker Affair: the Wackers being a pair of brothers, Berlin art dealers, who are charged with having created and sold a number of forged Van Gogh canvases (some thirty or so, I believe it was). The Wackers' defense seems to lie with the proposition that the works in question were acquired in good faith and sold in good faith. If there was deception, they claim, it was engineered by other hands somewhere further back along a rather nebulous chain of custody. Good luck to them. The art of connoisseurship has developed over the last century into something approaching a science, with nearly infallible methods of separating the wheat from the chaff.

Not that I pretend to any authority on the subject myself. Though I can bring the discernment of an enthusiast to an after-dinner discussion of Reynolds or Gainsborough, I confess myself largely ignorant of the school of French "Impressionists" and their ilk. My own tastes are more conservative; some have said more pedestrian.

I hardly gave the painting a thought when it first came to me. Holmes's taste in art had always bewildered me, and the portrait of the girl at the piano, crudely rendered against a background of bilious green wallpaper, only further fueled my suspicion that he believed painting to be some kind of joke. I was at that time entirely ignorant of any connection between my friend and the Van Gogh family.

However, there was a story that went with the painting, or a manuscript at least, which whetted my interest at first glance. You may imagine my disappointment when I discovered it to be written in German. Regrettably, my knowledge of that language reaches little further than the word *rache*. I set the manuscript aside to explore greener pastures.

Suffice it to say then, when the Wacker scandal first began to be bruited about, I was shocked to find out that the works of this once-obscure painter have increased in value from—well, you couldn't have given away his paintings while he was still living—to some very considerable sums. In fact, after sitting down with pencil and paper and working the figures, it became apparent to me that in today's cockeyed market, my Van Gogh might be worth as much as £12,000! Of course the painting held some sentimental value for me, but I have never been a man of means, and a sum of money like that simply couldn't be ignored. Yet there was still a story behind the painting, and I could not think of parting with it before I had done all within my power to learn what it was. I contacted my old friend Martha Pearce, whose fluency in German had proved so beneficial to us in the run-up to the war, and whose discretion is absolute. She was more than happy to oblige. I sent her the manuscript, and in less than a month a translation was in my hands.

I poured myself a brandy and soda and settled down in my best chair to read. I read straight through, finishing at about three in the morning, poured another brandy and soda, and sat down to read it again.

As a contribution to the annals of Sherlock Holmes, the Lermolieff manuscript is an oddity. The name Sherlock Holmes is never even mentioned in the manuscript, although our old friend Inspector Lestrade does come in for a mention. My own name crops up four or five times, although I was nowhere on the scene when these events transpired, blissfully unaware that Holmes had left his digs in Baker Street, much less crossed the Channel to France.

It is the only one of Holmes's cases in which he relies on the aid of another consulting detective—for whatever Lermolieff calls himself, he is a detective in his own right, using methods independently arrived at, but eerily similar to those of Sherlock Holmes. Without his rather unorthodox methods of producing evidence, Holmes would never have brought the case to a satisfactory close.

But what readers will want to know, since I have raised the question, is whether the Lermolieff manuscript reveals anything substantial about the private Holmes? I believe it does, if only in a roundabout manner. I have spent too long looking for Holmes among the rolling meads of Sussex, perhaps, ignoring his French antecedents. I have accused Holmes elsewhere of being a calculating machine, an automaton without a heart. I wonder now if that calculation was in fact the purest expression of love that ever man witnessed.

The narrative that follows, then, is substantially the work of Dr. Ivan Lermolieff, as he styles himself, from his contemporaneous notes, with emendations by myself. In my efforts to fill in certain lacunae left by Lermolieff's account, and make it more palatable to the popular reader, I might justifiably be accused of taking literary liberty with a few of the facts, at times even positing a person's innermost thoughts. Since, according to Holmes, half of what I write is fiction, anyway, I believe I have nowhere violated the trust of my fallen friend.

In that spirit, we begin our book, in a dark wood wandering.

# Chapter One

It was the third gallery Monsieur Vernet had dragged me to that sweltering morning. In his zeal, he had apparently forgot all about our promised luncheon beneath the cool awnings at Café Anglais, where I had hoped to sample the sole Dieppoise. I had a heel of cheese and half a paper sack of walnuts secreted in the bottom of my Gladstone, but it would hardly do to rummage about for them in the detective's company. Please don't think me a slave to appetite, unless it be an appetite for fine art, but it wasn't fine art we were likely to see. As had been our fate at the other galleries, we would be steered by some enthusiastic underling away from works by any respectable artists and into some dimly lit back room, where our eyes would be subjected to the latest embarrassments by the so-called Impressionists, or Intransigents, whatever they were calling themselves in the Year of Our Lord 1890. Paul Durand-Ruel, the chief of the Impressionist dealers, had actually been on the floor at his gallery, and treated us, ex cathedra, to a mind-numbing catalogue of his acquisitions, as if they were his ugly-but-beloved children. There were no other clientele at hand to rescue us from his depredations. At Georges Petit they left us to wander about like orphaned waifs; they sold Impressionists, but seemed loathe to admit the fact. Worst of all was the little paint shop owned by an old communard named Tanguy, where painters who couldn't even rate an exhibition with the Impressionists were hung proudly in the front window. The old man went mad with fury and tossed us out the door as soon as Vernet admitted he indeed had relatives among the distinguished family of painters that included Claude and Horace Vernet, who according to Tanguy were somehow complicit in revanchist conspiracies to bring back the Bourbons (if only it were true!). Tanguy's emporium actually boasted a dwarf in pince-nez, enthroned on the front counter, tossing back rotgut champagne and making ribald cracks at the clientele, like a jester at the old Hapsburg court.

Boussod et Valadon has a sterling reputation all over Europe. Its showroom in the Rue Montmartre certainly boasts the requisite deep carpets, velvet drapes, and soothing hushed atmosphere which declare a haven for serious art. I was hoping against hope that I might be treated to something new by Meissonier or even Gerome. But as soon as Vernet started dropping hints about "newer, lesser-known painters," Monsieur Boussod handed us off to a pink-faced assistant smelling of shaving soap, who led us upstairs to the mezzanine, where the Impressionists were penned.

It was a shadowless world, bereft of line or volume. Lurid pigments warred for attention with one another, leaving the viewer to guess at the paintings' subjects—which often enough were train stations or iron bridges or faded harlots, hardly lyric or heroic subjects. Rather than mixing their pigments on the palette, the Impressionists seem to like to mix them on the canvas, with predictable results. They paint in nervous, flat little strokes that bristle at the viewer like an alley cat among the dustbins. I could feel a familiar dull ache forming between my eyebrows.

There was really no good reason for me to be there at all, as I had complained to Vernet more than once. He was going to recite his inscrutable litany of questions, always circling round the same handful of Impressionists, whose names were beginning to stick in my head:

Monet, Renoir, Degas, Pissarro, Morisot, Cezanne. Each of them claimed space on Boussod's mezzanine walls. *Were they studio trained, or self-taught? Had they reputation enough to support themselves with their art, or did they rely on one or two generous patrons? Were they known among the American nouveau riche?* Then he would lard in a few Old Master names, like Fragonard, Watteau, and Poussin. His acquaintance with these painters was embarrassingly rudimentary, his ideas of their merits preposterous, but at least I understood the reason he hammered at those particular nails. He might have deferred to my expertise, but he seemed determined to prove himself a boor in front of every dealer we met. So I set my jaw and played the role of silent partner. He assured me repeatedly that I was indispensable to his method. What method? It almost seemed as if he didn't *want* to be taken seriously. Had I not been using an assumed name, my reputation would have been forfeit.

The dealer who had been foisted upon us spoke with a Dutch accent. He was in fact on the list of suspect dealers we had been given. Theo van Gogh was his name, I recalled. He was a slender reed of a thing, with a trembling lip beneath his clipped Calvinist moustache, and perhaps more passion for his subject than one would hope to see from such a straitlaced fellow. Vernet had him off balance, spraying questions at him, some of which seemed intended to test the depth and breadth of his knowledge, others insinuatingly personal, even asking his salary. The Dutchman bore up patient as a mule under all the rib-kicking, though his dignity must have been affronted several times over. He was a skilled enough diplomatist that I couldn't say for certain he felt anything but bored.

"What's that, a haystack?" Vernet pointed to a new mediocrity he had just discovered, in improbable shades of purple and blue. "Do people buy pictures of haystacks? Is that the latest mode?"

"This painter does a great deal of *en plein air* work. He's not so much concerned with the subject as with the play of air and light and color that possess it for a moment. You might say he's concerned with the conspiracy of eye and nature."

"But it *is* a haystack."

"Monsieur, it's only one painting," the dealer answered. "Monsieur Monet is not obsessed with haystacks, I assure you."

The Dutchman was perhaps being disingenuous; we had seen three Monet haystacks already that day. An idée fixe, apparently.

"I was led to believe these Impressionists handle a lot of—how should I put it—risqué subjects?" said Vernet, with a ferocious leer.

"Perhaps I could show you something by Degas?"

"And that's a fellow the Americans like?" The Americans seemed to combine obscene wealth with willful ignorance, which made them prospective marks ripe for fleecing by opportunistic Parisian dealers.

The Dutchman nodded wearily. "Monsieur Degas has made some inroads among American collectors. They tend to be a bit more adventurous in their—"

Boussod had appeared at the top of the stair and was trying to signal Van Gogh. Indeed, he had been there some time, but now his gestures were a trifle too histrionic to be ignored. He might have been directing traffic on the Champs-Élysées. Van Gogh raised a hand, both to acknowledge him and hold him off. "Please, messieurs, do look around, see what strikes your fancy . . ." He was backing away as he spoke. We could hear Boussod whispering urgently.

I could imagine their conversation. They'd wasted enough time on these two odd ducks, the proprietor judged. Neither myself nor the detective had the appearance of men of wealth. I was dressed in a charcoal morning suit of good Florentine wool, but certainly not in the latest Parisian style. As for the detective, he was got up as a comic-opera bohemian in a voluminous black frock coat, with a bright red scarf wound about his throat in defiance of the July furnace. I will admit he cut an imposing figure, tall and rapier thin, with the profile of a hawk and a silky reddish beard just coming in, that lent him rather the rapacious air of a Viking. Boussod had sized us up thoroughly and decided we were gawkers, not buyers. There was no profit in indulging our curiosity any further.

But his admonitions only managed to put the young man's back up. Van Gogh nodded toward us, gesticulating fiercely, his whispers become a growl. I doubt he was foolish enough to defend the proposition that we had deep purses. More probably he was arguing his prerogative to pursue matters according to his own instinct, whatever the upshot. He had more spine than I'd guessed.

In any case, he would never have the opportunity to part us from our putative fortunes, thanks to the arrival of a new character in our drama: a gangling youth in his early twenties who came windmilling up the stair at just that moment. He had hair of tousled straw and the vague promise of a moustache dotting his lip. He stood mopping the sweat from his forehead with a soiled handkerchief. His trousers looked as if he had walked a hundred dusty leagues in them. He was either too winded or too distressed to speak, but it was obvious that he had something vital to communicate to Van Gogh. He beckoned shakily toward him.

Van Gogh advanced on him and took him by the shoulders. "Hirschig? Tommy Hirschig?"

Those were the last words I understood clearly. This Hirschig was clearly a Dutchman as well, for both men dropped into that language. Dutch is not such a distant cousin of German that I was unable to follow the general tenor of their conversation; indeed, I could have guessed it even if they had been speaking in the dialect of Bora Bora, for the news flamed in their faces. Some sort of catastrophe had occurred, involving someone named Vincent.

The boy started slapping his pockets, looking for something he'd misplaced. Van Gogh, caught up in the urgency, hurled questions at him, which only rendered the boy more tongue-tied. Hirschig was finally able to produce a paper from his pocket, which Van Gogh tore from his grasp. He stepped away a few paces, scanning the pages while the boy tried to read over his shoulder, balancing on tiptoe.

Van Gogh folded the letter into precise quarters and put it in his pocket. His face seemed to pulse. He whispered something to Boussod.

"Urgent matter—again?" Boussod had no intention whatever of

whispering. He seemed to know all about this Vincent and wanted his opinion of the man published in block letters six feet high. But his thunder was wasted on Van Gogh, who was already halfway down the stair and a hundred leagues away. It seemed to me it must be an urgent errand indeed that made such a punctilious fellow take flight without even a word of apology to his prospective clients.

Abandoned by his lieutenant, Boussod was all contrition. For the moment he had forgotten that we were two undesirables. We were now rajahs whose magnificence had been wronged, and obeisance must be made. "Messieurs, if you'll come with me, I have some truly exceptional new works to show you," he simpered.

But with Van Gogh's flight, Vernet had dropped any veneer of aesthetic curiosity. He jabbed me between the shoulder blades, and then sprang down the stairs like a greyhound, out the door and into the street. I did my best to keep up with him, but once a man reaches forty his sprinting days are past. We left young Hirschig ogling Degas's chorus girls under the censorious eye of Boussod.

Theo van Gogh was just disappearing into a fiacre as we burst out the door behind him. It trotted away into the midmorning traffic on the boulevard. "Our bird has flown, Lermolieff!" cried Vernet.

"You think the boy gave him a warning somehow? What now, Vernet?"

I should note that Vernet was the name the detective insisted on being called, although as I understood it, Vernet was properly the name of his mother's family only. He insisted too on calling me Lermolieff, though that is most certainly not my name, nor is Russia my fatherland. He knew my name well enough—he had first become acquainted with Dr. Morelli through my wife's English translation of Morelli's works. He had become engrossed with Morelli's powers of observation, his revolutionary approach to seemingly insignificant detail. His own methods of detection dovetailed, Morelli had said.

Yet he insisted these clownish disguises were necessary to our success. He was a man, I would learn, to whom masks are second nature. Every drawing room, every street corner was to him a stage, and he was always playing to the gallery. Not a habit likely to inspire trust among his associates, you would think.

He commandeered a hansom cab while I was straining to follow our quarry down the boulevard with my eyes, but the fiacre had already blended into the anonymous morning traffic, one mackerel in a mighty school. I felt Vernet's arm hook my shoulder like a shepherd's crook, herding me into the cab.

"We've lost him!" I cried.

Vernet did not answer, but climbed into the seat beside me. "Gare du Nord! As swift as you may!" he called up to the driver.

His urgency must have infected driver and horse together; the nag's hooves struck sparks upon the paving stones. We might make good time, but to what end?

"Rest easy, Dr. Lermolieff," Vernet assured me as we were rocked from side to side. "Our target is still within our grasp."

"There are six railway stations in this city," I pointed out. "If he's trying to flee, could he not choose any one of them?"

"The Dutch are solid and predictable, my friend. Even their criminal class is unremarkable. If he's bolted, he'll head for the tulip fields of home. Gare du Nord is indicated."

His coolness was infuriating. "And if he's not the typical Dutchman? If his mind is deranged by panic? If he's a criminal mastermind who till now has eluded even the hint of official suspicion?"

"Oh, la! If he only seeks escape, Gare du Nord is still the closest railroad terminus. That shall be our north star."

His reasoning sounded specious, but Dr. Morelli had made me aware of his reputation in matters criminal, and I had no better-informed alternative to suggest. The churning of my stomach and the lurching of the cab left me too enervated to spar with him.

We were headed north on the Rue Montmartre. Vernet drew a watch from his waistcoat pocket and checked the time. "I don't suppose you know when the next train departs for Antwerp?" he said. My bewildered stare was all the answer I deemed necessary. Who would know such a thing off the top of his head? Was I a conductor of the line?

He only shrugged, as if he were willing to overlook my shortcomings. The Englishman's self-regard seemed impenetrable. For he *was* English, English as the lions of Trafalgar Square, no matter what nom de guerre he adopted. I knew the type well, having myself resided in London for several years.

But hadn't I witnessed the same level of self-assuredness in Dr. Morelli? And defended it against his detractors as a measure of strength? One can afford to be cocksure, I suppose, if one is always right; this detective had the name of being rarely wrong. It didn't make him any easier to tolerate, but that was incidental to the job at hand. Dr. Morelli had spoken often of his friendship with the Englishman, based on years of correspondence, without ever once meeting face-to-face. It was that friendship, I reckoned, that had led the detective to seek the doctor's assistance in this case. It was the doctor's arrogance that had allowed him to shift the burden cheerfully to my shoulders. And it was due to my own measure of pride, I suppose, that I believed I could substitute ably for Morelli.

But this haring about in cabs was well beyond the bounds of anything I had agreed to. There was a question of the authenticity of some paintings in the Louvre, Morelli had explained. It was a delicate matter, requiring a peculiar kind of expertise and a great deal of discretion. All well and good. I had come to Paris and met Vernet, who had detailed the nature of the problem. He struck me as eccentric, but then my work is full of cranks and cockeyed dreamers. He introduced me to a member of the consortium, Monsieur Eugene Dupuis, a very great honor, apparently, leading industrialist, financier, et cetera, all in the golden flower of youth. It was Dupuis who had thrown together the list of suspect dealers, which had so far proved of negligible worth. He had at least proved useful in introducing me to some of the city's most distinguished collectors—and more to the point, their most distinguished collections, which were essential touchstones for my comparisons. French painters are not my forte. I vastly prefer the Italians, as who does not?

I had met also Mademoiselle Valadon, a lovely young woman

with a gamin face and a shingled mane. She was, I assumed, Dupuis's mistress. (Frenchmen of a certain station must keep a mistress as they keep a coach and four.) Why he had felt it necessary to drag her along on our museum excursions I couldn't fathom, and then the way she had behaved! After all, who was supposed to be the connoisseur, the world's premiere authority on Leonardo da Vinci, or Suzanne Valadon, demimondaine?

Vernet's leads had proved rather more fruitful: after three weeks of close study, adhering to Dr. Morelli's methods, I was able to declare with confidence that nine—yes, *nine*—masterpieces by painters of the last century hanging in the Louvre and the Luxembourg were in fact fakes: a Fragonard, a Watteau, an Ingres, a Poussin, a Delacroix, a David, a Boucher, a Gerome, and a Cabanel, a roll call of giants. There were three more paintings I was less certain of, but I believed further study would prove them false as well. Of course, there might have been hundreds more fakes by other painters, but I was not in Paris to clean the Augean stables. Nine fakes of such stature were scandal enough to ruin the French art world and undermine faith in the Louvre itself; yet there we were discussing state secrets in the Salle des Sept Cheminées in front of the Valadon woman as if she were Joan of Arc.

I remember we were standing before David's *Belisarius Begging for Alms*, which depicts the great general, last of the Romans, old and blind, reduced to begging in the street.

"Do you see the fault in this painting?" I asked. I admit that I intended to bring Dupuis and his woman down a peg.

"The centurion's knees!" Dupuis cried out. "Obviously not neo-classical knees. Must be rococo, eh? Forgery."

He was mocking me, but I held my temper. "A fruitful area for study. Anatomical comparison is our first tool, but not our only resort. Look at the hills in the background. What color are they?"

"Blue," said Dupuis.

"Be more precise, please. The pigment?"

"Cobalt blue," piped up the girl. I'll give her credit for that one, though it was probably no more than a lucky guess.

"Yes, quite right," I said. "Except that this painting was made in 1781. A quarter of a century before the cobalt blue pigment became available to painters."

"Bravo, Doctor," said Vernet quietly.

"What about all these little cracks on the surface of the painting?" the girl asked, grazing the David with her fingertips, which made me wince. "Surely that means the painting must be old?"

"The skilled forger has methods at hand to induce craquelure in a new painting. There are a dozen ways. The simplest is to lay on the size thickly, then dry it rapidly before a fire. Indeed, some forgers specialize in aging paintings, just as others forge nothing but signatures." I had hoped that little lesson would be enough to silence her. But a woman, once she knows anything, thinks she knows everything. She went on prattling about varnish and glazes and dust, things far beyond her ken. I did my best to ignore her, though I couldn't entirely mask my irritation.

She dredged up another objection. "But what about all these girls? Are they forgers?"

Her gesture took in the copyists ranged up and down the gallery at their easels, some on stands, even a few on ladders. The majority of them were indeed young women, eyes locked on the paintings in front of them, brushes hovering over half-finished canvases, dabbing paint away from their shining cheeks with the sleeves of their smocks. Half of them were there not to capture the images of the Old Masters, but to catch the eyes of the young boulevardiers who stalked the museum's salons. Most of them, I pointed out, would never make a copy that could be mistaken for an original.

She refused to be instructed. "But some will, surely? Some of them have the talent, or at least the proficiency, to make a copy that could pass for the original."

"We can admire a fine copy as a piece of craftsmanship," I answered carefully, "and the copyist is guilty of nothing. But if your proficient demoiselle brings her copy to a Dirtier, to a Signer, a Sealer, a Genealogist, any of the specialists, if she enlists their talents, she has joined the ranks of forgers and thieves."

"Ah, but that kind of theft is no crime in France," said Dupuis vacuously.

"It should be."

The dilettante and the self-anointed expert are common hazards of my profession. They were galling, but I could ignore them. The true foe of the connoisseur is the collector. No collector wants to learn that the prize he paid thousands for is a fake. Few collectors want to hear that the prize they so desperately yearn to acquire is a fake. And there is always another connoisseur perfectly willing to tell them whatever they want to hear, as long as they collect a commission. Integrity is never as profitable as fraud.

Once I had identified the forgeries, I understood my work to be finished. Instead, Vernet cajoled me into visiting the galleries with him. I sent a wire to Dr. Morelli remonstrating. He replied with a letter urging me to cooperate with the detective in every respect. I acquiesced– perhaps not as gracefully as I might have. We toured the galleries, though I couldn't puzzle out just what he was seeking in these places, and he offered no explanations. None of them were known for their Old Masters. None of the artists they patronized had the requisite skill to forge one. Durand-Ruel was chief of the Impressionist dealers, and seemed to have little truck with legitimate artists. If gallery owners were assumed to be involved, Georges Petit would have been my first choice: at least he had a nodding acquaintance with the Old Masters.

None of it made sense. Forgers of such talent must already be known to the police. Receivers of such daring work must be known. Those were the sort of men we should have been questioning. In the meantime, the paintings themselves would be further away each day, finding their way into the vaults of unscrupulous collectors from whence they might never be recovered! Why we were chasing this cherub-faced Dutchman through the streets of Paris at breakneck speed, I had no idea. You could have dug up Père Lachaise plot by plot and not found a body more harmless. Of course, one must then ask— why was the man running? Could he be—?

"Pay the fellow, won't you, Ivan Ivanovich?"

I emerged blinking from my reverie to find that we were already being deposited at the rail station, with its great glass front soaring away above our mere mortal insignificance, like a modern-day cathedral, with its twenty-three female statues representing cities rather than saints. Vernet alit on the pavement before we were even halted, and tore off through the crowd without so much as a backward glance. I fumbled in my pockets, trying to sort out the proper French coins. Once I had overpaid the driver and was able to look around, I found all of Paris whirling round me as though I stood at the center of a cyclone. A tide of humanity streamed in and out the doors in unceasing circulation like a heartbeat. As for the detective? Him I had lost utterly.

# Chapter Two

I t was in those few moments, while I was trying to get my bearings, that my adventure truly began. I had not been commissioned to chase rogue art dealers through the streets of Paris. I could turn around, make the journey to the south alone, deliver my report to the consortium, and be quit of the matter with my integrity intact.

Then I caught sight of the red scarf bobbing in the crowd, and felt an alien prompting, a wild exhilaration well up in my heart. I might have been a boy playing at Katz und Maus. I pushed my way through the crowd toward Vernet. He didn't stop for me or even signal me, but once I gained his side, I felt I would remain there until we had seen the mystery through. We collected our tickets and sprinted aboard the train just as it was pulling away from the platform.

As soon as we had boarded, my ardor began to cool again. "So, we have gambled that the Dutchman is on this train. How do we go about finding him?" I grumbled.

"Van Gogh is a man in an inordinate hurry. He will not abandon his haste simply because he has nowhere to go. He will make his way down to the first car behind the tender, and seat himself on the side of the train closest to the platform. He has no luggage. He will deboard as soon as mortally possible, and continue his flight without hesitation. We shall find him in the first compartment in the first car, if it is not already occupied."

It sounded a highly implausible theory. By sheer happenstance, it was correct.

Van Gogh took no notice when we entered his compartment and took seats opposite him. His attention was on the two letters that lay in his lap. He took no notice when the conductor entered to check our tickets, then left. He was utterly unguarded, lost in the labyrinth of his thoughts. Even when he glanced up, his eyes were fixed on the middle distance. Anyone wishing to observe him at close quarters could do so now: the earnest scholar's face, the high intellectual brow, the faraway gaze. There was no mistaking the pallor of anxiety in that face. Was it guilt that so burdened him, or something else? Who was Vincent? Were we witnessing the devil making a rendezvous with his lieutenant? I felt my pulse racing. It was not an unpleasant sensation, I noted.

All the time I had been watching Van Gogh. I should instead have been watching Vernet, for the former's countenance, at first flushed with a kind of righteous triumph, now seemed full of chagrin, tinged with sympathy. He leaned forward to inflict himself upon the young man's reverie.

"Don't despond, monsieur," he said gently. "A doctor may be conversant with his patient's physical strength, and yet have no measure of the fortitude of his will."

The words must have chimed with the Dutchman's own thoughts. Indeed, they must have seemed to emanate from some inner mist, rather than a fellow traveler's lips, for a sympathetic light kindled in his eyes. "So I've found," he replied softly.

"I hope your brother may fully recover from his accident."

Van Gogh's mind snapped back to reality. He found himself staring into the unlikely eyes of the overinquisitive customer from the gallery. A side glance brought me into the picture as well. It must have seemed to him that he was dreaming. He drew himself up and crossed his arms upon his chest. He was fully alert to the moment; he had sifted out the fantastic from the actual—yet still there we were.

"What are you doing here? Have you been following me?" His gaze now was sharp and searching.

"I confess it," Vernet answered with a bright seeming of candor. "But our motives are pure. Wherever one goes in Paris, one hears that Monsieur Van Gogh is a champion of the new painters. As it happens, my associate here, Dr. Lermolieff, is a painter himself, in sore need of such a champion. We came to the gallery to feel you out."

I nodded like a spaniel, falling in line with this fresh lie, hoping I would not be called upon to support it.

"How did you find out about my brother? Do you know Vincent?"

Ah! Vincent was his brother, then! The matter began to unfold.

"Your brother is a perfect stranger to me," Vernet replied.

"Then how did—" Van Gogh looked down at the letters in his lap. He gathered them up and folded them hastily.

Vernet's lip curled into something that mimicked a smile. "I do have the ability to read upside down," he said in quiet rebuke. "But I would not idly peruse a gentleman's correspondence." A statement I very much doubted.

"Then perhaps you can explain your knowledge of my private affairs," Van Gogh demanded, still in high dudgeon.

"Observation and inference merely."

Van Gogh's icy stare required a fuller explanation.

"You're a gentleman of breeding and impeccable manner, as your profession requires. You bore up under my improprieties with grace and good humor. Yet the news you received from Monsieur Hirschig prompted you to depart without so much as a nod of courtesy in our direction. You are embarked upon a mission of some urgency."

Van Gogh shrugged. "Obviously."

"It is obvious once it is explained. Curiosity piqued, we searched you out on the train. We found you reading the letter which is the cause of your agitation. Disturbing news of a personal, rather than a business nature. A Parisian, as the cut of your clothes proclaims you, would hardly have urgent business interests in the little hamlets to the north. A death in the family? Death requires no such haste. A sudden illness or accident is indicated. It cannot be your wife—I see by your ring you are recently wed—a wire would have been sent. Your parents? Old enough that illness has touched them many times before. It would grieve you, but not upset you so. A brother or sister, then. After examining the first letter—written by a doctor, the script is nearly illegible—you take out another one, written by a man. A lady would never use such coarse stationery. Your close scan of the letters side by side leads me to the inference that the second was written by the subject of the first. Your brother, or one as close to you as a brother. Thus my condolences."

One had to admit it was a neat bit of reasoning. Vernet settled back in his seat triumphantly. Van Gogh was not a man to gawp, but I could see he was impressed. Yet it was not Vernet's deductive legerdemain, I think, that won him over; there was something genuinely sympathetic in the detective's nature that perhaps Van Gogh could not help but respond to.

"Your powers of observation are formidable, monsieur—I'm sorry, I've forgotten the name?"

"Vernet." We shook hands all around. "Lermolieff," I said self-consciously.

"Theo van Gogh. Monsieur Vernet, are you by any chance a painter yourself? I've known few with your eye for detail."

"I'm fond of painting, but I've never pursued it myself. My great-uncle was Horace Vernet. Perhaps I have his eye. Art in the blood takes the strangest forms, I've been told."

"Monsieur, you know so much. If you don't mind—"

"I'd be honored to receive any confidence you might place in me."

That was Vernet's real talent, I surmised, to put his interlocutors at ease, so that one minute they were guarded and mute, and the next they were unburdening their hearts to him. It is a talent shared by country priests and the better sort of prostitutes.

Van Gogh took out pipe and tobacco, and Vernet followed suit.

For some men, this ritual is preparatory to the sharing of confidences. I am not one of those. Soon the two were puffing away like steam engines flashing past one another through a gorge. And I was trying to suppress a coughing fit.

"Perhaps you could tell me something about your brother, monsieur?" asked Vernet, ingenuous. This was the very subject Van Gogh wanted to enter into, of course.

"As it happens, he's a painter. A genuine talent, if I may say so, but misunderstood, like so many of the painters I represent. The public always resists a revolutionary at first, then they rush to the barricades once the danger is past. He's always been at the front lines. Many times it has seemed the fight might be more than he could bear, but each time he has martialed his reserves and soldiered on. Two months ago, he came to Auvers-sur-Oise to make a new start. Two days ago, he attempted to take his own life."

Vernet didn't bother with the usual vapid condolences. "By what means?" he asked.

"He shot himself."

"Is he . . . out of danger?" It was a double-edged question.

"The doctors seem to disagree on that question. And every other."

I am a man of tender digestion. My stomach was hollow as a kettle and turning bilious. Many consider the effects of tobacco salubrious, but on an empty stomach I can hardly abide the smell of the most inoffensive pipe smoke. Both of these men smoked Dutch shag, the foulest leaf in the world this side of hemlock. They were soon bundled in smoke. My eyes were raw. My forehead began to feel clammy. The continuance of this subject line could only exacerbate my discomfort.

"Has your brother attempted to harm himself before?" asked Vernet.

"Two years ago, while he was living and working in Provence, he slashed—"

I shot to my feet. "Gentlemen, please excuse me. I believe I'll take a turn."

I had expected some reaction, sympathy or approbation. Neither man seemed to notice I had spoken. I tucked my Gladstone under my arm and decamped into the passageway. If I could find a quiet compartment where I could gentle my stomach, I might be able to bring some order to my comparative studies. They were the heart of my report to the consortium.

It was not to be. The coach was unusually crowded; there were no empty compartments. I roamed up and down the passage, pressing my face against windows, peering in like a forlorn little boy outside a sweet shop, surprising passengers in their private moments. Fingers were pointed at me; fists were shaken. The standees in the narrow passage made their annoyance plain as I bumped through, forcing them to perform feats of acrobatics to let me pass. To add to the confusion, there was a straggling line of boisterous schoolboys bouncing up and down the passage, shrieking and laughing, utterly indifferent to the nuisance they created. It was impossible to avoid them. Then one got an imp on his shoulder; he reached out as he passed and tried to tear the Gladstone from my hands. I jerked back reflexively, and for a moment found myself in a tug of war with a twelve-year-old. Then the horrid boy butted me in the vitals like a billy goat. I folded to the floor, the wind knocked out of me. There was a yelp from the boy as a hand reached out to box his ears; then the whole mob of little villains went romping away, no doubt to inflict themselves on some unsuspecting innocents in the saloon car.

I sat propped against the wall of the passage, feeling the rumble of the train rearrange my insides as though I were Aetna ready to erupt. My Gladstone had been wrenched open; there were sketches strewn down the corridor.

"Damned Freemasons! You've got to watch yourself every second!"

Green morocco-gloved hands, weaving in front of my eyes, beckoning for me to take them, helping me to my feet. The same hands had cuffed the boy; I remembered the stumpy green fingers. Now the hands were helping me gather up my sketches. Most solicitous, for French hands.

The hands spoke: "Ah, you're an artist? On your way to Auvers? Guess who I'm going to visit!"

My knees were water. I was in no mood to enter into parlor games.

"Dumoulin! I commissioned a portrait from him! My dog and wife!" crowed the hands.

I tried to assemble a congratulatory smile.

"Now you'll say Meissonier is the finest painter alive in France. Bosh! It's Dumoulin! You saw his exhibition of *Japonisme* last year at Georges Petit?"

I nodded dumbly, trying to remember if I had ever heard of Dumoulin. Since the French government had thrown up its hands and called it quits with the Salon ten years ago, it was hard to keep track of even the most serious French painters.

One of the hands reached out to shake mine. "Jules Brunelle, monsieur."

I was surprised to hear myself reply, "Dr. Ivan Lermolieff." The detective's penchant for masquerade had wormed its nasty little way into my heart.

"Ah! A Russian! The court of the czars!" He pumped my hand once again, which made me queasy. Apparently, he mistook my look. "You're admiring the gloves. I'm in the line. Van de Walles, out of Bruges. We make ladies' opera gloves, mostly, but those don't fit my paws. We're going to be great friends, I think."

My eyes traveled up the sleeve to the shoulder, to the face of Jules Brunelle. He was a dapper little man in spectacles, with a silky imperial. His shoulders were broad, his torso squat like a rolltop desk. He wore a cravat with an emerald tie pin. The gloves, which emphasized the smallness of his hands, seemed more likely to belong to some small forest creature—a badger, perhaps, if badgers wore breeches and gaiters.

"Come into my compartment! We'll talk Dumoulin for days."

Desperate to avoid the possibility, I mumbled something to the effect that I had friends waiting for me. I picked out a compartment at random and jerked the door open. There were two men inside, and they turned as one, glowering at me with such malevolence that I shuddered. If I could have guessed who these ogres were, and what part they would play in future events, I would have shuddered down to my toes. I nodded an apology and withdrew. I followed Brunelle down the passageway.

# Chapter Three

I stood waiting outside the train station in the little village of Auvers-sur-Oise, damp and disheveled, after enduring an eternal hour of Brunelle's opinions on art and life, all from a crackpot's viewpoint. To hear him tell it, the most important artists of the age were neither realists nor romantics nor the Barbizons nor the academics, but the Freemasons, Martinists, Rosicrucians, and sundry worshipers of Isis and survivors of the fall of Atlantis who called themselves Symbolists. As it happened, he was acquainted with them all, and was ready to enumerate the virtues of each. What all these supposed secret societies had to do with painting was obscure at best. But the French are apt to monomania.

He had insisted on seeing all my sketches, though he was obviously perplexed by them: what must he have made of dozens of iterations of ears, hands, noses, folds of drapery, bunches of foliage, which spoke volumes to the expert but said nothing to a man unacquainted with the Morelli method of authentication—especially one under the impression that they were studies for a work of my own. He came to that conclusion without my encouragement; neither did I trouble to enlighten him. I had feared all this was preface to him springing open his sample case in an attempt to sell me his fall line. Mercifully, I had been spared that ordeal.

Once I was finally released, I made my way back to our compartment only to find it empty except for the smoke. I remembered then that Van Gogh had said his destination was Auvers; Vernet must have gone to say adieu. By now he must be ready to return to Paris—with his tail between his legs. At least I fervently hoped so.

Vernet came striding down the platform toward me. "Dr. Lermolieff! Delighted to have found you. I trust your journey was not too dull. May I commend you on your tact?"

I had no idea what the detective was blithering about. Vernet's remarks seemed to hop about, omitting explanation in favor of some gnomic aphorism that the listener was invited to tackle like a cypher. Whether it was habit or strategy was a further puzzle to be pondered. Later. Much later. I longed for a cold compress, or better yet, a glass of Goldriesling.

He continued blithely, "You will have already judged that Van Gogh is not the quarry we had hoped to flush. My interview with the man was conclusive. His sudden flight to Auvers is due entirely to his concern for his brother, who apparently has a history of seizures."

"Vincent?"

"You've heard of the man?" Vernet raised his eyebrows as if it were the most unlikely of possibilities.

"We saw one of his pieces behind the counter in that shop we went to, Tanguy's." I had only just recalled it, but I could conjure it in my mind plainly now, a painting of an olive grove writhing beneath a lowering grey sky, with mountains rolling up behind. It had the unmoored air of a nightmare. The old shopkeeper had caught me staring at it, and mistaken my horror for admiration. He'd mentioned an entire room of paintings by the same artist; he could show me if I were interested. I begged off, promising to return when I had more time. As if Daniel would step again into the lion's den.

"What was your opinion of it?" Vernet asked.

I thought it no surprise the man who'd painted such a nightmare had attempted suicide. But I was not up to wading into the matter. "So, we return to Paris now?" I asked hopefully. "Or shall we go straight on to Montpellier to meet with the consortium?"

Vernet's forehead creased. "Van Gogh's story has raised some interesting points."

Were I a faithful student of Dr. Watson's accounts, I might have taken a warning in those words. Instead I gazed about the station. It looked a sleepy ruin in the afternoon sun, but surely there was a café nearby. "We can find something to take with us on the train to eat," I suggested, "and have our luggage sent from the hotel."

"The luggage will have to shift for itself. I propose we dine here in Auvers. Van Gogh praises the town for its beauty and serenity. Apparently, it's something of an artists' colony. You have perhaps heard of Louis Dumoulin?"

I believe I groaned. For an hour I had heard of nothing but Dumoulin. Whether he was an Orientalist or a high priest of Osiris I hadn't been able to keep straight.

Still, when Vernet led on toward the town, I dotted my brow with my handkerchief, shouldered my Gladstone, and followed in his wake. I had made my promise to Morelli.

To be strictly honest, it *was* a pretty town, the streets rising in terraces lined with chestnuts along the river Oise to the fields above, tumble-down cottages with mossy thatched roofs and gardens verging on wilderness. Its charms were obviously no secret to the world at large. As we ambled along, I spied at least six different painters in broad-brimmed hats hunched over their easels, capturing the shimmering light for posterity from their various aeries in the shade. On our way, Vernet filled me in on Van Gogh's story. Apparently two years ago his elder brother had been living and painting in the southern city of Arles, supported entirely by Monsieur Theo's generosity and forbearance, dashing off paintings as fast as canvas could be shipped and stretched. He had some wild-eyed scheme for establishing a studio of the south, where like-minded artists could gather under the spell of the southern sun and Do Great Things. He was eventually joined there by a fellow madman, a failed-stockbroker-turned-painter who was also dependent on Van Gogh's largesse. Painting was eventually supplanted on the syllabus by drinking and whoring and quarreling, till the brother had some kind of crisis of nerves, took a razor, and lopped off his own ear. He then carried it like a matador's trophy to his ladylove, one of the local whores on whom he had lavished his tender yearnings. The other vagabond, one Paul Gauguin, had the good sense to flee the scene before the gendarmes appeared and the whole town rose up in arms against this Vincent. He was carted off to the nearest asylum, where he spent a further year painting like a demon, stopping on occasion just long enough to eat his paints or assault the attendants. Two months ago, the brother had been released from the asylum—an unwise idea. Monsieur Theo had brought him to Auvers and placed him under the eye of a local nerve doctor named Gachet, who, like everyone else in town, was also a weekend painter. And the result was that he had blown his brains out—or not his brains; in fact he'd shot himself in the belly, just to prove that he could botch even a simple suicide.

I tried to crank up some sympathy for the fellow, but the well was dry. "A tragic story, certainly," I said. "But you mentioned something about points of interest?"

"You must have noted them yourself, Doctor! First, the quarrel in Arles that precipitated the brother's self-mutilation began immediately after he and the stockbroker Gauguin had visited the Musée Fabre in Montpellier. Second, the stockbroker was apparently something of a swordsman—no, I mean that literally. He had been trying to tutor the brother in the art of fencing, with lukewarm results. Thirdly, it was the brother himself who elected to go to asylum, stayed there a year, then declared himself cured. Finally, he attempted suicide by shooting himself in the abdomen, then immediately called for a surgeon to remove the bullet."

I *hadn't* noted any of these seemingly random details, but perhaps my attention had wandered. The detective apparently considered them clues of some import, but where was the mystery to hang them on? Van Gogh's brother was a madman; that much was obvious. What connection was there with our own investigation? If he had been in the madhouse, he had not been snatching paintings from the Louvre. We couldn't let ourselves be distracted by every little conundrum that sprung up in our way, no matter how it piqued the detective's curiosity.

Was I being too hard on Vernet? Perhaps a detective views a fresh corpse with the same mingling of excitement and suspicion that a connoisseur views a newly discovered Giorgione. I already knew what Dr. Morelli would say: apply the method. In the analysis of a painting, there is always a moment when any of a dozen details seem to swarm in the air like phosphenes before one's eyes, before those that are truly characteristic come together and fall in place. Could the method apply beyond the world of art? Was there truly an interleaving between the detective's work and my own? It seemed folly to even entertain the notion.

We turned into the main street, the Place de la Mairie, where the city hall stood like a solitary cracker box. Across the square was a row of small shops and a café with the name "Auberge Ravoux" painted above the door. It was toward this café the detective's steps wended.

From outside, the place appeared closed. The tables out front under the scant shade of a pair of tortured pear trees were deserted, but the faded curtains were open. As we stepped inside, the air was a stir of anticipation and anxious whispers. A stout fellow with a ruddy, affable face and spiky whiskers shuffled among the tables in waistcoat and shirtsleeves, picking up glasses and plates, scowling at them, and setting them back down just as they were. This must be the owner, Ravoux. A little girl, no more than two, trotted along behind him unnoticed, trying to catch the leg of his trousers. Only some secret sympathy between them kept her from being trod upon. A handsome young matron and a girl of perhaps sixteen, sitting together at a table by the counter, kept motioning him to sit. He paid them no mind; nor did the baby. The mother—Madame Ravoux?—was possessed of a good figure and dark complexion, with searching almond eyes. Her dress was that of the *haute bourgeoisie*, testament either to her own housekeeping skills or her husband's extravagance. The daughter was a copy of her mother, but in pastels rather than charcoals, with golden hair and eyes of aquamarine.

A few men sat drinking wine at one of the long tables at the back of the room. In their laborer's smocks they might have been boatmen or railway men or yet more painters. They were alert to every coming and going; they had been whispering to each other and trying not to stare since the moment we walked in the door. Two more, young fellows with the down still upon their cheeks, hung over the billiards table in the middle of the room, their fingers blue with chalk, contemplating a game whose progress our entrance had arrested.

Ravoux had been keeping us in the corner of his eye as well. He seemed uncertain whether to accost us or ignore us, the only two quivers in his bow. Now he growled: "Well, messieurs?"

"We're friends of Monsieur Theo van Gogh," said Vernet. Another lie.

Ravoux gave a curt nod toward the stairs.

"You must be thirsty, messieurs!" the woman said in a low, musical voice. She was not addressing us, but prompting her husband. "You must be thirsty, messieurs," he echoed grudgingly. His words were a charm that freed the daughter to jump up and pour wine for the newcomers, smiling prettily.

The stairs complained. Every eye in the room looked up. I expected to see Monsieur Theo. Instead, the man who descended the stairs was one of the oddest ducks I'd ever laid eyes on. He was wearing a fisherman's cap, and a blue artist's smock greatly dappled with yellow lake. His hair and beard were red as a new pfennig, though he must have been well over sixty. There was the melancholy of the circus clown about him. His step was jaunty, but his eyes were as deep and haunted as one of Goya's pilgrim's. He slouched to the counter and drank off one of the glasses of wine the girl had just poured for us. For a moment I felt a chill along the nape of my neck, wondering if I were looking at the suicidal brother, risen from his deathbed.

"How is he, Doctor?" asked Madame Ravoux.

This doctor—I never met a man who looked less like one—threw his hands up in surrender. He tapped the glass for a refill. If this were the guardian Theo van Gogh had set for his brother, one could only question how he had survived so long. The girl poured him another glass.

"Will he live?" asked the girl, anxiously. Her eyes glistened with tears unwept.

"Perhaps. His will is strong."

Vernet broke in. "Strange to speak of the will to live in a suicide." I thought it grossly bad taste for him to inject his opinion in a conversation he had not been invited to join, with people who were perfect strangers. It seemed obstreperous and ungentlemanly. If his words were meant to tease a reaction, however, he had succeeded admirably.

"Vincent is no suicide!" the girl shouted, the tears fleeing her eyes.

"Adeline! Forgive my daughter, monsieur," beseeched Ravoux. He snatched up the bottle and two new glasses and bore them to us. "This attack . . . is not like Vincent. It's not in his nature. It's as if he were visited by demons." He set the glasses in front of us and made a quick sign of the cross before he poured.

Vernet nodded sympathetically. "It was not my desire to upset your daughter. Your Vincent certainly seems to cling to life tenaciously. It's my fervent wish he may recover." He turned to the doctor. "Dr. . . . . Gachet?"

"That is my name," said the doctor, with a curt nod.

"Mine is Vernet. I understand your patient was wounded in the abdomen, Doctor? Where was the entry point located?"

"Are you a doctor?" asked Gachet, nettled.

"I have some experience with wounds of this type."

"And Monsieur Theo brought you up from Paris to second-guess me?"

Vernet's face was blank, betraying nothing. He would let Gachet fill the space with his own insecurities. Which he must have done. He answered testily: "The wound is level with the edge of the left ribs, in front of the axillary line. The bullet missed the vital organs."

"There was no shock? No suffocation?"

"No."

"No hematopsy?"

"No."

"No melanesia?"

"No, no, no!" The wine slopped from the doctor's glass when he struck the counter. "No shock, no hematopsy, no . . . melanesia. Vincent's got an iron constitution. He could live with a bullet in his gut for forty years."

Vernet's eyebrows shot up. "You didn't remove the bullet?"

The doctor turned sulkily defensive, "No. We believe the bullet is lodged near the spinal column. Surgery would be too dangerous. Everyone agreed on that."

"Pardon, monsieur, just what kind of doctor are you?" Vernet asked in the frostiest tone possible. For myself, I wondered who "everyone" might be. Auvers-sur-Oise was not a town likely to field a college of surgeons.

The doctor tried to turn the attack. "And what is your diagnosis, eh?"

The detective's face turned black. He kicked back his chair and made for the stair. I was behind him, trying to prevent him, but he slapped my hands away. I spurted past him at the top of the stair, blocking his path, with the good God at my back.

"A man's life hangs in the balance," he said.

"Perhaps. But one of your aphorisms Dr. Morelli is fond of quoting is to never make judgments in advance of the data. Have you gathered enough data to make so critical a judgment?"

"Lermolieff, do you know what melanesia is?"

"I know the doctor said there were no signs of it."

"Melanesia is a chain of islands in the south Pacific."

I stood aside and followed him up the stairs.

We were in an unlit garret at the top of the house. Two rooms led off the hall. One door stood open, letting in whatever semblance of fresh air there was. There were voices. Theo van Gogh, broken-hearted, asking, "Why, Vincent?"

A second voice, low and flinty like summer thunder, answering: "I asked the same question after the attack in Arles. Perhaps someone's jealous of my painting?"

"Who do you mean?" Theo asked. "Anquetin? Bernard?"

"God," he whispered in reply. "Don't look so cross, brother. I don't mean I'm the better painter. He's still the maestro. But He's jealous I won't paint in his image. I won't let Him stand in my light."

"You scare me sometimes, Vincent!"

"I scare everyone. Ask Gachet!"

"Ask him what?"

We both strained to hear a reply, but instead there erupted a long, hacking cough that sounded like ribs cracking one by one. Silence followed.

Vernet hauled me back into the shadow of the second doorway just as Theo van Gogh emerged from his brother's room and went downstairs. Vernet darted into the room behind him. I was shocked by his effrontery, but I could see nothing for it but to follow. In for a penny, as the English say.

Even with the door open, the attic room was suffocatingly hot, reeking of sweat and carbolic acid mixed with cheap tobacco and linseed oil. It was bare as a monk's cell. The smoky light of an oil lamp revealed Van Gogh's elder brother, huddled in fitful slumber on a mean iron cot shoved against the wall. There was a rush-seated chair playing the part of a nightstand, with a lit pipe sitting on it, the smoke curling up toward the canted ceiling. On the opposite wall stood a washstand with an empty bowl. That was the furniture in its entirety.

But the room was anything but empty. Canvases were stacked against every wall four deep, claiming almost every inch of floor space. Canvases were hung haphazardly above them, the town of Auvers and its environs painted from every conceivable perspective, every winding street, every red-tiled villa, every hillside vineyard dismantled and transported hither. If he'd only lived in the little town two months, the man must have rattled off a painting a day. In the smoky light, the garishly colored paintings throbbed to life, threatening to erupt from the walls. I could hardly take my eyes off them. Vincent's easel stood in a corner, a painting still strapped to it. It looked to be a field of golden corn beneath a louring sky, with a rain of black dashes slapped across it—birds of ill omen, perhaps? What kind of mind conceived such waking nightmares?

Vernet appeared oblivious to the paintings. He moved to the invalid's side.

Vincent van Gogh was a grim sight. He had been lying in the same clothes, among the soiled, bloodstained bed linen, for two days. Someone had attempted to wash him as he lay there, to little effect. His red hair and beard were matted, his flesh was grey. I couldn't help noticing that his left ear was mangled; it looked as if the lower half had been sliced right off.

This is what the confraternity of painters had devolved into, I thought to myself. The masters of the Renaissance had all been apprenticed in their youth to master craftsmen: Michelangelo to Ghirlandaio, Da Vinci to Verrochio. Every Giotto had his Cimabue. But these new painters, even the ones who started out in the studios, submitted to no masters. Each seemed to wander alone in his own fever dream, isolated from those who came before and those who would come after. It was the perfect formula for madness.

Vernet slipped a hand under the dressing, probing the wound. His own face seemed to take on a tinge of grey. "Too late, too late!" he muttered, more to himself than to me. "Why did they wait?"

The painter groaned, arching his spine beneath Vernet's hand. His lips worked, repeating the last words he had said to his brother: "Ask Gachet . . ."

"Ask him what, Vincent?" Vernet asked, soft but urgent. "Ask Gachet what?"

Vincent stirred again, but made no answer. Vernet hovered over him, his ear almost against Vincent's lips, waiting, willing him to speak.

". . . about Olympia."

"Who is Olympia?"

We waited to the breaking point of our nerves, but no further answer came. Those were the last words we heard from Vincent; perhaps the last he spoke in his life. Vernet brushed his lips against the dying man's forehead, a gesture both tender and unexpected.

"He's burning up with fever."

There were footsteps on the stair. We fled again toward the second bedroom, but the door handle started to turn before our eyes. Vernet hustled me back into the shadows at the end of the hall, putting a finger to his lips. As the Ravoux girl arrived on the landing, Tommy Hirschig popped out of the second bedroom, scaring her.

"Oh, Monsieur Hirschig! I didn't know you were back." So Hirschig was the occupant of the second bedroom, it seemed.

She carried a stack of towels under one arm and a pitcher of water in her hand. For his part, Hirschig was now decked in a clean, if ill-fitting, suit. His hair was damp from a quick wash. "Just got in. How's the old fellow, then?" He nodded toward Vincent's door.

For answer she only shook her head, her eyes on the floor.

"Don't you worry, Goldilocks. I think the old bear is only shamming. I could hear him clomping about in there just now, and talking to himself the way he does."

She looked at him strangely, biting her lower lip. She dipped her head and went into Vincent's room.

Once she was inside, we followed Hirschig down the stair. He was too preoccupied with combing his hair to notice we were behind him. Nor did anyone pay attention as we rejoined the company; any noise we made was swallowed up in the buzz of conversation and the clinking of cutlery. The room was beginning to fill up. We took an empty table. Madame Ravoux cast an inquiring look our way. I nodded eagerly.

Auvers is still a country town as far as mealtimes go. The Ravouxs had their hands full dishing out dinner to their boarders. There was a crowd of Americans at one table, always the loudest voices in any room, and a mix of cosmopolitan and Picardy accents emanating from the other tables. Hirschig joined Gachet at the table next to us. They nodded briefly to one another, exchanging desultory greetings, but

Gachet was already deep in conversation with a bottle of wine, while young Hirschig's eyes tended to follow Madame Ravoux as she glided around the room, serving her guests.

"Tommy, have you seen Monsieur Valdevielde tonight? Will he be dining with us?" the lady called across the room to him.

"Not he. He's afraid Vincent might take it into his head to shoot someone else—beg your pardon, Monsieur Theo." Hirschig's cheeks reddened when he realized Van Gogh was present.

Theo van Gogh stood at the counter, brow knitted, working through a stack of telegraph forms. There were bread and wine before him, and a bowl of broth going cold: all untouched. He did not appear to have heard Hirschig's remark. Indeed, he appeared unaware of any activity around him. His face was waxen, and his hands trembled. I realized then that he was more than simply affected; he was positively ill.

"Monsieur Hirschig brings up an interesting point. Where is the gun Vincent van Gogh used to shoot himself?" asked Vernet, turning to Gachet.

"I don't know." Gachet, morose, stared into the deeps of his wine glass.

"Do the gendarmes have it?"

"They weren't able to find it."

Vernet threw up his hands and turned away.

"Don't be alarmed, monsieur," the doctor jeered. "He doesn't have the gun now. He didn't shoot himself in bed."

Vernet turned back, with a sudden gleam in his eye. "Where did he shoot himself?"

Gachet waved vaguely. "Out beyond the cemetery, in the fields. They found his easel and paints up there."

"He took his easel with him when he went to kill himself?"

"I didn't say that. Perhaps he went out to paint, but fell into a spasm of despair and decided to take his life. With cases like his, the black mood may hit like a stroke of lightning."

"You merely reverse the conundrum. Why should he take a gun out with him to paint?"

Hirschig broke in, talking with his mouth full. "Scare crows."

Vernet turned to him with a look of amused astonishment. "Monsieur, please elaborate."

"Vincent had been working on some paintings of wheat fields—not much of a subject, as far as I'm concerned, just a lot of straight yellow lines, but he wasn't one to listen to advice. And he loved yellow—my God, he could go through six tubes a day!"

"Yes. And the gun?"

"Well, he didn't want to paint crows, but where you've got wheat, you get crows, and he couldn't bring himself to ignore them. So, he borrowed a gun from somewhere and shot it off to scare them away."

"What kind of gun was it?"

"Never saw it. Heard it, though. So did the crows." He mimed aiming a rifle at the sky and squeezing the trigger. "Boom!"

Gachet snorted in derision. "It was a revolver. One of those American guns. A Colt, I think they call it?"

Vernet whipsawed back again. "Doctor! He *did* show the weapon to you? Where?"

"I believe we were in my study. Vincent was fussing over a painting I'd acquired that hadn't yet been framed, he claimed the paint was cracking—"

"One of his paintings?"

"No, no, a friend of his—a Guillaumin, I think it was. Perhaps you know the fellow? Well, someday you will, all the world will know his name. I'm something of a collector. It takes a discriminating eye. But it also takes time and care. Sometimes I don't have that time. I have a busy practice in the city. Introducing some exciting new procedures. The mind is a fascinating- "

"I'm sure it is. Vincent? And the gun?"

"Oh . . . well, Vincent blew everything out of proportion. First he was shouting, then he was screaming. He pulled the gun from his pocket and waved it around like a man possessed."

"What did you do?"

"I—I stared at him, very firmly, you know—" Gachet assumed

what he must have thought a fearsome expression, though it nearly made me laugh out loud. He looked as if he had the toothache.

"And?"

"That was all. He lowered his head and skulked off."

"Truly, you must have been a matador in another life, Doctor. You made no attempt to disarm him? Were you unaware of his history of violence toward himself?"

"That violence you speak of, it's not Vincent. It's an aberration."

"I thought that could always be said of madness," I said. I hadn't meant to speak out of turn, but really, it needed to be said.

"I don't know what can always be said of madness," Gachet snapped back. "Are you an alienist?"

Vernet pursued doggedly: "No one asked what he did with the gun?"

"Everyone asked! The police questioned him till they were blue in the face. Ask him yourself! Monsieur Theo! Did he tell you anything about it?"

Van Gogh stared up with blind eyes. He collected his thoughts like shells upon a distant shore. He noticed the crowd, and the evening light turning saffron. He caught sight of the landlord, a familiar landmark. "Monsieur Ravoux, if you could see to it that these are sent as soon as possible?" He pushed the forms across the counter to him. "I should rejoin my brother."

Vernet stood and crossed to the bar. "I can take those for you, monsieur. I need to send a wire myself."

Van Gogh's eyes slid across Vernet's, and then mine, but there seemed no recognition in them. But he let him take the forms. Vernet fixed me with an imperative stare.

"But we have dinner coming!" I protested.

"Please, Doctor, I need your eyes. Before we lose the sun. We can find dinner elsewhere."

A handful of telegrams certainly did not require the efforts of two people. But I had no wish to quarrel with the man in public. I threw my napkin on the table and joined him.

We stepped out into the deepening summer evening. The post office was just across the square, and we had soon dispatched our commission. Vernet promised the telegrapher we would return before he closed to deal with any replies.

"Now, Doctor, we must take a little stroll. I would like you to think of this little town as a great open-air art gallery. We are searching for a particular painting. You have seen the original before. We must find the copy."

It sounded a mad idea. "You want to search the entire town?"

"Perhaps. Let us start out past the cemetery."

The yellow heat of the day was ceding to a sultry purple twilight. A barn owl screamed away in the distance. We took the track that wound uphill between the vineyards and walled gardens, the stone houses with red-tiled roofs and the cottages crowned with thatch, crowded by the heavy scent of flowers, out past the chateau and the cemetery, to fields still lit with gold in the waning sun. The scene was rife with tableaux suitable for a landscape. But there was nothing to prod me with its familiarity.

"Anything?" Vernet urged me. "Anything, my friend?"

We had arrived at the edge of a great field of wheat. Three paths met there: the one we had followed from the town, which continued on into the hills, another that sheared off toward the river Oise, and one that divided the stands of wheat into two neat rectangles and disappeared into the west. I gazed off into the fields, where the light seemed to clutch at the darkening sky like a man drowning.

"Quite a view," I said, taking in the panorama. Then I sucked in my breath, realizing where we were. The only thing missing from the picture was the crows.

"Vernet! This is where he was painting!"

"Capital! I knew I could count on you."

If Vernet was such a keen observer, it seemed to me he should have been able to discover the spot without my aid. He stepped about gingerly in the crossroads, examining the ground. In a moment he was on his knees, sifting through the dirt with a magnifying glass, searching for something. "See, here are the marks from his easel. The beaten earth around here would be unlikely to hold any footprints, of course; in any case they would have been trampled by the searchers. But observe these stands of wheat!"

I looked out across the fields, but saw nothing that spoke to me. Tall stands of golden wheat, unbroken and undisturbed. Hirschig's monotonous yellow lines. I confessed as much to Vernet.

"Precisely! Unbroken and undisturbed!" he cried. "Vincent did not go tramping off into the fields to dispose of the gun, nor did anyone search for it here, in spite of what our good Dr. Gachet assures us. No one wanted to trample valuable crops, after all. But you and I have no such qualms."

He was already wading slowly through the waves of grain on one side of the path, intent on the ground. "Couldn't he have dropped the gun anywhere along the path home?" I asked. It seemed the most likely explanation.

"We took the most direct route to this spot. The route a desperate man would take going home. If the gun were merely dropped some-where on his return journey, it would have been found already—by ourselves, if no one else. But if Vincent planned beforehand to hide the gun, this would be the obvious place for it. And a man who'd just shot himself in the gut could not have cast the weapon far."

I nodded and pushed into the field on the opposite side of the path. Though Vernet had not positively requested my aid, it seemed expected. I felt a bit foolish tiptoeing about in the grass, and the dust tickled at my nose, but I had a secret yen to find the blasted gun myself and score one off the detective. Between us, we made a fairly thorough search of the area near the shooting, though night was coming on fast. We did not find the weapon.

"Could it be that someone has found the gun and left it unreported?" I asked.

"This isn't London or even Milan, my friend. In a town this size, there will only be a handful of guns, and everyone will know precisely who they belong to. Even if the finder was unaware of the gun's importance, he would have returned it, either to its owner or the police."

He didn't say it then, and I refrained from saying it myself, yet the word seemed to coagulate from the ether. It seemed overly dramatic for a summer evening in the country, with the stars opening one by one in the sky. But if some person or persons unknown, as the examining magistrate might phrase it, had taken the gun away, it stood to reason that same person had brought the gun here to begin with, and used it.

The word we did not speak was "murder."

# Chapter Four

It was after midnight when we turned into the Place de la Mairie again. We had taken rooms for the night at the St. Aubin, a couple of streets away. We had actually sat down to a meal without interruption, though Vernet mainly picked at his food, staring off into space. I would have been content to sink into the soft white sheets of my bed, but he felt the need to speak to Monsieur Theo again, if possible.

Apparently, the detective didn't eat *or* sleep. His stoic habits would be the death of me. Like any good German, I'm accustomed to a regular regimen of meals and rest.

"You pumped him for an hour on the train. I thought you were satisfied."

"I am satisfied he was not attempting to escape us."

"The man is devastated!"

"So it would seem. But I would like to know his whereabouts on Sunday afternoon."

"What difference does it make?"

"My dear doctor. We have a Parisian art dealer supporting a new wife and infant son on a meager salary. Also supporting his brother, paying his brother's medical bills, subsidizing his brother's profitless career as a painter. A heavy burden to bear. Where can he look for relief?"

I didn't like where this was going. "But he has faith in his brother. He hopes for an eventual return on his investment."

"And what increases the value of an artist's work like his death?"

"You're implying that Van Gogh took the train to Auvers on Sunday, hiked across the fields, found his brother, shot him in cold blood, and returned on the afternoon train? Without ever being seen? It beggars belief."

"On the contrary, it's entirely plausible. But I'm not accusing Van Gogh of anything. I merely point to a thread that must be pulled on."

"Say what you will. I believe he loves his brother."

"Now, that is a very interesting thing you say. Interesting and perhaps important."

"What the devil are you getting at?"

"I think love may have played a crucial role in this murder. Remember what the gendarme said."

I had been with him earlier in the evening when he hunted down the gendarme, Rigaumon, at his home. This was the man who had questioned Monsieur Theo's brother about the shooting. The officer was cross at being caught out in his undershirt, in the middle of his dinner, in a cloud of garlic. His answers were grudgingly short:

*I visited the alien Van Gogh after his attempted suicide was reported. It's against the law to take one's own life in France, whatever they do in Holland.*

Had he attempted to take his own life?

*Yes, perhaps, who knew? The devil had hedged the question every time he was asked. Said it was his own damn business, his own damn fault. He'd nearly become violent.*

Had he, Rigaumon, made further investigation?

*What was I supposed to investigate? The man was alone. No one had helped him. No one had witnessed it, no one was within earshot, no one had found the gun, had they? My dinner's getting cold. Good night, messieurs.*

"I don't recall that love was Rigaumon's theme."

"No, but you can see the painter wanted to be certain no one else was accused."

"Because he alone was responsible!"

"Or—perhaps because he was protecting someone else."

The gendarme's report had put to rest my darker suspicions. Now here was Vernet raising the specter of murder once more. "Do you sincerely believe this sophistry, or will you clutch at any pretext for murder?" I asked scornfully.

He hardly blinked an eye. "Suicide is so much simpler for everyone," he said. "We all share the guilt, but only one soul bears the responsibility. With murder, suddenly each of us is a suspect, a potential killer, all our history caught in the crosshairs of the law. Then the vast machinery of justice must be brought to bear, and that machinery is as likely to crush the innocent as the guilty."

"And you are determined upon bringing that machinery to life."

"Oh, I am not an officer of justice. I'm only an instrument of the truth."

The trill of the nightjar broke the stillness of the air. But it was a note of another kind that brought us to a halt. At first it seemed so intertwined with vespertine birdsong that I couldn't unravel it, and then it came to me: the catch and release of a young woman weeping. It came from the town hall, across the square from Ravoux's. She was standing in the porch, almost invisible in the shadows. But the moon picked out the porcelain edges of her face, and the golden curls piled high upon her head. Her eyes were liquid with tears. We stole upon her as one does a skittish fawn.

"May we be of assistance, mademoiselle?" Vernet asked softly.

She was taken all unawares. She took a step toward us, then shrank back and cast about nervously from side to side. She was dressed as a gentlewoman, in something with primroses on it, with a high collar and gigot sleeves. Like a countrywoman, she wore a bonnet rather than a hat. She could hardly have been more than nineteen.

"Oh! Monsieur! I thought you were—but you're not Monsieur

Theo. Are you another of his brothers?" She seemed confused, perhaps even feeble-minded. So many of these country girls are raised like livestock.

Vernet held up a reassuring hand. "Only a friend. Are you close? Have you had news?"

She started, ready to take flight, then she seemed to gather herself. "Vincent? I hardly know him. He's—he's—he's a madman, that's what they say. I was crying because I've turned my ankle." She took a limping step forward to prove it. It was anything but convincing.

"May I look at it for you?" Vernet made to kneel in front of her.

She shied away. "It's better now. Thank you. I have to get home."

There was nothing wrong with the young lady's ankle. She was obviously shamming. The only question was why Vernet let her get away with such an outrageous falsehood. He merely stepped aside. Once released, she darted away like a rabbit, disappearing into the shadows of the road.

We crossed the square to Ravoux's. The lamps were still lit, the door standing open, though the curtains were drawn. Ravoux was sitting out front, sharing a carafe of wine and a game of dice with a few bibulous neighbors. Gachet had returned and taken possession of the other table, in quiet conversation with a young man who resembled him like a son—which, I would learn, he was. The conversation at either table was intermittent and staccato, as though each word were doled out. This was not a warm summer night's entertainment. It was a deathwatch.

Ravoux nodded to us as we mounted the curb. Gachet looked up. "The gentlemen from Paris!" he said, with a false joviality bolstered by drink. "It *was* Paris, I think? We thought you'd taken the train."

"And yet here we are. How fares your patient, Doctor?" Vernet returned.

"Monsieur Theo tells me you're a painter yourself." Gachet said this to me. Then he cast a hard eye on Vernet. "But he didn't tell me what you are."

"I'm something of a collector myself," Vernet returned coolly.

"Ah. Paintings? Sculpture?"

"Enigmas. Puzzles."

"Doctor!" It was a cry of anguish from above. Monsieur Theo.

The cry pulled us all inside the café, even as it drew the women from the kitchen, Madame Ravoux and a couple of friends. Gachet started up the stairs. Vernet would have followed, but I laid a hand on his shoulder. "Now is not the time," I pleaded. He nodded, subsiding grudgingly into a chair. One by one, the men followed suit, though the women remained standing at attention, ready to take charge of the body and perform the rites that have belonged to them since Eve found Abel lying in the fields.

No one spoke. No one moved. At long last we heard a tread upon the stair. We saw the drawn countenance. Monsieur Theo came to a stop in the middle of the room; he seemed lost as to where to go next. One of the men drew a chair for him. He sat reflexively. He drew out a pipe, the one we had seen on the rush-bottom chair. His brother's. Released from his spell, the women hurried upstairs.

"Ravoux, is there a carpenter?" asked Theo van Gogh, his voice creaking rustily.

The landlord cleared his throat. "Monsieur, the priest might not allow it. In sacred ground, at least."

"You needn't concern yourself with suicide. The man upstairs was murdered," said Vernet, as confidently as if he were pronouncing that the man upstairs was a redhead.

An untimely pronouncement, to say the least, that naturally provoked an upheaval of protest. I thought for a moment the men might lay hands on Vernet. Instead they all turned to Monsieur Theo, who seemed to be searching in a mist for the answer.

"My brother shot himself," he whispered.

"He refused to say so plainly to the gendarmes. Did he admit it to you?"

"Yes. Of course. Perhaps not the exact words—"

"What were his exact words?"

"He said he'd botched it again . . . that it was his fault."

"Again? You told me that he had never before attempted suicide."

Van Gogh fell into a brown study, unwilling to engage any further.

Vernet leaned back in his chair, a professor lecturing refractory scholars. "A man takes a gun out to the fields to scare away crows—yet there are crows in the painting. He decides on a whim to shoot himself. Not in the head or in the heart or the head, but in the belly. Having done so, he hides the gun where he is sure no one will find it, and comes trudging home to die. And his first words when he arrives at the inn, according to the police, were, "Who can cut this bullet out of me?" I cannot accept such illogic, monsieur, not if your brother were Mad King Ludwig himself."

"If someone attacked Monsieur Vincent, why wouldn't he tell us who?" asked Ravoux.

"Indeed, that is a question which must be answered."

I thought it a rhetorical question. I didn't know Vernet.

Van Gogh took a long pull on his brother's pipe. His face was grey with grief and exhaustion. "Ravoux, if you could find out about that carpenter, we will need a coffin, whatever the priest may say. And I'll need to get word to my family, and Vincent's friends in Paris."

"Vincent had friends?" Hirschig blurted it out in surprise, not spite. A fellow of negligible intellect, but not actually malicious.

"My brother had a great many friends," answered Theo van Gogh, his voice clotted with sorrow. "He was a much-loved man."

Vernet and I returned to our inn in the wee hours. I was dead on my feet. We agreed that we would rise early to return to Paris in the morning, and then on to Montpellier in the afternoon. At least that was my understanding. But when I startled awake the next day, the morning was wearing away, and Vernet had vanished. I almost thought he had forgotten me, but a question to the landlord revealed that he had bespoken our rooms for another night. Why?

There was nowhere for me to point my steps but the Auberge Ravoux. Vernet wasn't there. Ravoux had not seen him. The restaurant was closed, but he would gladly bring me some coffee. I accepted with gratitude.

The funeral party had begun to trickle in. The coffin, hastily banged together by a neighbor, still smelling of fresh pine, lay on the billiard table in the middle of the room, with a sheet draped over it. Theo van Gogh's brother-in-law, another Dutchman named Bonger, had hurried up from the city to pitch in. He and Van Gogh spent most of the day hanging Vincent's paintings on the walls, debating the placement of each canvas as if they were mounting an exhibition at the Louvre.

With nothing to do until Vernet put in an appearance besides stay out of people's way, I let my eyes wander over the paintings. They were not nearly so alarming in the plain light of day as they had been in the shadows of the attic room. The effect of seeing them hung *en masse* on the café walls forced me to reconsider my antipathy toward them. Not that they weren't crude; they all appeared to have been executed extempore, without any preparatory studies at all, subject to momentary inspiration or lack thereof. But they were so absolutely drenched in color that there was something bravura in the performance, as though every painting were a swimmer crossing the English Channel, wearing a millstone round its neck. You had to applaud them even as they sank beneath the waves. One painting especially arrested my attention, bringing to mind something the strange girl had hinted at the night before.

"You appear mesmerized, Dr. Lermolieff." Vernet was standing behind me, as if he had precipitated out of thin air. Part of his bag of tricks, no doubt.

This was where I was meant to rebuke him for so cavalierly deserting me, further delaying our appointment in Montpellier, and I had rehearsed just such a dressing-down. But my mind was on another matter just then. "You do resemble him, you know."

"Who?"

"Vincent."

"My dear doctor! How can you say such a thing?"

"Not as he lay dying, but there—look at that painting!"

It was a self-portrait of the painter, positively glaring at us from the canvas, his red hair and beard fiery against a swirling blue-green background. I hadn't entertained the notion until I had seen the portrait, and remembered how the mysterious girl had taken him for Vincent's brother the night before, but there was indeed an uncanny resemblance between the detective and the man we had seen dying in the attic room. The same hawkish profile and lantern jaw, the same whippet-thin frame, the same probing eyes, gray-green and deep as the ocean. Had Vernet recognized the resemblance himself? Had it perhaps stirred his unconscious sympathies for the poor fellow?

Vernet studied the painting. "That's him?"

"A self-portrait, I think. Very like."

"No! Look at that devil-red beard!"

"Your beard is red—reddish, at least."

"Is it?" He rubbed his chin thoughtfully. "I wish I'd never grown the confounded thing. It itches damnably in this heat. Well, at least it's not henna red, like Dr. Gachet's."

There was a portrait of the doctor there, too, head in hand, the picture of melancholy. His hair was indeed henna red, and he, too, somewhat resembled Vincent.

But Vernet had made me curious about the beard. "Why *did* you grow it?" I asked.

"I fancy Vernet as a bearded man, don't you? Vernet is French. A bit of a rake, a bit of a swindler, a bit of a fox. The beard makes the man. Don't know how you stand that great bushy thing in this heat."

"My beard is not bushy," I objected, stroking it fondly, though there was grey beginning to show in the black. "It is luxurious."

It struck me that for him the beard, like all the rest of his accoutrements, was meant simply as a disguise. The "Monsieur Vernet" I had mistaken as solid flesh was a prop built of beards and scarves and stories snatched from the ether. I wondered what sort of man lay beneath the mask. Perhaps he was all surface, like a painting, with only the illusion of depth.

Ravoux had been right about the priest. With Vincent's death officially registered as a suicide, he would allow neither a church

service nor the use of the parish hearse. In this instance Vernet actually set to and made himself useful. Once he was made aware of Monsieur Theo's predicament, he sent a blizzard of telegrams to various
connections until another hearse was procured and sent over from
a nearby town. He refrained from mentioning again his contention
that Vincent had been murdered, and was awarded a wary gratitude
from Monsieur Theo. As for the lack of a church service, Van Gogh
seemed unconcerned, perhaps even relieved. Vincent had once been
a missionary, we were told by the brother-in-law, Bonger, but he had
rejected the church, and perhaps even God, as the years exacted their
toll on his psyche. Theo van Gogh had never been a missionary, unless
you counted his proselytizing for Impressionists. If he believed in a
god, it was a deity in the image of his brother. Vernet was mad to
consider him a suspect.

Adeline Ravoux and her little sister came in from the fields with
an apron full of wildflowers to strew upon the coffin. Between their
bouquet and Vincent's bright canvases the room lost its somber atmosphere and took on a festive air. The girls capered about till even the
undertaker laughed. Madame Ravoux opened a box of madeleines and
kept the coffee coming. When her husband cracked open a bottle of
the local abricotine, things became almost merry. Theo confided some
happy tales of his boyhood with Vincent to the company. So does the
eager earth send up shoots through the burial mound and cover it in
green. The bones of men are buried beneath every house in every street
and along every country ride. The coffins are stacked one atop another
all the way down to the center of the earth. Yet mourning is not the
natural mold of man. The heart is buoyant as a channel marker.

Vernet confided in me that he had received a wire from his cousin,
Lecomte, calling it positively urgent that we drop further inquiries and
come to Montpellier at once.

"Then shall we not heed his summons?" I said.

"Of course, Doctor, you must do what you think best, but I have
further inquiries to make here. I would welcome your assistance."

We were decided. What profit was there, after all, in arguing with the great English detective? He would have his way. I would feel a fool arriving in Montpellier alone.

I returned to the St. Aubin and spent the time at a sidewalk table in the shade of an awning, putting my report in order. I had offered to show Vernet a preliminary draft, but he demurred. "You've already informed me of your results; I have perfect faith in Dr. Morelli's method." Fairer words could not be said.

I was sitting therefore, sipping at a glass of wine, going over my notes on Fragonard's *The Lock*, detailing the exuberant, nearly tumescent upsweep of long, fluid brushstrokes, the tension of the line like an arrow notched in a bow, the lover's hand straining for the latch— ah, but that hand was never painted by Fragonard! Fragonard's hands are round and plump, creased at the wrist like a baby's, fumbling for its mother's teat. This hand was long and splayed, one of El Greco's claws!—when I suffered a strange delusion. I was studying the Fragonard with the mind's eye; the canvas lay plainly before me. But as I did so, a watercarrier passed me on the street, tall and thin and brown, his heavy buckets yoked across his shoulders, yet he was moving in what could only be called a jig. And though he was certainly walking away from me, he was just as certainly coming closer.

I squinted, and brushed the rheum from my eyes; the world righted itself. An unframed painting was approaching me along the street, in the hands of—well, the hands were all the clue I needed, stumpy fingers sheathed in green kid gloves. I could barely see his eyes between the painting and his homburg hat.

He slammed the canvas down on the pavement in front of me. "Well! What do you think?" Jules Brunelle asked. His face was flushed, his little eyes bright with righteous indignation.

It was inoffensive enough. An Oriental scene, I gathered, a native water-bearer making his barefoot way down a shade-dappled street in Siam, or Tonkin, perhaps. It appeared to have been hastily made, a compromise of sorts between the labored Salon style and the myopic slapdash of Impressionism. Meant to suggest exoticism, I suppose, though the scene could have been Provence as easily as Cochin China.

"Very fine," I said to placate him. "But didn't you say you had commissioned a portrait of your wife?"

"My wife and her dog! Do you see my wife? Do you see the dog?"

I neither saw nor cared, but I humored the man. "What does Dumoulin say?"

"Monsieur Dumoulin says nothing! Monsieur Dumoulin says *au revoir*!"

His hands were trembling. I waited for him to collect his savoir faire.

"Dumoulin has gone to Japan. Left on Sunday. There were only a pair of hired men—a pair of poltroons!—closing up the house, putting things in storage, they said. They wouldn't even let me look for my painting. They fobbed this off on me instead. One painting good as another, they said. They pushed me out the door! I'll give this thing to the fire!"

"Keep the painting," I counseled soothingly. "When Monsieur Dumoulin returns from abroad, I dare say he'll make restitution. At the worst, if this Dumoulin has the reputation you say, you could always resell this one for . . ."

I looked at the painting again, appraising it. I was certain I had never seen a single work by this artist before, and yet the more I looked, the more familiar it seemed. I felt a wild electric tingling at the base of my scalp. Then it came running at me. I nearly jumped out of my chair in excitement. "Monsieur Brunelle," I said, struggling to keep my voice level, "do you mind if I make a few sketches of this painting? It poses interesting . . . aesthetic problems."

"You like this painting? You think it's good? Perhaps I should keep it."

I nodded vigorously to everything he said. In the end, he let me make the studies I needed right there at the table—I always keep a charcoal in my bag—though he never stopped carping from beginning to end. It was conspiracy, he railed, Jesuits or Zionists or the Black Hand. For my part, I was almost beginning to think we were fortunate indeed that Vernet had ignored Lecomte's urgent summons. Here was a real clue to the mystery of the forged paintings, fallen in my lap. Once I had what I needed, I was able to turn aside Brunelle's dinner invitation, citing a previous engagement. Feeling a bit feverish, I retreated to the quiet of my room, laying a cold compress on my forehead. I was just dropping off to sleep when Vernet came barging in without so much as a knock.

"Try this with your toast and tea, Doctor!" He slammed something down on the night table.

I sat up and swung my legs over the side of the bed, rubbing the sleep from my eyes. I picked up the object and brought it into focus. A jar of honey. "You've been shopping?" I asked.

"I've been snooping. At least that's what Mademoiselle Gachet tells me."

"Gachet? There's a daughter?"

"There is indeed. You met her last night."

My mind was a blank. Then I recalled the mysterious girl in the shadows of the Place de la Mairie. The revelation of her identity rendered her even more mysterious.

"You've been to see Dr. Gachet? I can't imagine he welcomed you with open arms."

"I did not go to see Dr. Gachet, or his son, or his daughter. I followed the bees."

"I'd heard your methods of investigation are unorthodox, but I didn't know you interrogated bees."

"Would that I could. Oh, what the bees could tell me! I hope one day to retire and spend my days keeping bees. But today I merely observed a profusion of bees upon the road west of the village, and followed them to the rather unkempt garden in which they are hived. There I happened upon the beekeeper."

"Our mystery demoiselle?"

"And most mysterious she appeared, floating among the skeps dressed head to toe in black, a black boater with a veil down to her waist, and a smoker in her mouth. Quite alluring, if you're a bee enthusiast."

"A smoker?"

"For stunning bees with smoke."

"I see. Like tiring the bull with lances. So, you spoke to her?"

"She had other visitors. I didn't want to intrude."

"But you didn't mind . . . observing."

Vernet flashed a sudden grin. "You're beginning to grasp my methods."

"What did you observe?"

"Two men. One short, in muttonchops, one tall, with a moustache like a Tatar, both exuding a rather thuggish air. Indeed, Mademoiselle Gachet must have thought so, too."

"They were on the train!" I said, for Vernet had described exactly the evil-faced men I had encountered when trying to avoid Brunelle. I had only seen them for a moment, but they had impressed themselves upon my memory.

"You seem to have made all sorts of acquaintances. At any rate, they asked for her father, and she answered not a word. Something about a painting in his possession. They were quite insistent upon it, but they may as well have been speaking to the ghost of the Richmond murderess. The short one began to make threatening gestures. I thought I might have to intervene. Did she seem a meek young girl to you last night?"

"The word insipid springs to mind."

"She was mighty among the bees. As soon as she was threatened, she blew smoke in their faces, sending them both into coughing fits."

"Brava. And then?"

"She threw a skep at the short one. Which he caught, wonder of wonders! But when he realized that what he had caught was a hive full of bees, he dashed it to the ground and started kicking it. I have read a number of celebrated beekeeping manuals, and none of them recommend such a procedure. Exit, pursued by a swarm of bees. But even in midflight, the Tatar called back, 'Tell your father to order his affairs. Tell him to close the house down!'—to which our mystery mademoiselle answered that she would look after her father."

"She sounds imminently capable of doing so."

"She was perfectly prepared to unleash her wrath upon me once I made my presence known, but I won her trust by helping her set her skeps aright. By the time I was offering to purchase some of her honey, I believe I had allayed most of her suspicions."

"And what did you learn?"

"I learned that besides bees, Marguerite Gachet keeps a goat, a tomcat, a turtle named D'Artagnan, some ducks, and an ever-expanding family of rabbits. And that Vincent van Gogh was part of her menagerie."

"You mean to say that she and the painter were intimate?"

"I won't hazard to guess what degree of intimacy they achieved, especially since her father apparently had some rather strenuous views on the subject, but I believe Vincent was dear to her. She broke down crying as she spoke of him."

"What else did she tell you?"

"At that point, unfortunately we were interrupted by the arrival of one of her father's students, one Mademoiselle Derousse."

"A medical student?"

"An art student. The doctor, like every other denizen of this enchanted hamlet, suffers from the delusion that he is a painter, worthy to train other painters. Did you know that he had drawn a postmortem portrait of Vincent?"

"What, as he lay dying?"

"As he lay dead. Mademoiselle Derousse set about making an exact copy of the thing as I stood there."

I wasn't sure what Vernet had achieved from this rather outré encounter, but he seemed to consider it quite a coup. My own revelation would trump his, I thought.

I recounted the story of my serendipitous reunion with Brunelle. Vernet listened without interruption. When I finished, he said simply, "So you're certain this Dumoulin was the forger?"

"I'm certain at least that the painting I saw this afternoon was made by the same hand that executed the fake Ingres I showed you in the Louvre."

"Then I suggest we visit chez Dumoulin forthwith."

He rose and rapped the floor with his stick. I slipped my boots back on. "Dumoulin left for the Orient on Sunday," I reminded him.

"Before or after murdering the Dutchman?"

I opened my mouth to speak, then shut it again. It was only the twinkle in his eye that made me realize he was joking. Or if not joking, at least not entirely serious.

"At any rate, he's gone," I answered.

"He left his paintings behind, I trust."

The hotel clerk was able to give us directions to Dumoulin's villa; he was a well-known figure in the village. Auvers-sur-Oise is rather vain of its painters, the successful ones at least. We made our way on foot as quickly as possible; it seemed all I could do to keep the detective from breaking into a sprint. But as we came in sight of the villa, a tall white house in the violet chokehold of clematis, he came to an abrupt halt, gazing up sourly at the sky. I urged him on, but he continued only reluctantly. "I thought we were in a hurry!" I said, impatient with his sudden despondency.

"Look at the chimney, man," he replied.

Smoke was rising from the chimney stack. On a hot July afternoon. We were too late.

Vernet rapped on the door with his stick. No answer returned. He tried the handle. It turned; we walked in. There was no light in the hall or in the shuttered parlor, but the fireplace in the kitchen glowed red, and a horrid reek stung the nostrils. There had been a great fire in the chimney; the embers were still smoldering. Every canvas, every stretcher, every sketch had been incinerated methodically in the grate. The hearthstone was littered with bent nails. There was not a scrap we could save.

We fought our way out to the street, coughing and hacking. The heavy brick-oven air felt like wine after the poisonous atmosphere inside.

"What do you make of it all, then?" I asked, once we were well away from the house and its treacherous fumes.

"I think it time we depart for Montpellier, my friend," he replied dourly.

Just when I was certain we should remain in Auvers.

# Chapter Five

W e did not leave that night, nor by the morning train. I had thought my discovery of one of the forgers had made Vernet forget about the travails of the dead painter, but the man suddenly got it in his head that we should witness the funeral. When I say witness, I don't mean that we actually attended—no, that would have been too bourgeois for Vernet. When the coffin was loaded on the hearse that afternoon, we were watching from across the square. I had thought perhaps that Vernet wanted to refrain from upsetting Van Gogh any further by his presence, but that of course was not his concern. He didn't try to conceal himself; he explained that he simply wanted to remove himself from the frame, to observe the scene without being part of it. If we were noticed, we would be noticed like the hills on the horizon or the barges on the river. A man who carried a magnifying glass with him everywhere might have realized the advantages of observing his subjects up close, but Vernet could not resist being a contrarian.

The funeral was sparsely attended. What would you expect? It is only the very old and the very young whose funerals people flock to, in genuine grief or greedy expectation. The funerals of suicides are especially avoided, out of pure embarrassment. Those who do attend want to give each other comfort, but they really want to say: *Not my fault! I did what I could. We were never that close. Not my fault, not my fault, not my fault!*

There was near a straggling score of them altogether, so far as I could see, villagers and city dwellers, most dressed somberly, yet carrying bright flowers. Sunflowers, drooping awkwardly on their tall stalks, seemed to be the preferred offering. The mourners followed the hearse up the hills to the cemetery. Dr. Gachet was weeping like a watering can, leaning on his son's shoulder. The daughter was not in attendance; I wondered what Vernet made of that. Van Gogh and his brother-in-law walked together, their faces set as if against a north wind. Others conversed in low voices, laughing sometimes, sharing memories of the dead man, perhaps. Most of them must have been painters (and not the prosperous ones) or their camp followers. I recognized old Tanguy from the paint shop among them, and, oddly enough, Mademoiselle Valadon, all in black silk like Death's *maîtresse-en-titre*. I pointed her out to Vernet; he merely nodded, unsurprised. A peasant girl, incongruous in white, trailed nonchalantly in the van, picking wildflowers. I couldn't decide whether she was one of the mourners or had simply fallen in with the crowd. She might have been the angel sent to roll back the stone from the grave, were she not embarrassingly early for such a chore. At the tail of the procession Adeline Ravoux danced with her little sister, scolded by their mother.

We kept pace with them, staying well back from the road. Vernet navigated among copses and hedges and garden walls, keeping us virtually invisible. He had a marvelous knack for moving from cover to cover, that seemed almost instinctual, like Natty Bumppo in the stories.

But we weren't the only ones shadowing the funeral. As we dodged among the tombstones in the cemetery, we caught sight of another figure standing spectral in a curtain of yew between ourselves and the mourners verging the grave. He was a big, broad-shouldered man with unkempt dark hair, dressed in a suit of dark velvet that had seen better days. Vernet moved up behind him. I hung back a step.

"You were a friend?" Vernet asked quietly.

The big man whirled around, startled. "Ah! No, monsieur. Had no idea. Just out for a stroll." He gave a wink as though he was taking us into his confidence. I had no doubt that Vernet was no more taken in by his nonchalant air than I was. This was one of the men from the train, the men who had threatened Mademoiselle Gachet.

Now that I could study his face up close, there was something that put me in mind of Mongols plundering across the steppes, scything a trail of death and destruction in their wake. Perhaps it was only the drooping black moustache and the pendant lip, or perhaps it was the eyes, slits curved like scimitars against the dazzle of the August sun.

"You live in the village?" Vernet asked him idly.

"God, no, Paris. Just up here for the day. A little country air. Who was he?" He nodded toward the funeral.

"A painter named Van Gogh. No one you would have heard of. You're a painter yourself, though."

"What put that in your head? I'm a stockbroker." He extended his hand to shake. "Name's Schuffenecker. You?"

Vernet took his hand and turned his wrist. "Tell me, Monsieur Schuffenecker, how does a stockbroker get flecks of cadmium yellow and Prussian blue on his sleeve?"

The other man snatched back his hand, then chuckled, trying to make light of it. "You one of those carnival palm readers?" He lodged a cigarette in the corner of his mouth, and struck a match. "Guess my weight?"

"By your gait, I would say you were a sailor for a time, and by your wrist I'd say you were a fencer." Schuffenecker dropped the match in the grass and stared, as if he had seen the devil in Vernet's eyes. Vernet stepped toward him and stamped out the flame.

Schuffenecker returned the cigarette to his pocket. "Found me out. Good eye. It's true, I'm a weekend painter. Just a few daubs. Nothing like that fellow."

"You've seen his work?"

"Should I?"

A wail rose up from the gravesite. Dr. Gachet had been stumbling through a maudlin eulogy, but had become so overcome with emotion or drink that he had to be led away. They began lowering the coffin into the grave, a chancy proposition without the help of a proper church sexton. The girl in white strayed toward us from the crowd, in pursuit of a flock of purple gentian. Schuffenecker took the opportunity to doff his hat and back away. Vernet did not attempt to detain him.

We could hear the sough of the spades. "Shall we go pay our respects to Van Gogh?" I asked.

"No need. He is coming to us." Indeed, the Dutchman had broken away from the group he was talking to and was coming to meet us. I blenched to think what Vernet might say to the man this time.

But Vernet rose to the occasion with unlooked-for grace. "Monsieur, let me offer my profoundest sympathy. Your brother's paintings affect me deeply. I wish I had known the man," he said simply, taking Van Gogh's hand. I offered my sympathies as well, in more conventional tones.

Van Gogh cast his eyes to the ground. "Monsieur Vernet, you appear to have made a few acquaintances among my friends. They tell me that you may not be what you seem. That you're in fact a detective of some kind."

I had no doubt it was Mademoiselle Valadon who had put that flea in his ear.

Vernet was unruffled by his unmasking. "I represent a consortium that has certain interests in the Parisian art world, and suspects those interests may be threatened by a criminal conspiracy."

"And you believe my brother was involved?"

"I believe your brother was no suicide. Whether his death has any connection to my investigation, I cannot venture to say. But I am not a great believer in coincidence."

Van Gogh had approached us with something particular to say, and now decided to say it. I prepared for a tongue-lashing. "My brother once said that to commit suicide was to turn one's friends into murderers. I am no murderer, messieurs. Please, do what you can to discover the truth. If I can be of any assistance, don't hesitate to call on me."

Needless to say, it was not what I had expected. He turned away, suddenly shy, and retreated to the safety of the crowd. I started to register my surprise, but Vernet put a finger to his lips. He led me away, taking another road, and we were soon walking among the beeches and the drowning willows down by the river, taking a half hour's holiday from the world. One question nagged at me.

"Did you mean what you said?" I asked Vernet. "About Vincent's paintings?"

"I did. But I have been told by experts that my taste in art is execrable." He chuckled at some private memory.

"Yes? And how do your tastes tend?"

"I'm fond of the Belgian moderns. Karel Ooms. Jan Verhas. My friend Du Maurier introduced me to their work a few years ago, and I was smitten."

Verhas! A man who'd made his name painting portraits of the apple-cheeked children of the petite bourgeoisie. I tried to picture this man, whose daily work was blood and depredation, passing his hours in front of *Children Blowing Bubbles*. The idea was so grotesque as to be laughable. I recommended Constantin Meunier, another Belgian, to him; he promised to acquaint himself.

We left Auvers on the afternoon train and stayed the night in Paris. The detective had some mysterious business to see to there, which he did not invite me to join in. I opted for dinner with some German friends, whom I hadn't seen in years, not since our old days at the court of Prince Frederick. I tried to dismiss Vernet's investigations from my mind for a few hours; I failed miserably. I found myself paying attention to the minutest details of my surroundings, the waiter's fingernails, the weave of the tablecloth, the drape of my friends' dinner jackets, as if the world were a problematic canvas. Though my dinner companions, both members of the German diplomatic corps, had moved to Paris shortly after the fall of the Commune twenty years earlier, they spoke of nothing but Germany, the shocking fall of the Iron Chancellor, the surprising pick of Caprivi as his successor, and the inevitability of his failure. Since we were dining in the Brebant, at the base of Eiffel's iron tower, and none of us had visited Germany in years, it was the idlest speculation. The saddle of lamb was uninspired. The conversation turned awkward when they asked me what business had brought me to Paris. I sated their curiosity by telling them I had been called in to authenticate some paintings in a collection. I omitted to mention that the collection was the Louvre.

Every time I closed my eyes, I saw the face of the dying Dutchman, every pause in the conversation whispered the enigmatic name "Olympia." I wanted to ask them if they'd ever known a man who'd shot himself. Self-destruction was not so rare, especially in Germans of a certain class, that it would have shocked either of them. If a man wanted to shoot himself, Vernet had said, he'd put the gun to his temple, or his mouth. He might even shoot himself in the heart; cast-off lovers often did. But it should be obvious to anyone that to shoot oneself in the abdomen would be extremely painful, without necessarily leading to the desired result. For a right-handed man to shoot himself in the left side would be absurdly awkward. And then the path of the bullet had showed a downward trajectory. Vincent had been shot from above. Perhaps he had been on his knees in front of his executioner? And the fact that the bullet had not gone through could only mean the shot had been fired from a distance. Only a foot away perhaps, but how does a man shoot himself from a foot away, and from above? Or perhaps it was perfectly possible, for all I knew. I had learned human anatomy from Da Vinci and Raphael, not Galen or Vesalius.

I might not have been so fractious had I been able to pose my questions to Vernet, but he had been singularly uncommunicative in the train, warning me repeatedly against forming theories in advance of data. I agreed it was a reasonable admonition in the forgery case; there was a great deal more to learn from the consortium in Montpellier. But the mystery of the painter's death had begun to prey upon my mind. Had we left a killer behind us in Auvers? Might he kill again? Vernet seemed entirely indifferent.

Next day at break of dawn we were boarding the train at Gare de Lyon for the south. I was bleary-eyed after too late a night and too much Bénédictine, but the detective appeared buttoned down and eager for the journey. We would not arrive in Montpellier until late morning of the following day. I had convinced Vernet to book us berths on a Wagon-Lits coach, and let his cousin, Monsieur Lecomte, foot the bill. I don't think the luxury appealed to him per se, a man so careless of his own comforts, but the chance to annoy his cousin most certainly did. I expected to recoup my rest during an uneventful journey.

It was not to be.

It happened as I was returning to my sleeper after lunch, anticipating a nap. I noticed the door was ajar. I assumed the porter was inside, putting things in order. As I pushed the door open, powerful arms pushed back, sending me flying across the passage. The door was flung open and a stranger erupted into the corridor. I had but a moment to capture his features: short and stout, moon-faced, with a shock of fair hair and muttonchops—the other ogre from the Auvers train! He was hugging my Gladstone to his chest. I grabbed for it, spilling some of its contents yet again, but he drove a fist into my sternum, slamming me back against the partition wall. I must have cried out; Vernet appeared in the doorway of his own compartment, just down the passage. He took it in at once: me gasping for breath, the drawings on the floor, the intruder's wild eyes flashing between us. Then the intruder was on the run with my bag, Vernet flying past me in pursuit. One after the other they slammed through the door at the end of the carriage. I hobbled after them, wheezing like a bellows.

I pursued them through one carriage after another, stopping at whiles to reach down and retrieve some of my sketches the thief had let drop in his wake. I arrived at the luggage van just as the far door slammed. I made my way dodging among steamer trunks and stacks of crates that swayed and threatened to spill on top of me with the rocking of the train. I opened the far door.

Vernet stood on the observation platform, leaning against the rail, his pipe clenched between his teeth. Schuffenecker lit a match with a steady hand, shielding it from the wind, and helped the detective to a light. They might have been two old Etonians lounging in the foyer of a Pall Mall club.

"Ah! Dr. Lermolieff! You remember our acquaintance from Auvers, Monsieur Schuffenecker?"

It was a small platform with the three of us standing there. There was not an inch of concealment. The thief had vanished with my drawings. I saw pages flying in the wind behind the train. I nodded dumbly toward the Frenchman.

"You cut short your stay in the country?" Vernet asked pleasantly.

"Business called me away." Schuffenecker was not a man of elaborate explanations.

"One of your Parisian clients?"

"Toulouse. An elderly countess who requires the personal touch."

The train gave a sudden jerk. Vernet stumbled against Schuffenecker, then righted himself. The broker patted his coat with a look of dismay.

"Some clients are easily alarmed by sudden shifts in the market," Vernet remarked pleasantly.

There was more desultory conversation about the journey, about the weather, about nothing at all. Yet harmless as it all seemed, I had the feeling of watching two bare-knuckle brawlers trading body blows, till they were at an impasse. Silence overcame us, save for the clicking of the wheels and the buffeting of the wind. After a decent interval, Schuffenecker made his excuses and retreated back inside the train.

"Vernet!" I burst forth, as soon as we had seen his back. "What happened to the thief? How did he elude us?"

"He didn't. I followed him to the end of the train. But he had already disembarked."

I looked at the steep embankment along which we were thundering. "He threw himself from the train?" I asked in horror.

"Was thrown, more likely. Schuffenecker is a man of quick decision and ruthless application."

We were thundering along at nearly fifty miles an hour. A fall like that could break a man's neck.

"You think they were in league together?"

"I'm certain of it. They were the two men who visited Mademoiselle Gachet. And I extracted this item from Schuffenecker's lapel pocket."

He handed me a diary, the very diary this account is taken from. It had resided in the bag with my sketches. I seized it eagerly.

"You'd have made quite the Artful Dodger," I said, admiringly. But then I was stricken by a terrible realization. "All my drawings, all my documentation—gone! I have nothing to show the consortium."

"A bad business that," Vernet agreed with perfect equanimity. "But your conclusions are more important than your proofs, which would hardly be admissible as evidence before a magistrate. And the fact that someone felt it necessary to purloin those proofs validates them."

His points were logical as always, but cold comfort. I pointed out the forced lock of my compartment to the porter, who brought in the conductor to adjudicate, who in turn practically accused me of breaking down the door myself, before finally giving in and moving me to another compartment. I bolted the door on the inside and dragged my trunk across the door as a barricade in case there were more attackers lying in wait. Then I composed myself for my long-delayed nap. And found myself wide awake.

I don't think I'm a physical coward. I have done my service in the military. But the cloistered world of galleries and museums affords one little chance to test one's mettle. I hadn't expected to risk life and limb in this enterprise, even when the possibility of murder had been introduced into the equation. I considered my wife and children, and my responsibilities to them. Was this playacting at being a detective not a betrayal of their trust? Once I had delivered my report to the consortium—and what a fiasco that would be, now that I had been robbed of my studies!—I would return home to my family, no matter what questions remained unanswered. I tossed and turned through the night, wrestling with my decision. The miles clicked by in the dark.

By early next morning, we had truly arrived in the south, the shimmering valley of the Rhône, in which each blue atom of the sky jostles against the one next to it. But with the south came also the mistral, the furious wind that blows from the mountains to the sea. It's a rare occurrence in the summer months, so our attendant in the dining car told us, but all the more dangerous for that; it withers the crops and can turn the spark of a wagon wheel on paving stone into a raging fire. But watching the wind slam doors shut and spin the dust of the street into cyclones was oddly exhilarating, as though there were devils in the air. When the train stopped in the town of Arles to refuel, we learned we had an hour's delay. Vernet suggested we get out and do battle with the elements. I was tired of the stale air in the compartment, and readily agreed.

I rued the decision almost immediately upon disembarking. The wind howled at us, slapping our faces red and raw. There were women in the streets moving side to side in a slow ballet, sprinkling water on the cobbles to keep down the dust, the wind playing mischief with the hems of their skirts; all they effected was to turn the dust into spiraling sprays of mud.

Across the road the station café beckoned. I put my head down and bulled my way toward it. Then I realized Vernet was not with me. I turned around; he was standing in the middle of the street, oblivious to the elements, staring up at the tobacco shop next to the café, his coat flapping about him. A perfectly ordinary shop, painted bright yellow with a green door. The shutters were locked; it was too early for business. I called out, but my words were thrown back at me by the wind. I gestured emphatically toward the café and pushed toward it. Damn the man anyway.

I tripped over the threshold into the café, cutting a slice out of the early-morning silence. An old billiard table commandeered the center of the room, the baize worn down to the slate. It was flanked by a dozen granite-top tables. One of last night's patrons was passed out facedown at a table near the door, with the reek of vomit rising from him. A small bar stood at the far end of the room beneath an old station-clock; its drip-drop tick-tock was the only answer to my call of good morning. Next to it stood a potbelly oven, a battered pot of coffee on top sending up a curl of steam. Eventually I heard slippered feet on the stair, and the café owner, as I assumed he must be, appeared in the doorway.

He was a small man with thinning black hair, watchful eyes, and a face coarse as a slab of beef. He was holding his boots in one hand; perhaps he feared to wake the house. He said nothing, but looked at me askance. There was that look in his eye, common to southerners, as though poised between taking the stranger into his heart or stabbing him in the ribs.

"Coffee, please," I said, and then added, "and a brandy." The mistral gets into one's bones.

The owner seemed in no particular hurry to accommodate me, but in due course coffee and brandy were set before me. The coffee had probably been on the stove since the night before, and the brandy had the distinct taste of kerosene, but I was grateful nonetheless. I squinted up at the bottles behind the bar, coated with the dust of centuries.

A painting on the wall above the bar caught my eye, an unframed portrait of a man, almost hidden behind the bottles. I don't know how long I stared at it. I must have set the coffee down and made my way to the street door and outside. I cast my gaze up and down the street, the wind starting tears in my eyes. Where had he gone? That greengrocer's? The police station with the tricolor whipping wildly out front? Back to the railway terminal?

The café owner was at my elbow, with a heavy hand on my arm. "Monsieur, you owe for your—" Then he stopped dead. "Who's got in?" he cried.

The door of the tobacconist's shop stood ajar. The café owner brushed past me and plunged inside. I followed him, already sure of what he would find.

The shop was empty. One of the shutters had been opened, stamping the red flagstone floor with a bar of yellow light. We heard a noise from the room above our heads. I followed the owner back out to the hall and up the stairs. I nearly ran over his back when he stopped short at the top.

There was a large room given over to storage, and a small kitchen off to the side, like an afterthought. Vernet had opened the shutters here, too, and shoved chests and crates away from the western wall. He was crouched on the floor, peering at something through his magnifying glass. There was a faded Japanese poster on the wall above his head, a geisha holding a fan before her face like a shield. A dull brown stain spattered the wall below it.

"Monsieur, this is private property! You cannot—"

Vernet held up a hand, silencing the man. "This was his studio? Where he painted?"

There was that imperative in his voice that made the café owner answer his question, rather than demand his own answers.

"Vincent, you mean? Yes. He always said the southern light was worth the fifteen francs."

Vernet had known the answer to the question before he asked. Theo van Gogh must have told him. A yellow house with green shutters on the Place Lamartine, across from the station, he must have said, adjacent to the park, and Vernet filed away the information in the cabinet of his memory. He hadn't been gazing out at the scenery as we pulled into the station—he'd been watching for the yellow house. He'd seized the opportunity to search it. He wasn't stretching his legs, or taking in the fresh air—who but a fool would think of such a thing in the middle of the mistral? He was plotting, he was questioning, he was hunting. I had misjudged him, his intent and his intelligence both. He had never abandoned his obsession with the painter's murder.

"Look here," he said to me, handing me the magnifying glass. I squinted through the lens at the floorboards, just as I had seen him doing, but I saw nothing.

"As plain as if it all occurred yesterday!" he said, exulting. "The bloody trail leads down the stairs to the shop. He had his bedroom down there?" he asked the café owner. The man nodded, mystified, outraged, fascinated.

It came into focus for me, a few flecks of brown across the floor. It could have been anything, as far as I was concerned. But if any man knew a trail of blood when he saw it, however old or faded, that man would be Vernet.

"Of course, it's more difficult to pick out on the tile downstairs, but I'm sure you observed there was no blood by the window. Nor in the foyer by the door."

I nodded as if agreeing, though I had observed nothing of the kind. Who could observe something that wasn't there?

"You're police?" the café owner asked.

I shook my head.

"Friends of Vincent? How is the old fellow?"

Vernet turned his attention to the man. "You're Ginoux?"

"Joseph Ginoux, yes, monsieur."

I found my voice at last. "There's something else you must see," I told Vernet.

He took a last look through the window, out upon the park next to the station, the cypress trees bent double like old pensioners, mastered by the wind. He nodded, closing the shutters. "We've seen enough here."

We all went down. Ginoux lingered at the street door, examining the lock carefully, trying to discover how Vernet had got in without leaving so much as a scratch. We left him to it and retreated to the café. I didn't know how to preface my discovery to Vernet: I merely pointed up at the picture behind the bar.

"Ah!" he said, greatly pleased. He strode up to the painting as if to interrogate it. The subject of the painting spied on us from heavy-lidded eyes beneath a stormy brow. The heavy moustache bracketed a concupiscent mouth. The background was an incongruous bright yellow—Vincent's yellow, studded with white flowers.

"I see, yes. A fine likeness, Monsieur Ginoux!"

Ginoux, who had come in behind us, eyed Vernet as if he were unhinged.

"That was his pal," he sneered.

"His pal?" Here was a clue it seemed Vernet had not anticipated.

"Vincent. That's his pal. Vincent's a fine fellow. Give you the shirt off his back. Not that he had anything besides the shirt on his back. His pal—" Ginoux spat on the floor.

"Then why do you keep the painting on the wall?"

Ginoux waved his hands in surrender. "Wife won't let me take it down. Vincent put it up there, so we'd know him when he came in on the train. I should've sent him packing as soon as he got here."

At the sound of our voices, Ginoux's wife poked her head out of the back room and immediately set about berating her husband for not offering his guests anything. She was a woman of fine Roman profile, with dark hair piled high on her head and the shoulders of a stevedore. We bowed to her, a tribute she accepted like a duchess. We fended off her offer of wine and stuck to brandy. When Vernet attempted to pay, Ginoux refused his money. "Friends of Vincent pay nothing!" he insisted.

Madame Ginoux was immediately on her guard. "Friends of Vincent? Who says so?"

"Madame Ginoux, my name is Vernet. I regret I am the bearer of bad news. Vincent van Gogh is dead."

The reaction was not as I expected. It was Monsieur Ginoux, not his wife, who broke out in great sobs, covered his eyes with his apron and retreated to the back room. Madame Ginoux took the news as calmly as a general on the battlefield.

"You had already received this news," said Vernet, appraising her.

She nodded. "Monsieur Theo wrote us. I didn't know how to tell my husband. He was fond of Vincent, you see."

"I'm sorry to have intruded. If I may ask, madame—Monsieur Schuffenecker sat for Vincent? They were acquaintances?"

"You ask me? Who is this Schuffenecker?"

Vernet pointed to the painting. "Monsieur Schuffenecker. Well captured, if rather crude."

"Shuff—? No, monsieur. That's Vincent's pal. Gauguin. Half man, half wild Indian. All devil."

Vernet's eyes narrowed, like a hunter sighting his prey. "Forgive my mistake, madame. So that is Paul Gauguin, the painter who shared the house next door with Vincent?"

"They used to tramp all around the town like peddlers, with their easels on their backs. There was never any trouble till he came."

"Yet you keep his portrait on your wall."

"In case he comes back. The girl who works here in the evening has never seen him in person."

"Why would he come back?"

"Things he left behind. Some clothes. His swords."

"His swords?" Vernet's face lit up, as though a sword-fighting painter were the exact beast he needed to complete his menagerie. "Monsieur Gauguin is a fencer?"

I was about to remind him that he himself had informed me of this fact, but a look from Vernet silenced me.

"So he claims. He tried to teach Vincent a few times, right out there in the square. I thought sure they'd kill each other."

"And yet he left his blades behind? Curiouser and curiouser. I'm something of a fencer myself, madame. Might I have a look?"

Madame Ginoux called for her husband to bring the swords. After a few minutes he shuffled in with a long case of some dark wood in his arms. He had dried his eyes, and though there was a great deal of snuffling, he seemed to have got rein of his emotions. He set the case on our table and popped the latches, revealing a pair of French naval sabers—shorter than rapiers, and thus more dangerous in a duel—slightly curved, with ornate baskets that suggested Spanish make. "He was a sailor once, or so he claimed," Madame Ginoux explained, unwilling to place a grain of faith in anything Gauguin had told her. Vernet lifted out one of the sabers, examined it, swung it in his grip, and made a few swift passes. "A good blade," he said, "and keen as the north wind. But what's this?" He picked up the second saber and sighted along the length of the blade. Then he sliced the air before me, nearly trimming an inch of my beard. I hopped back in a panic, nearly losing my balance.

"It looks as if it had indeed led to bloodshed," he observed.

With the sword point quivering under my nostrils, I could see what he meant. I could almost smell it. There was dried blood all along the edge.

"Here, if you're a swordsman, why don't you take them?" said Ginoux. "We don't want the damn things, and we don't want him coming back for them, either."

"Perhaps you could send them to Theo van Gogh for me. Ask him to hold them till I come to Paris."

The Ginouxs were amenable to the suggestion, and even more so to the gold Napoleon Vernet dropped in Madame Ginoux's palm. We poked our heads out the front of the café. The mistral was still knocking on every door like the police in the night. Vernet consulted his watch.

"Our train departs in ten minutes. We can be in Montpellier by lunchtime. Or . . . we could spend the day taking in the sights of Arles. There are some spectacular Roman ruins, I've been told." This was said with a conspiratorial smile, as though he were inviting me to a gambling hell or a high-priced brothel. He stepped into the street with the jaunt of the pied piper. I followed. Deliver me from temptation.

Halfway across the street all my doubts returned, redoubled. I grabbed him by the tail of his coat, shouting in his ear. "What are we looking for?"

The wind swallowed up my words again. Vernet pulled me into a fruit stall. We crouched behind a table full of figs, somewhat out of the gale. He spoke as if we were seated in front of a fire in his study.

"Our problem hinges on the question of whether Vincent was mad or sane. If he was mad, then we can accept the improbability of his suicide, laying the bulk of his misfortunes at the door of the asylum. We can posit that he shot himself, ignoring any evidence to the contrary. But if he was sane, then we must re-examine every event with a skeptic's eye. Did he have incriminating information about the works of your forger Dumoulin? Or this fellow Gauguin? The tale of madness begins on the night Vincent hacked off his own earlobe. If we go back to that night and review the evidence—"

"But how? It was almost two years ago. Where do we even begin?"

"With the evidence of the blood trail, which I had hoped against hope to find. According to his brother's account, Vincent seized a razor from the washstand, and slashed at his ear, severing it in two. Then, bleeding all the way, he carried the ear out the door and down the street to his ladylove at the Maison du Tolerance. But what do we see instead? The trail of blood?"

"Leads from his bedroom up to the studio," I said, beginning to follow the labyrinth of his logic.

"Say rather that it leads from the studio to the bedroom. Remember the blood spattered on the wall? That was where the injury was accomplished. Then he goes downstairs, lies down on the bed, wraps himself up in the bedclothes, and presumably loses consciousness."

I looked up toward the attic room. Behind the shutters, two men stationed at their easels, furnished not with brushes and palettes, but the sabers Ginoux had shown us. One challenging, threatening, offering the point of his blade, the other refusing to take the bait, or offer more than the most perfunctory defense. Is it cowardice, or a refusal to be bullied? Does he lower his head like the dying bull? Is the offer of his bared neck too tempting for the Tatar to refuse? Is the pass meant merely to cut the air? Or cut his throat? But then the sudden spurt of blood brings them both back to earth. They drop their blades. One runs out into the night, seized with guilt or shame or panic, the other with no more aim than to stanch the flow of blood and keep the shameful secret.

"But he took the ear to the prostitute!" I said.

"That contention is yet to be proved."

"Do we attempt to follow the blood trail down the street?"

"Let us turn our attention to the paper trail instead."

He nodded toward another door, just a little way down the street. The tricolor danced in the wind outside a brick façade with mullioned windows. The brass plaque on the door discretely announced a police station, as though only meant for a select few.

He plunged into the road. I followed, and then stopped again in the middle of the street. "Our luggage?" I roared against the wind.

He pointed west. "Sent on!"

Of course, he had already arranged it. Vernet was the puppet master, I the puppet.

# Chapter Six

The police station was dark and smelled of mold, the paint peeling from the walls. The anteroom presented a tall counter like a pulpit, with a fat yellowed ledger and a dry inkwell. A long, stanchioned barrier divided the room, suggesting that it was better to be behind the barrier than before it. There was a bench along the front wall and a few dusty file cabinets standing at crooked attention to the side. A gendarme, unshaved, with his tunic open at the throat, stood over an open drawer at one of the cabinets, smoking a cigarette, leafing through files, ostentatiously ignoring us.

"Good morning, officer!" Vernet trumpeted.

The man's look seemed to contest the proposition. He didn't return the greeting.

"We need to speak with someone about an incident that occurred here some months back, involving an alien named Van Gogh," Vernet continued, undeterred.

The gendarme cast a sidelong glance at us. "Vincent? The crazy Dutchman? We get all kinds around here. What's he done now?"

"He's been murdered."

The gendarme took a long drag on his cigarette. "Small loss. Is that what you came to tell us?"

Vernet was not a man of volatile temperament. Still I could see that this impudent officer was working his nerves. "Perhaps if I could speak to your superior?"

"Chief doesn't see people this early. Who are you, anyway? Haven't seen you before, have I?"

"My name is Vernet. Tell your chief that I am a detective working with Monsieur Goron of the Sûreté on a matter of national importance. I wish to speak with him—*now*."

The name Goron was unfamiliar to me, but it acted as a magic talisman on the gendarme. He dropped the file back in its slot, slammed the drawer shut, and disappeared through the door into the back office, with only a sidelong squint at us before he went. We waited.

The bench had been polished by the backsides of every ne'er-do-well in Arles. It was nevertheless beginning to look inviting by the time the door opened again, and a second gendarme gestured us inside. "Messieurs, if you'll step this way, please?"

This officer was as different from the first as chalk from cheese. His uniform was spotless, his eyes bright, his moustache constructed like a Euclidean proof. He led us through the common room, that held a half-dozen desks, only one of which was occupied. The first gendarme sat there with his chin in his hands, dreaming perhaps of supercriminals savvy enough to match his colossal wits. There was a row of cells along the back, too shadowed in the early morning to see if they held any prisoners. Our Virgil brought us to a side door, and knocked.

"Enter!" rumbled a voice, in a Corsican accent.

"Leave the door open, Auguste," the voice continued as we entered. Our man bowed stiffly and went off to pursue his duties with an avidity no doubt equal and opposite to his fellow officer's glum inertia.

"Gentlemen! I'm d'Ornano, chief of police." He rose to greet us, but did not offer his hand. We recognized this not as a lack of manners but an accession to practicality. Our hands would not have met across the vastness of his desk.

Chief of police d'Ornano was a little brown dumpling of a man, barely five feet tall and nearly as broad. There were crumbs from breakfast upon his cheek. An empty plate and a firkin of butter on his desk stood testament to his minute attention to business—of a kind, at least. Having exercised as much courtesy as was physically possible, he sat down again and took a swig of coffee. He was hedged in on either side by stacks of files in buff folders; either he was a very busy man or he couldn't reach the drawers to file them.

"Chief Goron sent you?" he asked. He waved to a pair of cane chairs in front of the desk, directing us to sit. We complied with the best grace possible.

"We're assisting the Sûreté with an investigation," answered Vernet. It was another lie, so far as I knew. Vernet held no brief for the truth when a lie would suit his purpose better. We introduced ourselves, using our noms de guerre.

"And you want information on"—he wiped the crumbs from his mouth with his sleeve and glanced down at the file Auguste had laid before him—"Vincent van Gogh."

"You recall the incident?" asked Vernet.

D'Ornano barked, "Do I remember Van Gogh? Vincent? I'm not likely to forget him or that bastard Gauguin. When I first laid eyes on them, I said to Auguste—"

He called out to the unseen officer: "Remember, Auguste? I said one would end up in the nuthouse and the other one be hanged?"

"Yes, monsieur!" rang out the reply from the outer office.

"Why did you think so, monsieur?" asked Vernet.

"Gauguin was one of those insinuating devils that dare you to craziness. Vincent was just the kind to let him get under his skin. I said so, didn't I, Auguste?"

"Yes, monsieur!"

"Now Vincent's locked up over in St. Remy, and unless I'm an idiot, you're Paris cops here after Gauguin."

We neither of us felt it necessary to correct the police chief.

"See, you can't fool d'Ornano. It's about Christmas Eve? Two years ago, thereabouts?"

"The night Van Gogh mutilated his ear?"

"That's a good word for it, eh, Auguste?"

"Yes, monsieur!"

"Sliced the damn thing off, flush with the head, then brought it to the girl at Number One, wrapped up like yesterday's fish. What was her name?" he muttered to himself, scanning the file.

"Flush with the head? You're saying that Van Gogh cut the entire ear off?" Vernet and I shared a look of misdoubt.

The inspector produced a pair of wire-rimmed spectacles with thick lenses from his coat pocket and settled them on his nose. He scanned the file again. "Gaby! That's her name." He whipped off the spectacles and looked up at us. "If you told me Gauguin did the actual cutting, I'd not be surprised, the way he used to switch around the square with that cavalry saber. But Vincent would never lodge a complaint against his pal. I've seen it before. He was the corporal, Gauguin was the captain."

"You observed this ear yourself, monsieur?"

"The ear?" He appeared irritated that Vernet kept coming back to it. "I saw it, Auguste saw it. You want to see it yourselves?"

"You *have* the ear?" Vernet was utterly confounded.

"Got the undertaker to pickle it for evidence. Scares the urchins out of their wits. 'You want to wind up like this devil?'" He laughed immoderately. "Auguste, bring the ear, eh?"

Presently the fastidious Auguste entered with a gallon jar in his gloved hands and set it before us on the desk with an apologetic air. The ear floated in a murk of formaldehyde. We stared at it in stunned silence.

"The ear of the Dutchman! Bring me Gauguin's head, I'll have the set." If d'Ornano expected general mirth, he was disappointed. I closed my eyes, envisioning Vincent once again on his deathbed. The mangled left ear, missing the lower lobe. But not this, not this!

"Monsieur, you might rethink your methods of evidentiary collection," Vernet said flatly.

"Or your choice of profession," I added, hoping it would sting.

"I tell you, he was bleeding like a stuck pig!" d'Ornano retorted, belligerent. "They had to haul him off to the hospital, raving!"

We rose together. Vernet turned away without a word. "Good morning, monsieur," I mumbled. "Thank you for your assistance."

"Well, whose ear do you think it is? We don't have a surplus to go around!" d'Ornano spluttered.

The immaculate Auguste ushered us out. As we readied ourselves for the tempest of the street, he eyed Vernet narrowly.

"Monsieur . . . Vernet, you said your name was, sir?"

"I said so, yes. Was there something you wanted to tell me, monsieur?"

It seemed that the officer indeed had something on his mind, but he merely smiled in self-deprecating fashion, and shook his head. "Enjoy your stay in Arles, monsieur. I hope you find everything you are looking for." He favored me with another of his searching stares. "And you, too, Doctor."

I supposed we were done, but Auguste had one more thought to convey. He touched Vernet on the shoulder. "You'll want to find the Maison du Tolerance No. 1. It's in the Rue Recollet. Ask for Madame Chabaud."

Vernet looked at the man with fresh eyes. "You're a man of some perception, Monsieur Auguste. Thank you."

Auguste saluted crisply.

If it was early in the morning for cafés and police stations, the street of "tolerance" might as well have been a mausoleum. Still Vernet persisted, banging at the door of Maison No. 1 till curses were flung from windows up and down the street. Finally, a pair of shutters opened above us, and a blowsy girl wrapped in a bedsheet looked out, yawning.

"Go home, idiots! We're closed!" she yelled.

"Police business! We're here to see Madame Chabaud!" Vernet called back.

She looked down on us with a jaundiced eye, but a girl in her profession knows she cannot take chances with the law, whatever her suspicions. She tied up her hair behind her and disappeared from the window.

A few minutes later we heard the bolts being drawn back, and saw the beak of a sallow little bird pushed out of the crack in the door. He was still strapping on his braces over an undershirt. "Police?" he asked. This was the sentry—hardly an imposing figure. He obviously wanted to demand our papers, but he hadn't the courage to go eye to eye with Vernet, who had assumed the face of outraged authority. Since we gave no answer, he could only let us in or bar the door. He chose the more prudent course, leading us down a dark hall ripe with the odor of venery to a frowsty little parlor, where he deposited us.

The parlor was obviously Madame Chabaud's sanctum, languid with thinning damask drapes and moldy Persian carpets. There was a striped chaise longue for the lady, and a horsehair sofa with broken springs and sprouted stuffing for her admirers, which we first attempted and then avoided.

Once again we waited for an unconscionable time, but women cannot be hurried, and women of Madame Chabaud's profession gather a certain gravity about themselves that makes them ponderous and slow to move, like a barge in a canal. When she entered, it was with an appearance of dishabille, as though she had risen fresh from her couch only a moment before, and thrown on the peignoir and mules that she wore. She carried a tortoiseshell brush in one hand, as though to intimate that she had just raked it through her Titian locks. But it was all no more than art. She held out her hand; I kissed it reflexively. Vernet declined to follow my lead.

"You're not the local police," she said, deciding to address herself to me.

"Neither local nor police, as I'm sure you've guessed, madame," said Vernet.

She tossed her head. "You told Marius you were police."

"I told him we were here on police business. We are private detectives on the track of a man named Vincent van Gogh."

Her brows lifted in surprise. "Vincent, the Dutchman? A monster!" She prostrated herself on the chaise, the very figure of the Divine Sarah, plus about twenty pounds. "Won't you sit, gentlemen?"

We would not. Vernet moved about behind her so that she had to twist her neck to see him. The extra effort was irksome to her.

"A monster?" asked Vernet. "Was his behavior so odious? Did he abuse your girls?"

"Oh, no, hardly that. He was such a shy fellow he could barely raise his eyes to them, and whenever he heard a ribald story he would blush to his fingertips. Not at all like that brute, his friend."

"Gauguin? The stockbroker?"

"Stockbroker? Beggar, you mean. He tried to pay my girls in paintings!" She was still scandalized by the enormity of such an affront.

"Then why do you call Vincent the monster?"

She sat up straight, abandoning her pose, and took a pinch of snuff from a box on the table. "Haven't you heard about that thing with the ear? Well, there you are! Who but a monster would do such a thing! Poor Gaby nearly jumped out of her skin when she saw the thing."

"He must have been a spectacle himself."

"I'm sure he must have been." She began to brush her hair absent-mindedly.

"You didn't see him yourself?"

"Oh, no, he never came inside. Gave it to Marius to give to Rachel. Wanted her to 'take care of it,' he said. A keepsake!"

"I thought you said the girl's name was Gaby."

"Marius gave it to Gaby to take to Rachel. Gaby's the girl who tidies up after the *michetons* have finished. It was wrapped in a hanky. I think she was a little jealous. She got too curious. Serves her right."

"May we speak to the girl?"

"Long gone. Once she got her name in the papers, everyone thought the same as you, that she was a *fille soumise*. Her whole lousy family considered themselves dishonored. They packed up their rags and moved away."

"What about the other girl—Rachel?"

"She never saw the thing at all. Didn't even hear about it till the next day. Rachel stays busy."

"Was this Rachel a favorite of Vincent's?"

"Him and his friend both. Mad about her. Skip a week's worth of dinners to spend an hour with her. I'm surprised they didn't throttle each other."

"Might I see the girl, madame?"

"I told you, she never saw a thing. The police took the ear away that very night, as if it were a prize from the bullring. Men!"

"It's not necessary that I speak with her. I only wish to see her for a moment."

"Well . . ." A sly little smile edged into the woman's face. "If that's how you indulge yourself . . ." She picked up the bell from the table and rang. The sentry Marius appeared again, having only strapped on one of his braces so far.

"Tell Rachel to come down. Tell her not to dawdle, you hear?"

Rachel was not a woman of gravity. She came pattering down the stairs in short order, breathless, dressed only in a transparent shift, her bare feet blue from the cold floors. She was a tall thin girl, her unbound blonde hair streaming down her back, her skin pale as moonlight.

Vernet inspected her briefly. "Your hair, mademoiselle." He gestured piling imaginary hair up on the back of his head. She nodded and followed suit, baring a shapely neck.

"Yes."

"Yes?" Madame Chabaud was ready to do business.

"No."

With that word he was finished with the girl. The madame looked rattled, but she waved the girl away. Before I could tear my eyes from her retreating figure, he was already making our farewells to Madame Chabaud. She rang the bell and Marius came trotting in once again to see us out.

"Marius, the night Vincent brought you his ear . . ." Vernet hinted as we followed the sentry to the door.

Marius seemed to be searching his memory, as if body parts were delivered to the establishment on a regular basis. Perhaps they were. In the south, violence always seems as much a matter of art as of temperament.

"Oh, yeah, the ear," he said dully.

"The man must have been covered in blood. You didn't think to call the police as soon as you saw how he had wounded himself?"

"Never saw him."

"You said Vincent brought you the ear."

Marius stopped to glare at him. "No, you said that. The boy brought the ear. Said it was for Rachel from Vincent. It was wrapped up in a rag. Never saw him, never saw the ear."

"The boy?" I asked.

"Poulet. Used to run errands for them. A bit soft in the head. But then they all were, weren't they?" He snorted and snapped his braces.

That was enough conversation for the less-than-loquacious Marius. He blew his nose in his hand and saw us out, retreating into the echoing emptiness of the brothel.

Vernet had one more stop marked on his itinerary: the Hotel-Dieu, the hospital where Vincent had been brought after he was found Christmas Eve morning, lying in his bed, wadded in bloodstained sheets. We put the river on our right and turned our steps to the south. It was only a fifteen-minute walk, but the constant harrying by the wind made it feel like a day's trek.

The great stone walls flanking the Hotel-Dieu lacked only watch towers at the corners to evoke a medieval fortification, but once we passed under the Greek pediment at the front, we were rewarded with a view of wide galleries on three sides, surrounding a bright, shaggy garden with a fountain burbling at its center. It was so wild and so calm at once that I couldn't help the notion springing to my mind: what an ideal scene for Vincent to paint!

Then my scalp prickled. Bobbing among the flowers were minatory slashes of black, terrible as Vincent's crows. I stopped. Vernet strolled on ahead blithely, hallooing, and one of the crows moved out toward us, transforming itself into one of half a dozen Augustine nuns stooping, not crows but nearer to scarecrows, knives in hand, cutting flowers for the wards: irises, oleander, poppies and primrose and forget-me-nots, gathering them against their dark bosoms.

The sister who approached us was young, but old enough that the constant stooping had put a bend in her back. Her reddened knuckles stood out above the backs of her hands. She asked us our business. I don't recall whether Vernet told her we were from the police, or the board of health, or were papal nuncios, but she seemed satisfied, if not entirely convinced. She led us up the garden walk and inside the main wing of the hospital. There she surrendered us to an older nun, presumably her superior, who was pushing a cart full of freshly laundered bedding from ward to ward. As soon as we mentioned Vincent's name to her, she pursed her lips in disapproval and said, "Dr. Rey."

We waited for a more forthcoming statement. She offered it only grudgingly.

"Dr. Rey treated that patient. You must speak with Dr. Rey." With that, she cut us loose. Then, as we started to drift: "Not that way. That's the women's ward. Upstairs." She troubled herself to point.

"Bless you, sister," said Vernet.

She clicked her tongue against her teeth in disapproval.

We climbed the stairs to the men's ward. This turned out to be a cavernous room of twenty beds or so, rendered ghostly by the screens of muslin that flanked each bed. Morning light lanced down from high windows. Here we came upon a third sister, manning a table by the door: a squat creature with bulging eyes, almost hidden behind two tall stacks of paper. She was armed with an ink stamp in either hand, and another between her teeth. This last gatekeeper leered at us with clenched teeth in lieu of a smile. When we mentioned Dr. Rey, she nodded eagerly, with her entire body, but she didn't take the stamp from her mouth, or cease for a moment in her labor: examining the top page of the first stack, pouncing on it with one stamp or the other, flipping it onto the second stack, freshening each stamp on an ink pad after every application. She seemed to take an absolute glee in this meaningless make-work. The French find a romance in bureaucracy that surpasses even the Germans.

At length we ran Dr. Felix Rey to ground ourselves. He was making his rounds in the ward, moving from one bed to the next, probing wounds, peering into orifices, asking questions with a professional directness that knew no modesty. He was a dark young man, shockingly young in fact, in his mid-twenties, with chocolate eyes, neat silky hair, and a shovel beard. He asked us our business without once pausing in his own. Vernet asked if he remembered Vincent van Gogh, which elicited a crooked smile.

"All of Arles remembers Vincent, messieurs, even though most of them never laid eyes on the poor man."

"What was your personal impression of him?"

"Anton! Stop pulling at your dressing! I explained about infection, didn't I?"

A nun hurried over from another bed over to prepare a fresh dressing for Anton, a robust young peasant who appeared to have burned the insides of both arms badly. We left her chiding the young man, who appeared mortified at rousing the ire of his physician.

Rey stopped and turned as we followed him between beds.

"Say what you really mean, monsieur. You want to know whether Vincent was of sound mind. That's all anyone wants to know about him. They don't ask about Vincent the philosopher, or Vincent the raconteur. They don't ask if he was a good or bad painter, a genius, a journeyman, an amateur. Is he mad?—that's what they want to know."

My curiosity was piqued. "Was he a good painter?" I asked.

"He was a terrible painter! I have a portrait of myself downstairs to prove it. A waste of good canvas. Yet somehow I can't part with the damned thing."

"You were close to him in the aftermath of his attack?" asked Vernet.

"Vincent was a friend to anyone who would befriend him. But it was a difficult operation. He had no shell, he had no hide. He was all nerve and blood and sinew, so you had to handle him carefully, the same as that young fellow's burns. It's not something many people are willing or able to do."

"So we come back to the original question," said Vernet.

"You're a stubborn man." Dr. Rey weighed the question carefully. "I'm not an alienist. But to put it bluntly, I would say he was *not* of sound mind."

"No?" It was not the answer Vernet had hoped for.

Rey stopped at a bed where another nun was removing a bandage from the ribs of an old man with milky white eyes. A long row of stitches stood out against the walnut skin of his belly. Rey prodded the wound, but the old fellow didn't let out a peep.

"Hardly anyone here is of sound mind. This is a poor town. The poor rarely receive proper nourishment. They drink too much, and what they drink is not Napoleon brandy. The women they consort with are raddled with disease. Vincent suffered all these afflictions, as well as another. He was ambitious. He wanted to paint the world in its entirety, whether it was a pair of worn-out boots or the sweep of heaven over the Rhône. He'd stand at his easel for hours in the sun and wind and rain, even beneath the stars. It made him stand out, his ambition, made him a figure of fun. Even before his attack."

He nodded to the nun, who began to bathe the old man's wound with a sponge. "No more knife fights, eh, Lucien?"

The blind old man grinned toothlessly, nodding.

Rey concluded his diagnosis: "In Arles, to be ambitious is unsound."

"He did suffer from attacks, though?" pursued Vernet.

"When his friend Roulin first carried him in here, he was off his head. He insisted someone was trying to kill him."

"So he was mad?"

"Eh"—the doctor shrugged—"unless someone *was* trying to kill him."

"Who would want to kill such a man?" I asked.

Rey plunged his hands into a bowl of water, and then dried them scrupulously, all the while staring at us, as though taking our measure.

At last he relinquished the towel, shrugged, and said simply, "Who indeed?"

Finished with his rounds, Rey scanned Vernet from head to toe.

"You know, you resemble him."

"The beard?" Vernet darted a look at me.

"The eyes. Full of questions. You're not a relative, are you?"

I felt vindicated in my opinion. Vernet let a smile wander across his lips.

"Come!" With Rey it seemed more of an order than an invitation. We followed him downstairs to a small surgery. Over the examining table hung a wooden crucifix. On the wall opposite hung a portrait of Dr. Rey himself, showing eyes as piercing as arrows. It didn't take an expert to recognize Vincent's hand. Its roughness suited its subject.

Rey threw on a coat and hat. Then he took a rather curious item out of a cabinet, an old straw hat with blots of white wax set round the rim. He handed it to Vernet.

"That was the hat he wore at night, when he wanted to paint under the stars."

Vernet examined the hat minutely, as if it were a sacred relic. "Candles?"

Rey nodded. "He would light the candles and paint for hours, till the candles guttered. Anyone seeing him working like that would be convinced he was mad. Try it on."

Vernet set the hat on his crown. "Ingenious. But surely dangerous?"

"Extremely so. Shall we take a stroll?"

It was an odd suggestion. The wind outside still marched up and down angrily. But Rey seemed to have some object in mind, and Vernet was willing to humor him.

"Keep the hat on, please, monsieur." Odder still.

Dr. Rey was obviously an old hand at navigating the mistral. He led us through back streets and alleyways where the wind's searching fingers could barely find us. Along this route we would run into the occasional locals going about their business, railway workers making their way to the yards, boys trotting along making deliveries for various shops, doffing their caps to the doctor, staring at the strangers with naked curiosity.

Then the attack came, just as Dr. Rey must have anticipated when he lured us out of doors. We were in a narrow lane where the spume blown off the river flung itself over the rooftops, wetting our shoulders. Then, as if from nowhere, a crowd of boys surrounded us. Rey grabbed me by the arm and pulled me into a doorway. A flurry of missiles was launched: cabbages, aubergines, potatoes, stale heels of bread, even a few stones, all aimed at Vernet, with practiced and demonic accuracy.

The detective reacted as anyone would under such an assault, shielding himself with his arms while trying to chase off his attackers, shouting and cursing heaven's thunder at them. He got hold of one urchin by the collar and was bitten for his troubles, which made him curse all the more. The boy tore free, and the next boy slipped his grasp as well. Then a gendarme broke in upon the scene, laying about liberally with his baton, shouting, "Hooligans! I'll have you all behind bars!" The boys broke ranks and fled pell-mell down the street, laughter and catcalls floating down the wind.

Vernet stood rasping, mortified, trying to brush the debris from his clothes. The gendarme, whom I recognized as our friend Monsieur Auguste, whipped out a clean handkerchief and wiped Vernet's spattered face.

"A thousand pardons, monsieur. The ragtag of the streets. Vicious and ignorant."

Vernet frowned across at Dr. Rey, who had held me back from giving any assistance. Not that I had put up too vigorous a struggle. Rey's dark eyes twinkled.

Vernet's face broke into a smile, like a ragged light through the clouds. "Quite the demonstration, Doctor. Did I look like a madman?" He handed the straw hat back.

Rey took the hat and gave a little bow, his work done. "If you'll pardon me gentlemen, I'm only allowed an hour for my midday meal."

"One question before you go, Doctor," I begged. "Can you tell us anything about the man Paul Gauguin?"

I knew Dr. Rey for a man of science, else I'd swear it was the sign against the evil eye that he arrested midgesture. "That gentleman was never a patient of mine. For which I am grateful."

And there he left us, strolling away down the street as if basking in the sun rather than battling the mistral.

Auguste seemed pleased to see him depart. "May I have your ear for a little minute, gentlemen?" he asked.

We fell in walking on either side of the gendarme, ready for whatever news he might divulge.

"You were surprised to see that we had Vincent's ear?" he asked.

"Quite surprised," replied Vernet carefully. For my part, I might have used the word "flabbergasted."

"But you were not shocked. I could see that. You've met Monsieur Vincent, then?"

"We've seen him," Vernet answered.

"And you observed what the superintendent never bothered to. That the lobe of Vincent's left ear had been severed, but otherwise the ear was intact."

"It therefore follows the ear you have in evidence—" Vernet began.

"—that does not resemble Vincent's ear in the slightest—" I added.

"—could not belong to him," Auguste agreed. *Quod erat demonstrandum.* "Yet, I assure you, this was the ear delivered to the prostitute. Have you asked him about that night?"

"Vincent is dead," Vernet answered.

"Ah! Poor fellow. We'll never know."

"Did you not ask him yourself?"

"He would tell me nothing. But this I will swear on my honor: he was as shocked to see this ear as the girl was."

"You think perhaps this ear was substituted for some trinket he had purchased for her? As some kind of macabre prank?" I asked.

"He and the other fellow, that Gauguin, they were both mad for her," Auguste said, and shrugged. "I requested permission to inspect the bodies in the mortuaries, but, alas, I am not the chief of police!"

"Vincent had nothing to say about all this? Surely it would have saved him a world of suffering," Vernet suggested.

"They were friends. He hung on to his friends like a bulldog."

Vernet nodded. We had heard this sentiment voiced before. "The boy who actually delivered the ear to the brothel. Did you question him?"

"Boy?" Auguste stopped. "Ah, you mean Poulet. A simpleton. We could learn nothing there."

"Might we interview him?"

"He's not here. He went with Vincent."

"Went with him?" Vernet's voice was electric.

"Yes, when he went to the madhouse in St. Remy. To help look after him."

The alarm was plain in Vernet's countenance.

"Yes, that concerned me, too," said Auguste. "But what would you? Vincent needed help. Few were willing to supply it."

Our steps had taken us back to the police station in the Place Lamartine. We were facing Ginoux's café and the tobacconist's. The shutters of the shop were open now. Business as usual. What truly had happened inside that house at Christmas a year and a half ago? Had Vincent van Gogh gone mad and taken a razor to his own ear, as the police record told it? Or had there been some quarrel that caused Paul Gauguin to attack his friend with a saber, leaving him bleeding on the floor, as Vernet seemed to hint? I realized my head was throbbing, and had been for some time.

Vernet turned to Auguste. "Monsieur, you're a man of acute perception and intellect. You've restored my faith in the French constabulary."

The gendarme blushed prettily. "You've been a model for me for years, monsieur. I've read every account of your cases—in the English! Good hunting to you!"

He stood on tiptoe and planted an immaculate kiss on each of

Vernet's cheeks. Now it was the detective's turn to blush. Auguste made an about-face to me. "And the good doctor! One must not forget the Boswell, eh?" Auguste had mistaken me, I think, for a fellow named Watson. He shook my hand vigorously, sparing me the kisses. Then he marched away down the street with a firm grip on his baton, keeping an eagle eye out for all the malefactors in the world.

In that moment I caught a glimpse of how those stories in the Strand might shape a certain kind of man—not boys, but boys at heart, knights of the Grail, celibate as monks, who viewed life as a gantlet to be dared, with a horde of foes lining either side, jabbing at their sides with long sharp spears, vying to bring them down before they came to Calvary. Was Vernet one of those boys himself? Were we engaged upon a commission, or a quest?

At all events, our business with the good citizens of Arles was concluded. At last, we were on our way to Montpellier.

# Chapter Seven

Strictly speaking, we were on our way to Al Hambra. That was what Monsieur Lecomte had christened the chateau he had reimagined in the Moorish style on the outskirts of Montpellier, on an eminence east of the town. "He's a dedicated Orientalist, my cousin Michel," Vernet explained.

"A modern Marco Polo?"

"Quite the opposite. For forty years he rarely strayed more than twenty miles from Paris. Then, when Grévy ascended to the presidency, he journeyed into exile here. During the last ten years he's never left Al Hambra."

"Exile? You're joking."

"Self-imposed. Lecomte always considered himself a servant of the crown of France, even after France had toppled the crown. But Grévy's ascendancy finally convinced him that his hopes were dashed; there will be no restoration of the monarchy in his lifetime. So, he retreated to our one-time family estate and tricked it out in Moorish costume. I think he fancies it the last outpost of a faded empire."

"From what post did he retire?"

Vernet looked out the window. We had bid the mistral farewell, and opened the windows of our compartment to the lazy breezes from the sea. Hillsides garlanded in woad and madder rolled past, tiny yellow flowers massed together in streams of gold. "He used to audit the books in some of the government departments. Extraordinary head for figures."

I will confess I felt certain misgivings at the prospect of facing Lecomte and his consortium without any of the proofs I had worked so diligently to accumulate. But Montpellier was also the home of the Musée Fabre, that had grown from a gift to the city fifty years earlier to one of the finest collections in France outside of Paris. Once I had discharged my commission, I hoped to have the opportunity of viewing their collection for the first time. That opportunity would present itself sooner than I expected, and in a most unusual fashion.

If Lecomte had made a career as a minor government functionary, then he must have inherited a dragon's horde of money somewhere along the way. Al Hambra was more than just a name. Turning off the main road into the park, we rode the station diligence up the drive through groves of orange and tamarind. The camphorous scent of eucalyptus lulled our senses. A blink of the eye and we were in the Andalusian gardens of antiquity.

The estate had been far larger when the chateau was first built by Horace Vernet, an immensely popular painter of battle scenes and mythological tableaux, great-grandfather to Lecomte and Vernet both. Then, when the family's fortunes dwindled, Eugene Dupuis's father, a budding industrialist, had purchased the land along with the chateau, devoting half its acreage to industry. Fields run wild with madder and woad were replaced by mills dedicated to processing them into dyes. Then, with the burgeoning development of the new aniline dyes, the mills had been largely supplanted by chemical plants, with laboratories devoted to the birthing of an ever-increasing number of synthetic dyes. (I recalled Titian's dictum that a real painter needed only three colors: black, white, and red. God knows what he would think of the carnival colors of modernity.) On Lecomte's retirement, he had somehow persuaded Dupuis to sell back part of the estate. But the soot-blackened chimneys of the dye plant still loomed in the east, marring the Edenic prospect.

Our first sight of the chateau was akin to the Moor's last sight of Granada. The stoic melancholy of old Spain oozed through every ruddy brick of the facade. The three wings of the chateau, originally shaped in the Baroque style, must have put Lecomte in mind of the Palace of the Lions. The courtyard, once a greensward, had been tiled over and a splashing fountain anchored in the center, guarded by sleepy stone lions. The facades were bolstered with horseshoe arches, the lintels incised with Arabic script. The motto above the entrance, however, though Arabic in style, was in fact Latin: *Ego autem non movebor*—"But I shall not be moved."

No sooner had we arrived than Vernet turned the household upside down. Dupuis and General Normand, the other two members of the so-called consortium, had come down earlier in the week and had been waiting impatiently several days for this conclave. They had waited lunch for us. But then lunch had begun to get cold, and then they had not waited. The heat of the day was coming on, and they were grown lethargic in the still air.

But Vernet, fresh off the train, even before proper introductions were made, insisted we at once pay a visit to the Musée Fabre, which lay in the heart of the city. He had the diligence still waiting in the court. He promised it would "prove instructive," which he seemed to think was ample reason for all and sundry to abandon their plans for naps and bow to his whim. And, of course, in the end, everyone did, for no one ever had such an iron whim as Vernet. But no one was cheerful about it. Mutiny was threatened every minute.

Heaven forbid I should object to the chance to see such a collection of paintings for the first time! But I suspected this would not be the pleasure visit I had looked forward to. *Ars gratia artis* doesn't require the kind of punctilious examination implicit in the Morelli method. I could only assume I was the show pony Vernet wanted to put through his paces before our clients. With most of my studies still blowing in the wind over the valley of the Rhône, we undoubtedly needed another means of winning the gentlemen's confidence. Not that I expected to find forgeries in Montpellier, but the process of authentication must ever be systematic and rigorous, no matter the circumstance.

Thus was I crammed inside the diligence with the gentlemen of the consortium, once again mourning a missed lunch, while Vernet sat up free and easy on the box with the driver. Worse, I was placed next to Michel Lecomte himself, a gentleman whose girth encompassed a considerable amount of real estate. He was nearer seventy than sixty, a tuft of white hair hanging on to his scalp, with a bulldog demeanor and boiled-gooseberry eyes enlarged by wire-rimmed spectacles.

Across from us sat Dupuis, whom I have mentioned before in connection with the Louvre and the Valadon woman. Next to him was General Victor Normand, whose discoveries, I was told, had somehow been the spark for our investigation. One could hardly fault Dupuis for his patrician good looks or his meticulously fashionable dress, and yet I overcame all obstacles to manage it. An air of superiority is even more grating when paired with a mordant sense of humor that seeks only to milk every sacred cow. He quickly became tedious.

Normand's reputation and complexion had both been burnished in the French campaigns in North Africa. He was gaunt and rugged, with a fierce white moustache ensuring that no one would ever mistake him for a frivolous man. He had retired only a few years earlier; one could imagine phantom epaulettes upon his shoulders and a cutlass dangling by his side. Except for the occasional flippant remark from Dupuis, that fell on stony ground, there was no conversation in the offing with such men. We might have been packed into a tumbril rattling through the streets of Paris to the Place de Revolution, rather than a four-wheeler rolling through the palm-lined boulevards of Languedoc—a view which I would have thoroughly enjoyed in better company. The city put me in mind of Florence with its medieval architecture, or Bologna, with its ancient university. Still, I breathed a sigh of relief when we were delivered to our destination.

The Musée Fabre is not the Louvre, and for that I was thankful.

Though it had grown tremendously from the thirty paintings bequeathed by its original patron, the painter Francois-Xavier Fabre, over sixty years ago, it was still a collection one could view comfortably in a single day. No trudging from one echoing gallery to another, to be mesmerized by the sheer number of canvases on display. It was hardly an intimate gallery, but at least one did not feel oneself unmoored and cast out on an endless sea of objets d'art.

But many of the painters whose works I had scrutinized in Paris were also represented in this museum, so I couldn't help my eyes being drawn to the Poussins, the Ingres, the Davids. As we moved through the galleries, I sensed the other men looking over my shoulder, as if I were a carnival conjurer and they were waiting for me to produce a flock of doves from up my sleeve.

Vernet stopped in a corner to admire a painting. I stopped as well. Was he trying to signal to me that there was something suspect about this painting? The caravan hove to behind us, in a clump. Since there was already a student planted at his easel in front of the painting, and since it was by no means a work of great size, we were quite as rucked together as we had been in the coach.

The painting was a depiction of a southern seacoast in a golden morning mist, and a ship becalmed in the shadow of a promontory; the day promised to be hot and windless. Admirably executed, but certainly nothing unusual about it. Who was the artist, then? Ah! The signature was Vernet—whether Carl or Claude or Horace hardly mattered. Only one of them had specialized in these naval tableaux, but paintings in similar style had been the lifeblood of three generations of Vernets and their in-laws and cousins, uncles and nephews and probably even nieces. The detective's interest was probably no more than familial vanity, shared by his cousin, whose eyes rested upon the scene with an abiding affection. I wondered idly whether Vernet's mother in her youth might have been one of those copyists in the Louvre, and even whether he daubed in watercolors in the privacy of his chambers when he wasn't tracking down safecrackers and blackmailers and second-story men. He and the copyist (no sylph with milk-white complexion, but a small, middle-aged man with alarming blue eyes behind thick spectacles and a long, waxed moustache like a meat skewer) traded comments extolling the painting's virtues as if it were a newfound Correggio. I moved on, and my caravan shuffled behind me.

Then I happened upon it. It almost seemed that it happened upon me. I felt the hair stand up on the back of my head. I had come face-to-face with a phantom. It was ostensibly a portrait by Delacroix of Alfred Bruyas, one of the museum's most famous patrons. Nothing strange in that, you'll say: there are several portraits of Bruyas in the museum, all by different painters, originally part of his private collection. As portrayed by Delacroix, Bruyas was tall and cadaverous, with flaming red hair and a heavy beard. He is dressed in black, with an embroidered waistcoat in gold. He is seated in an armchair. But Delacroix had died in—what I saw there, it simply wasn't possible.

"Dr. Lermolieff? What is it, man?" asked Lecomte, who had caught the spark of my excitement even as I tried to tamp it down. I looked around wildly. Where had Vernet got to? I went tearing about, searching for him, even as the consortium stood gawking like peasants at the Bruyas portrait, wondering what the fuss was about.

He was still in front of the Vernet seascape, leaning over the shoulder of the copyist, who had broken out in a sweat and seemed out of breath, unnerved no doubt by the unlooked-for attention. I beckoned to the detective wordlessly, urgently. Vernet and the copyist exchanged a curt nod. He joined me and we hastened back to the Delacroix.

"Not, not, not a Delacroix," I said, stuttering in my excitement.

Vernet took just one look at the painting. "You've outdone yourself, Dr. Lermolieff."

"I don't understand," protested the general. "I know he's supposed to be a connoisseur, but he hasn't even seen the documentation on this painting. How can he make such an offhand determination in the space of a moment?"

"Oh, please don't ask, General! I've already been subjected to this dreary lecture," said Dupuis with an exaggerated show of ennui.

"I expected nothing like this," I said into Vernet's ear.

"Imagine what Vincent must have thought," Vernet answered.

Dupuis heard the name and was suddenly curious. "Who's Vincent?" he asked.

Who was Vincent? Eugene Delacroix had died thirty years ago, Alfred Bruyas perhaps ten years later. Yet the red-bearded patrician staring out from the painting in front of us was unquestionably Vincent van Gogh. There was no need to apply the Morelli method; it was self-evident. What Vincent must have thought, indeed!

"Gentlemen, we have kept you from your repose too long," said Vernet with abrupt solicitousness. "Our business here is finished. Dr. Lermolieff's methods can be enlarged upon at length over dinner. Shall we depart?"

"Wait!" General Normand objected again. "How do we know this is the only fake? Hadn't we better have your expert examine every painting in the museum?"

"That would be the work of hundred-eyed Argus, General. I believe Dr. Lermolieff has already satisfied himself as to the authenticity of the artists whose works have fallen under suspicion. There will be a time for revelations."

"Come, gentlemen, we have placed our trust in my cousin's judgment. I see no cause to withdraw it at this juncture," said Lecomte. "I, for one, am nearly overtaken with fatigue. Let us retire."

No one balked at the suggestion. Presently we were once again packed into our sardine tin and rolling back to Al Hambra. Vernet had stopped to say farewell to his ancestor's painting, an excess of sentiment which even his cousin found cloying. At least the poor put-upon copyist had made his getaway while we were occupied.

I was anything but fatigued. The bed in the room I was installed in was softer than swan's down; the only noise was the soft cooing of somnambulant pigeons. They had no charm over me. Hunger paired with curiosity kept me wide awake all the afternoon. I wrote reams of letters to my wife, my children, Dr. Morelli, and half the names in my address book. I wandered the mazy halls of Al Hambra, trying to find a helpful servant who would show me the way to Vernet's quarters. I may as well have been exploring Sleeping Beauty's castle. All the world, it seemed, was fatigued. All the world had retired.

By the time I tracked Vernet to his own room, the first bell had rung for dinner. As he opened the door I burst forth at once with the question uppermost in my mind. "Today at the museum, did you expect me to find that Delacroix forgery?"

"How could I anticipate such a thing? A bizarre choice for the thieves, don't you think? Among all the depictions of mythological debauchery and royal courtesans, one portrait of a straitlaced art collector is purloined, and replaced with—well, what shall we call it? A parody? A monumental joke? But recall that the quarrel between Vincent and Gauguin occurred shortly after they visited this same museum. Perhaps it was this painting that sparked the quarrel?"

"You don't think it was . . . an intentional provocation, do you?"

"It would be a considerable risk to run merely to get a man's goat."

"But why then did you insist we visit the museum?"

"Ah. That you shall know presently." He would say no more on the subject.

A knock came on the door. Vernet gave a nod, and I opened it. A servant in livery stood in the doorway. He carried a telegram on a silver tray and a long cylindrical parcel done up on brown paper under his arm. The servant was a frail old man, almost elfin in appearance, yet upright as an oak.

"Père Alphonse!" Vernet jumped to his feet. His face was flooded with unalloyed joy.

"Young master," returned the servant, "it is a pleasure to see you." His own feelings were betrayed only by the color which crept into his pallid cheeks.

"Dr. Lermolieff, let me introduce you to Alphonse Tireauclair. He's been in service here since Napoleon was a corporal. When this was still Chateau Vernet."

"The young master is too kind." Père Tireauclair used the English "young master" for Vernet, and never called him anything else.

"What have you got for me, old friend?" Vernet took the parcel and set it on his bed. I looked askance at him, but he ignored me. He took the telegram from the tray, tore it open, and read it quickly. The contents seemed to satisfy him. He turned his attention back to the old retainer. "How does my cousin treat you, my friend? If he abuses you, I'll flog him!"

"I am perfectly content, young master, thank you. My duties are not as burdensome as once they were. I have ample time to stroll the park in the evening and contemplate the mysteries of life."

"I spent three summers here when I was a little lad," Vernet said to me. "Père Alphonse was my particular friend. He used to tell me stories of the days when my mother spent her own summers here."

"A charming young lady she was, young master, and a talented violinist. Her Schubert sonatas were particularly affecting."

"I still have the violin you gave me."

"She would have wished it so." For a moment the old fellow seemed overcome with emotion. Then he collected himself. "Will you be answering the telegram?"

"No, thank you. I won't keep you."

The servant turned to go, but hesitated. He looked into Vernet's eyes as if he were searching for the little boy inside the man. "I've been told you still like to solve riddles, young master."

Vernet grinned. "From time to time. Remember how we solved the mystery of the missing case of claret?"

"The old hunting lodge, young master."

"My first case," Vernet explained. "Is it still standing, or has Michel had it torn down?"

"It stands yet. May I look in upon you this evening before bedtime?"

"I am entirely at your disposal, my friend."

Père Tireauclair bowed genially and took himself away.

My curiosity was piqued. "So what was the case of the old hunting lodge?"

"No one would have even noticed had it been a *vin ordinaire*. But when the old steward Raoul discovered six bottles of our best Côte du Rhône missing from the cellar, suspicion fell on the domestic staff, especially Alphonse, who was known in those days to have a weakness for a good plonk. About the same time, my great-aunt's spaniel was found dead near the old lodge, poisoned by apple seeds, it was said. There were apple cores strewn about its corpse. No one connected the two events."

"Except yourself, of course."

"Myself and my mentor, Père Alphonse. The dog certainly didn't drink six bottles of wine. And it was arsenic that poisoned the poor creature, not apples. Alphonse and I looked into the lodge and found enough evidence to force one of the kitchen maids to confess that her brother was a naval deserter and she had been hiding him there for over a fortnight, pilfering food from the larder to feed him. She had no idea the wine was so dear. The brother had cleared out before we made the discovery, else my first case might have resulted in a hanging, I'm afraid to say. Mind you, since he had poisoned the spaniel when it came sniffing round the lodge, perhaps he deserved hanging. One might argue that the spaniel was my first teacher."

He took the parcel from the bed and tucked it under his arm. "Now let's find our way down to the Hall of Abencerrajes."

The name made my heart skip a beat. "The Hall of Abencerrajes? Isn't that where the sultan massacred his enemies?"

"My cousin will have his little jokes."

It was a relief to discover that Lecomte's Oriental mania did not extend to the dining room accommodations. The entrance arches were hung with prisms in the Moorish style, like stalactites in Aladdin's cave, and one wall was lined with paintings of sloe-eyed damsels in a myriad of Oriental costumes, but we were not subjected to cushions on the floor round a communal bowl. The table and chairs were Louis Quatorze. Crystal and silver glittered on the tabletop.

"My harem. They're all originals, if that's what you're wondering," said Lecomte, who entered the room behind us as we were staring up at the paintings. I half-expected to see him in a caftan with a cloth-of-gold sash round his munificent belly, but he was attired in proper evening wear.

"And all by the same artist, I'd wager," I said.

"You'd win that wager. The artist is my brother Emile. Always trotting about the globe to see what he can see. It seems a terrible waste of energy. But I am fond of the results."

Lecomte's Andalusian affectations may have been no more than the fantasies of a man who had never been further east than Monte Carlo, but I couldn't quite dismiss the idea of swarthy open-shirted Mamelukes bursting forth from recesses in the wall with scimitars ablaze during the cheese course. That we were supposed to be allies rather than enemies afforded me little comfort.

We discovered we were only four for dinner. "Monsieur Dupuis begs our indulgence. He was required at the dye plant," Lecomte explained.

"I was under the impression Dupuis was a financier?" I asked.

"I think he's largely withdrawn from that arena, after sustaining some rather heavy losses on speculation. But he still owns the dye works. You may have seen his chimneys on your way in. Its reeks play havoc among my rose beds."

"Coal tar derivatives, I believe he said?" put in the general.

"The future of the twentieth century, he assures me."

I had never heard of coal tar, to say nothing of its derivatives, and said so plainly.

"Coal tar is a byproduct of the carbonization of coal," said Vernet. "It's a fascinating substance chemically, a compound of aromatic hydrocarbons, aromatic acids, and nitrogen compounds." I recalled that Vernet had a reputation for dabbling in chemistry. He warmed to the subject, making this coal tar stuff sound like a universal panacea. He rattled off a dozen different applications for its derivatives, everything from the preservation of wood to shampoos and soaps, artificial sweeteners and headache cures. Included in that list were the synthetic dyes that were threatening to replace natural pigments on the painter's palette.

"I understood coal tar to be a German monopoly," said Normand.

"Indeed, they boast the lion's share of the market," Lecomte replied. "Dupuis has carved out a niche in aniline dyes and the new synthetic pigments. He's poured all his money into the development of a synthetic indigo. The Holy Grail of pigments, he calls it. Since the Indigo Rebellion in Bengal, Europe has been convinced of the wisdom of developing our own resources. If he can bring an inexpensive dye to market before the Germans, he'll be richer than Croesus."

"These synthetic pigments are gaining popularity with the painters?" I asked. The Renaissance masters who were my special province had ground their own pigments, or paid assistants to do it for them. Their palettes were limited to the pigments found in the earth, or in the natural flora and fauna. Blue, originally derived from woad or from lapis lazuli, had always been difficult and outrageously expensive to manufacture. Once England had established herself in India, thousands of acres in Bengal had been given over to the cultivation of indigo to feed an insatiable hunger for blue cloths.

"Popular with his Impressionist friends, certainly," said Lecomte. "Dupuis grinds his own pigments and packages them. It's those little tin tubes of paint from Dupuis et Cie that allow artists to set up their easels by the riverbank and go mad. Without the little paint tubes, there would be no Impressionists. Dupuis would have to go collect seashells on the beach instead."

"Dupuis is a collector?" I asked.

"Obsessed with these mongrel painters. Another unwise investment." He smiled as though cheered by the thought.

This struck me as odd. From the way he had scoffed at the Impressionist dealers, I would have said that Dupuis deemed Impressionism the greatest folly of the century. But then Dupuis was happy to scoff at anything. He seemed one of those men who skated across the surface of the world, without ever leaving a line upon it.

Once we had taken the edge off our hunger, Vernet asked General Normand to tell his own story. "I've heard something of it from Lecomte, but we should like to go over every detail, if you don't mind."

Up to that point I had heard nothing at all of General Normand's story. It was in its way perhaps the strangest tale I have ever been privy to in the art world.

"Well, then, where to begin?" said Normand, affecting diffidence. "I was in Washington last winter as a guest of Ambassador Roustan, whom I had first met during the fighting in Tunisia. I'd been given letters of introduction to some of New York City's most avid collectors. America is becoming quite civilized if you'll believe it, none of that Buffalo Bill nonsense, and their best citizens seem determined to prove it. I received an invitation to a New Year's dinner at the home of Henry Havemeyer, the sugar baron, which I gladly accepted. Havemeyer's collection is one of the finest in America, by all accounts. When he promised to show me some of his newest acquisitions after dinner, I found myself barely able to swallow my food, my anticipation was so great. We stole away from the after-dinner conversation, just the two of us, brandy in one hand, coffee in the other, up a set of spiral stairs to a kind of turret-room. And when I tell you what he showed me there, you'll understand perhaps why they were segregated so. Six paintings he showed me, his latest acquisitions from the Paris dealers. He was bursting with pride. Shall I tell you the names of the painters? I wrote them down the moment I was alone, so as not to forget, since the names were strange to me." Then he actually produced a crumpled paper from his pocket, and laid it out before him as though it were orders from the war office. "I have the list here: Monet, Degas, Renoir, Pissarro, Cassatt, Sisley. A rogue's gallery, fit only for the gallows. You're a connoisseur, Dr. Lermolieff—perhaps you've heard of one or two of them, and can guess my reaction, but they were wholly unknown to me at the time. I wish to *le bon dieu* they had remained so. Those are the so-called Impressionists! What are their subjects? Are they saints in the throes of martyrdom or nymphs in Arcady? Portraits of great men, depictions of famous battles? No, they're crowds of sweating bourgeoisie massed in the streets, picnickers in the parks, grisettes, *mousmés*, pimps, and prostitutes! Steamships in the harbor, trains in the station, where's the poetry in all that iron-mongery? Not a single draughtsman among them, either; where's the Giotto who could draw a perfect circle with a single motion of his wrist? Where's Piero della Francesca, with his mastery of per-spective—"

Lecomte coughed discreetly. "General? If you could confine your-self to the events as they occurred?"

"Yes, of course. Pardon my raillery. My blood gets to boiling. Well, then. Havemeyer praised the Impressionists up and down, as if they were the Dutch masters, till I was sure he was off his head. But at the same time, I couldn't shake the feeling that he was secretly having me on, that every word from his mouth meant just the opposite. And then he said the tower was only a temporary harbor, that he meant to give them a place of honor in the grand salon! The best I could manage was a diplomatic silence and a hasty retreat to my hotel, where I consumed half a bottle of port before I could get to sleep.

"Well, what's one madman, I said to myself, or one season of madness? I'd glimpsed many fine paintings in Havemeyer's halls and drawing rooms and dining room. There's every prospect he might wake up one day and chuck the damn things out the window. Prayers rise up to heaven.

"Then, two nights later, I attended a second dinner party, at the home of the iron magnate Alfred Pope. The man's name is synony-mous with quiet good taste. He knew I'd been to Havemeyer's and told me he only hoped his collection wouldn't prove a disappoint-ment by comparison. I told him earnestly that would not be the case. Pope is a man of great subtlety and tact. He showed me many fine paintings, including a magnificent Poussin I'd give my eyeteeth for. Enough is as good as a feast, but the time came when I begged him outright to show me his latest acquisitions. I might not have been so forward, but my experience with Havemeyer had left me queru-lous. Then he must point them out, almost invisible among the Courbets and Corots: five new paintings, just as god-awful as any-thing Havemeyer had shown me, by those same foul daubers, along with another, the most obscene thing I have ever seen, a picture of some Montmartre prostitutes by a man named"—he consulted his list again—"Anquetin."

"I canceled my next two dinner appointments, pleading illness. Both were with men of sterling reputations. I had no desire to see those reputations sullied. I took in the museums instead, which were safe enough, though dull, mostly full of American painters no one will ever hear of. But I couldn't help being haunted by the thought of their walls being crowded someday with Impressionist works, donated by noble captains of industry without an ounce of taste among them.

"At last, just before I was due to leave the country, I took the train to Philadelphia to spend an evening with James Stillman. I've known the man personally for years. He's practically a Parisian himself, having taken a house in Parc Monceau a few years ago. I confided in him my experiences with Havemeyer and Pope. He laughed out loud. 'You think Pope's gone soft in the head? I hear he's taken up with a nineteen-year-old stenographer. From Boston!'

"I'm not one to countenance public scandal, but neither am I one to judge. Better a touch of the syphilis than those foul daubs of haystacks and whores. And that's just what I told him, in just those words. 'Let me show you something,' he replied. The same words I'd come to dread in New York.

"Stillman had recently added a new wing to the house, so new you could smell the paint drying and watch the wood shavings curl in the corners. That was where he steered me, down hallway after hallway, to an anonymous door I would have guessed was a broom-closet.

"'Do you trust me, old friend?'

"What could I answer but yes?—even as my heart sank at the question.

"'You'll see how much I trust you.' He unlocked the door and we went in.

"There were no windows; Stillman threw a switch somewhere in the dark and electric light dazzled my eyes.

"It was a room about the size of a lady chapel, with oak wainscoting, forgettable wallpaper, and three electrical fans suspended from the ceiling, ticking round slow as fate. There was a sideboard, with a few bottles of American whiskey and some cut-glass tumblers. Two overstuffed armchairs stood side by side in the center of the room, with a small table wedged between.

"On the far wall hung five modern monstrosities. I didn't even bother to notice the signatures. They were the same paintings of stagnant ponds, drunken boaters, half-naked whores, and iron bridges I had come to expect.

"Stillman didn't even give them a glance. He went to the sideboard. 'Glass of bourbon?' he asked, and poured each of us a tumbler. He handed me a whiskey, took me by the elbow, and installed me in one of the chairs, sinking into the other one himself. He puffed on his cigar, taking in the paintings one by one, as if they were suspects in a police lineup.

"'Pretty damn disturbing, aren't they?' he said, chuckling to himself. He raised a hand to forestall my answer. 'I'm getting used to them, though. Almost come to like them. Don't look at me like that, Victor. Pope and Havemeyer don't know you from Adam. But I trust you as a man of discretion.'

"He drew my attention to a small metal box with a switch on the table between us. 'Flip that switch,' he said, and winked. I half-expected to be electrocuted, but I did as he told me. There was the hum of a dynamo, then the whole section of wall behind the center painting slowly pivoted on a rod, replacing the Anquetin—by then I knew the most offensive of the bunch would always turn out to be an Anquetin—with Delacroix's *Shipwreck of Don Juan*.

"'Now what d'you think?'

"I sat bolt upright. I couldn't get a word out. He grinned and pointed to the whiskey in my hand. I took the hint and downed it. He poured me another and I drank that, too. 'I saw this painting three months ago in the Louvre!' I finally gasped.

"He was delighted by my reaction. 'You didn't. That's the real

McCoy there. The world can't know, of course. But what's the good of owning something nice if you can't show it off to your particular friends?'

"'In the name of heaven, how did you get hold of it?'

"'Won it in a lottery. No, sir, I'm not kidding. There are ten of us in it now, I believe, all men of means who are willing and able to take a flutter. Only five of us have won so far—Mellon twice, damn his eyes, a Poussin and a Gerome both. We each of us ante up for a consignment of these . . . lottery tickets. They're divvied up between us, blindfolded as you might say. Only one painting in every shipment conceals a treasure like this one.'

"'And these—things?' I waved vaguely at the other paintings.

"'Discarded tickets. But we are sworn as gentlemen to display them as if we were proud of them.'

"'But this painting belongs in the Louvre!'

"He gave me a stern look of reproval, as if I were a wayward corporal. 'How much did the Louvre pay for it? Not a thin dime. Does a treasure like this belong to the unwashed masses who trample through the public galleries on a Sunday, eating garlic sausage and drinking sour wine, leaving cheese rinds littered across the parquet, or to men who have the discernment to recognize great paintings, and the wherewithal to preserve them for posterity?'

"He had a point of course, and I fell silent, although by 'posterity,' he undoubtedly meant his posterity alone. My silence he took for approval. So I drank his bourbon and I contemplated his lottery winnings, and I went away. But before I went I let him talk, and he let drop the names of some of the other artists whose works had been stolen—he used the word 'appropriated'—from our shores, though he didn't name the actual paintings. He swore me to secrecy. I saw the ambassador before I took sail, and told him nothing. I crossed the ocean, and my fellow passengers named me General Lockjaw, because I was so tight-lipped. Had I not given my word?

"But gentlemen, I am for France! I have fought for France for forty years. When it came to it, I even betrayed Boulanger to defend France.

Once I saw the harbor of Marseille rise out of the morning mist, I knew what I must do. Before I even unpacked my trunks, I wired Lecomte to seek his advice. That is my tale, gentlemen."

# Chapter Eight

The four of us sat in silence. I could hardly have credited the story Normand had told, had I not discovered the forgeries myself. Now I understood how Vernet had compiled his list of suspect artists; now I understood his lack of urgency in trying to locate the stolen paintings. He already knew, more or less precisely, where they could be found. Twelve priceless works, the patrimony of France, had fallen into the hands of some of the most powerful men in America. Such an enormous scandal could undermine the brotherly ties between the two nations. And there were only we few, "the consortium," to prevent it. It made no sense.

I cleared my throat. "If I might ask, General, why did you bring your problem to Lecomte rather than the foreign ministry, say, or the Sûreté?"

Normand raised his eyebrows in surprise. "My dear sir! Do you not know who Monsieur Lecomte is?"

Vernet sat back, chuckling. Lecomte allowed himself a modest smile.

"I . . . I understood he was formerly employed by the government of France."

"Say rather that formerly he *was* the government of France! I've seen the president of the republic leave his office in the Élysée Palace and trot down the Rue de Duras to knock on Lecomte's door when faced with a crisis neither the government nor the army nor the church could solve. If Louis Napoleon had heeded Lecomte's counsel, he might yet be emperor today. The proper question is, why did he bring my problem to you?"

"The answer, General, is that I felt the need for an agent with a more energetic approach than is my wont," said Lecomte. "I called on my cousin here, who has his own considerable reputation for solving little puzzles of this sort. No one bustles about with more alacrity than the English."

Vernet smiled at the backhanded compliment. "And I brought in Dr. Lermolieff because he possesses a peculiar set of skills that has been essential to the unraveling of this mystery," he added.

"Oh, yes, the magical ability to tell a fake from an original at a glance." Normand was having none of it. I might have been offended had I not faced his kind of bullheaded skepticism often enough before.

"If you could sketch out your methods, Doctor," Vernet suggested.

"Simplicity itself. My method is the Morelli method."

The general's face darkened. "Morelli? One of Garibaldi's redshirts, wasn't he?"

"He's a senator of the Italian parliament, among other things." I wanted to avoid a political dispute, if at all possible.

But how to begin? I eyed the odalisques along the wall, Lecomte's harem, hoping for inspiration. It was granted me. I rose from the table and picked out a portrait of a girl in vaguely Oriental costume with a tambourine in her hand, in her eyes the serenely knowing look which was common to all her set. She would be my *point de depart*. I took the painting down and placed it on the table for all to view. I noticed Lecomte squirm a bit as I handled it.

"You say your brother Emile painted these, Monsieur Lecomte?

Before Morelli, if you wanted to be certain you had in your possession an authentic Emile Lecomte, the 'experts' would offer sage opinions, based on some nebulous 'stylistic similarities,' backed perhaps by a sheaf of yellowing documents supposed to supply provenance, but in reality as easy to forge as the paintings themselves. Morelli offers proof, based on the paintings themselves. As Cuvier can examine a fossil tooth and tell us whether it belongs to a carnivore or an herbivore, Morelli can look at the drape of a peasant's skirt and tell you whether it's Breughel the Elder or the Younger."

The general snorted in derision. I soldiered on. "Monsieur Lecomte, how would you distinguish a gentleman from his groom?"

"The cut of his clothes."

"And if you dressed them the same?"

"Every gesture betrays a man's station in life," snapped the general.

"Yes! Every unconscious gesture."

"Unconscious? Artists don't paint in their sleep!" The general was being willfully obtuse.

"The poet Coleridge calls the unconscious the seat of the imagination, those 'caverns measureless to man' through which the sacred river of inspiration runs."

"Coleridge was addicted to opium, I believe," said Lecomte drily.

"Which does not invalidate his conclusions. The painter changes his motifs, his composition, his palette. But he won't change the curve of an earlobe, a courtesan's ankle, or a saint's halo. He won't change the orchestration of his colors. These are the habits of the hand. He *can't* change them—he's unaware of them. These automatic details he repeats over and over. He doesn't see them, thanks to the habits of the eye—nor does the forger, who has his own unconscious habits. Morelli observes them. He recognizes in these seemingly insignificant details each painter's individual personality. The same hands, the same folds of drapery, ringlets of hair, the same leaf and twig. These comprise a master's true signature. They can't be discovered at a glance, of course, but the more one studies a painter's oeuvre, the easier it is to determine whether a particular painting is consonant with the rest. It's the same as Bertillon's identification system or Cuvier's anatomy. Is this the jawbone of a sauropod or an ass? Analysis and comparison are everything. Think of it as a morphology of art.

"This painting, monsieur, is an authentic Emile Lecomte—unless all the others on your wall are fakes. I think not, though. Notice the shape of the nostrils, the prominence of the knuckles on the hand"— then I saw it!—"remarkably like your own! This girl is as much a Lecomte as you are."

"Well"—Lecomte made a stiff little bow toward the portrait— "welcome to the family, mademoiselle." He tried to retain his bulldog demeanor, but I think he was pleased. He took the painting from my hands and carefully returned it to its place. "You might teach a forger a thing or two yourself, Doctor."

But the general was still unconvinced. "You're talking anatomy, not art! Did you trot up and down the halls of the Louvre, spotting forgeries with your eagle eye?"

"A distinct possibility in the Louvre," said Lecomte, trying to be droll.

Vernet interjected: "I suggested Dr. Lermolieff confine his investigation to the French painters mentioned by your American friends. They seemed particularly enamored of the Roccoco and the Romantic."

"Or perhaps it's that our thieves hold a grudge against the French?" Lecomte suggested.

The general was not ready to concede. "So all you can do is compare one painting with another. What if all the paintings you examine happen to be forgeries?"

"It's true, there are no absolute certainties," I conceded. "If all of Shakespeare's plays were written by another man, we could never know. But what's in a name?"

"I can't abide Shakespeare. Give me Racine any day," Normand grumbled.

"So what's the result of all this wizardry?" asked Lecomte. "Did you merely confirm what Normand had already witnessed with his own eyes?"

I removed a paper from my pocket and handed it to him. "That, and more."

Lecomte looked down the list, his eyes growing wide. This is what I had written:

Fragonard — *The Lock*
Poussin — *Venus and Adonis*
Watteau (2) — *Judgement of Paris; Pierrot*
David — *Belisarius Begging for Alms*
Ingres (2) — *Mademoiselle Caroline Rivière; The Source*
Boucher — *Madame de Pompadour with Her Hand Resting on a Harpsichord Keyboard*
La Tour — *The Cheat with the Ace of Diamonds*
Delacroix — *The Shipwreck of Don Juan*
Cabanel — *The Birth of Venus*
Gerome — *The Cockfight*

"This is twelve paintings!" he said, disbelieving. "Normand, you only mentioned six!"

He handed the paper to Normand, whose face went ashen as he read it.

"Did you think these forgers would be idle between last winter and today?" said Vernet.

I took up the tale. "Between the Louvre and the Musée de Luxembourg, I found twelve separate forgeries—executed, I think, by two or possibly even three different painters. For instance, I can say with certainty that the Boucher *Madame de Pompadour* and the Ingres paintings were all the work of the same hand. There's the same pendulous earlobe in all three works, which was absent in the other forgeries."

"Earlobe?" The general's look was one of genuine anguish. He could no more accept my methods than he could the French Republic, or the German *motorwagen*.

"Weren't there supposed to be studies of some sort to corroborate your findings? Isn't that what we agreed upon?" Lecomte peered at me over his spectacles like a headmaster with a delinquent schoolboy. I felt the flush of embarrassment rise to my cheeks.

"Dr. Lermolieff was attacked and his life threatened at gunpoint for possession of those studies," said Vernet. "Which is itself conclusive evidence that they fully supported his findings."

I was grateful to Vernet for coming to my defense, and for the way he phrased it, even adding a gun to heighten the peril. The other men had been looking at me as though I were a mountebank selling aqua vitae. Now I saw respect creep into their eyes.

"All right, then, you found twelve forged paintings," Lecomte acceded.

"Don't forget the Delacroix yesterday in the Musée Fabre," said Vernet.

"Surely you're not saying that was the work of this same Paris gang!" scoffed Lecomte.

"I believe it may be," I answered gravely.

"But how?" bawled the general. "No one simply walks out of the Louvre with twelve paintings! It's unthinkable."

"On the contrary," Vernet replied. "People walk out every day with paintings. Copyists."

"Only what they bring in," insisted the general.

Vernet shook his head slowly. "It takes but a moment of diversion. Dr. Lermolieff actually missed one obvious forgery yesterday at the Musée Fabre. The Vernet seascape."

"A Vernet? That's not possible!"

We turned to see Dupuis leaning in the doorway, looking discomposed and a bit out of breath. His boots were muddied, and his normally immaculate sleeves grimed. He must have recognized our apprehension at his appearance. He cracked a smile. "After all, who'd bother to forge a Vernet?" he joked.

Lecomte was not amused. "My father donated that Vernet to the museum. I'll vouch for its authenticity."

Vernet picked up the cylindrical parcel that had been resting against his chairback. He tore off the wrapping to reveal a rolled-up canvas. With a flourish, he rolled the canvas out on the table.

"You are perhaps thinking of this Vernet."

I stared at the painting, unbelieving. "This must be a copy."

"I can assure you it is not."

It was the Vernet seascape.

"But we were with you the entire time!" I protested.

"Not the entire time. With the proper tools and a bit of nerve, it only takes a few moments. The copy is waiting upon the student's easel, the tools are in his paint box. The transference is rehearsed and timed to the exact second. A distraction is helpful. You provided that admirably, Doctor."

I recalled the copyist at the museum, with his bizarre moustache. I recalled the friendly way he had with Vernet. Again the detective had been staging a play. I had been taken in.

"The copy on the easel was only half-finished," said Lecomte. "Are you telling me that a half-finished forgery hangs in the Musée Fabre and no one has noticed?"

"You saw only one side of the canvas," answered Vernet.

"This should be returned to the museum at once," I said.

"Have no fears on that score, monsieur. I'll see to it myself," said Lecomte. He began rolling up the canvas carefully.

By now the general was fairly sputtering. "This means nothing. Monsieur Lecomte might walk out of the Musée Fabre with a Botticelli under his arm. Who would search him, or even suspect him?"

"No one," Vernet acceded cheerfully.

"Well, it sounds to me as if Monsieur Vernet has wrapped up the mystery quite neatly," said Dupuis. "What say we get up a hunting party in the morning?"

"The only game you'll bag near this house are the gardeners," said Lecomte.

"Sounds like good sport to me," Dupuis replied.

"There's still the small matter of discovering the names of the thieves and forgers, and effecting the return of the stolen paintings to France," Vernet reminded them.

"Hear, hear!" cried the general. "Now we're getting somewhere. How do you plan to catch these people?"

"Money."

"Money? You mean bribes?" asked Dupuis.

"I mean simply that money abhors a vacuum. In a case involving the theft of valuable assets, someone is certain to wind up with far too much of it. It's impossible to keep hidden for long."

"What on earth has all this to do with these damned Impressionists?" asked Normand.

"You've placed your finger upon the crux of the mystery, General," said Vernet.

"Oh, as to that," Dupuis remarked casually, "I've done a bit more spadework, and I think I may have turned up a new suspect for you. Do you know Paul Gauguin?"

Vernet sat stone-faced. "Should I?" I would hate to play cards against the man.

"Perhaps not. Another one of Theo van Gogh's protégés, a talentless hack by all accounts, but with a streak of larceny. He's telling everyone who will listen that he's planning a voyage to the tropics, to create a 'studio of the south.' Now where does the money for such an enterprise come from?"

The question hung in the air. After our experiences in Auvers and Arles, I knew Vernet must suspect Gauguin of a great deal of mischief indeed. But he confided nothing in Dupuis. If Morelli's accounts of him were true, he would be sure of all his cards before turning them face up.

Lecomte rose ponderously. "Gentlemen, I think our business is done. I suggest we leave this matter in the capable hands of Monsieur Vernet. Doctor Lermolieff, thank you for your assistance. My secretary should have your fee ready in the morning."

He turned dismissively. The general rose and granted us a stiff bow.

"General, one last question," said Vernet, "since we're dealing with forgeries. What makes the Americans certain their paintings are the originals?"

"They have their own pet expert," answered Normand, with a disparaging look at me. "Fellow name of Shinn. Don't think he subscribes to the Morelli method, but Stillman swears by him. And Stillman is nobody's fool." His insinuation was clear, though whether he considered me Morelli's fool or Vernet mine was debatable. He gave another bow and departed.

Lecomte and Dupuis both followed him from the room. Vernet sat musing to himself, chin in hand. For myself, I realized that at some point in the last hour I had come to a decision. I would write my wife. She would have to understand.

"Where to now?" I asked. "Paris?"

Vernet looked up with a smile. "Doctor! You still wish to hunt with me?"

"Your cousin seems to think my services are no longer necessary." I must confess that his dismissal of me, as though I were a groom or footman, had nettled me. But it was more than that. Vernet's sense of mission had infected me. A great wrong had been done, and more than one. I wanted to see the world put to order.

Vernet reached out and shook my hand warmly, sealing our comradeship. "Paris, yes. But first I'd like to stop at that asylum in St. Remy where Vincent was committed."

I shrugged. "We won't find Gauguin there."

"Monsieur Gauguin can wait. I want Poulet."

I had near forgotten Poulet, the fellow who had accompanied Vincent to the asylum to tend to his needs. A simpleton, by all accounts. I doubted even Vernet could get much from that quarter. But I held my peace.

We said our goodnights and went our ways. Before turning in, I decided to take a solitary walk in the garden among the eucalyptus and mimosa. The twilight's last exhalation of rock rose and sage filled my nostrils. As I moved away from the lights of the house, pine trees and cedars stood up and crowded around me.

Then I saw a light moving toward me from the direction of the house. At first I fancied it a will-o'-the-wisp, its motion seemed so arbitrary, but as I stood watching, it came closer and resolved itself into a lantern in the hands of a servant—old Père Tireauclair, in fact. The light had seemed to dip and flutter simply because it was in the none-too-steady grasp of a feeble old man. I moved to join him. On hearing my footsteps, he stopped stone-dead and cried, "Who's there?" in a quavering voice.

"Père Tireauclair, it's I, Lermolieff! Were you sent to find me?"

"Ah, the Russian gentleman? No, monsieur. There's a weasel's been getting into the henhouse. I wanted to check the traps while there was still light."

There was no light. The last bars of violet in the west had thinned into infinity, the cicadas had gone silent, and it was now quite night. But a man who has trod the same paths for a lifetime carries an interior light that the interloper cannot share. And now that I had named myself an interloper, I decided to turn back to the house and leave the night world to Père Tireauclair. I had forgotten about the interview he had requested with Vernet, and would not have assigned it any importance even had I remembered.

We were having coffee in Vernet's room the next morning. Vernet had elected to avoid the rest of the company; for that I was grateful. I was tired of Lecomte's condescension, Normand's disbelief, and Dupuis's sardonicism. We were decided upon making our departure before noon, so that we might reach St. Remy in the afternoon. A little kitchen maid with a face like a kitten's had poured our coffee and set bread and butter before us. She stood waiting to be dismissed. Vernet asked her name.

"Therese, monsieur," she said shyly.

"Therese, where is Père Alphonse this morning?"

The girl's eyelashes fluttered, and her mouth went tight. "I don't know, monsieur."

"Would you find him and ask him to attend upon me as soon as he's available?"

Therese only nodded. She went out quietly.

"Were you and he up last night trading reminisces?" I asked.

"He never came to me last night."

Therese's footsteps in the hall came to a stop. She reappeared in the doorway, her face pale, her lips trembling.

"Oh, monsieur, we don't know where Père Tireauclair could be! He hasn't slept in his bed!" Then she broke down crying. It was some time before we could get anything sensible out of her. When we did, she told us that Madame Loyer, the housekeeper, had sent two servants out in search of the old man, but they had come back empty-handed. Père Tireauclair had taken to wandering the grounds at night lately, and the servants were deathly afraid something might have happened to him. The master had not yet been told.

Then I remembered my encounter with the old servant from the night before. I told Vernet about it.

It was amazing to see how quickly Vernet could light a fire under people when necessary, and how surely he could take command of the entire household, not merely the servants but also Lecomte and his guests, who suddenly found themselves torn from their breakfasts and launched out upon the grounds to search for some doddering old servant they had taken no notice of the day before. Presently the local gendarmerie joined in the search.

But of course, it was Vernet who found him, for it was Vernet who knew where to look. As he had said, it wasn't the dog who drank six bottles of wine. The gamekeeper's lodge, what remained of it, was no longer strictly part of the Vernet property. The land now belonged to Dupuis's dye works, though there were no walls or fences, only a tree line to mark the boundary. It was unclear whether Père Tireauclair had known that. But he had noticed the food stolen from the pantry, as was later established, and he had looked for an intruder hiding in the lodge. It was his misfortune to find him.

The lodge itself was the oldest structure on the estate, a modest two-room affair built of rusticated stone, without a stick of furniture save the pegs on the wall in what must once have been the gun room. There was a large hearth that may have belonged to an even earlier building, and outside the window a stack of firewood moldering against the moss-stained wall, with a rusty axe sticking up out of one of the logs. The old man's body was lying in a clearing near the lodge, not far from where he had found the dog twenty-five years ago. His neck was broken. We whistled for the police, who came tramping through the trees with Lecomte, destroying any possibility of finding footprints. They formed a ring around the body, as if defending it from any further harm.

"What was the old fellow doing all the way out here, monsieur?" asked the police inspector.

"He had an absolute mania about the old hunting lodge. Always certain every tramp in the countryside wanted to take up residence there. Mentioned something about it last night when he was serving the brandy, didn't he, Dupuis?" said Lecomte.

"Did he? I'm afraid I wasn't paying attention. Tramps are welcome to a little shelter, as far as I'm concerned."

The police inspector stared down at the body, nodded twice, and concluded that Alphonse Tireauclair had tripped over a branch and fallen. He was after all a frail old man, brittle as a dry twig. Never mind that there was no branch to trip over. Death by misadventure. Lecomte was satisfied with the verdict. The search party broke up and headed home with the body on a stretcher, congratulating themselves that justice was served. It was a case of outrageous negligence. I expected vehement protest from Vernet, but he merely shrugged. "If one expects nothing from the gendarmerie, one is rarely surprised," said he.

We inspected the lodge, of course. There was no sign of habitation whatsoever. I made the error of pointing out that fact to the detective. He merely laughed contemptuously. "I see footprints everywhere."

I stared dumbly at the floor. There was not a single footprint.

"No dust, Doctor," he said.

Of course! The floor was clean as if newly swept.

There was also no lantern, near the body or anywhere else. That was a clue even I couldn't miss. The man who had killed Père Tireauclair had taken the lantern. But no one besides myself had seen him with the lantern, and Vernet begged me not to mention it to anyone. The police would have no use for information that contradicted their easy verdict. "As for the killer," Vernet promised, "I shall deal with him. Had I taken the time to listen to my first partner yesterday, he would be alive today. But Père Alphonse shall have justice." His face was pinched with sorrow, at least sorrow I thought it. How deep the man's feelings could plunge, through what bottomless black waters his soul could swim, I had no inkling. Had I thought him all surface, like a painting? I had forgotten how many layers a painting may hide.

We returned to the chateau to pack for our departure. An hour later, I knocked on Vernet's door.

He was sitting on his bed, staring into space. The burning vitality that marked him out from other men seemed extinguished. I extended my deepest sympathy. Then, because it had to be asked:

"Do you think this murder is related to your investigation?"

"Doctor, what do they call it when the same element crops up over and over in a painter's work?"

"A motif?"

"Violent death is always an interesting motif."

He handed me a wrinkled paper that he had been holding. I stared at it in disbelief.

"Where did you get this?"

"I searched Père Alphonse's pockets before the police arrived. It is yours?"

"Yes, of course." It was one of my studies from the Louvre, repeated iterations of Ingres necks, famously out of proportion. "Then you think Alphonse somehow happened upon my attacker from the train?"

"With mortal consequences. And I think we can give a name to the murderer."

I raised an eyebrow. He said it in a spectral voice that made me shudder: "Poulet."

We finished packing and departed from Al Hambra without making any farewells.

# Chapter Nine

The asylum of St. Paul-de-Mausole, just north of the little town of Saint-Remy, was something less than fifteen miles distant from Arles. It might have been a different world. Nestled in a valley delved in the sheltering arms of the Alpilles, this new vista opened up before us green and sparkling as an Alpine meadow as our train wound its way out of a tortuous declivity. The asylum itself, a collection of grey buildings quarried out of old Roman ruins, had originally been a monastery, and had passed through the centuries from Augustinian to Benedictine to Franciscan hands before dwindling belief in signs and miracles had turned it into a mental hospital. It lay quiet as a grave among green fields and well-tilled gardens, groves of almonds and olives. If Vincent had come here in hopes of regaining his peace of mind after the catastrophe of Arles, he had chosen well, I thought. An air of retirement lay over the scene, cattle still as statues, crumbling garden walls mortared in saxifrage, stands of pine limned in the perpendicular light of the mountain sun. It was perhaps disconcerting that the first inhabitant of the asylum we met wore a starched white collar, black riding boots, and nothing more, but he was kind enough to give us detailed directions to the office of the director, Dr. Peyron.

Theophile Peyron, the director of St. Paul's, turned out to be an ophthalmologist rather than an alienist, but at least he was a doctor. His treatment regimen consisted mainly of rest, fresh air, and cold-water baths twice a week. When Vernet let slip that he had a wealthy uncle who was, well, a bit bothered in the head, Peyron put himself at our disposal. The asylum was woefully short on patients, and therefore woefully short on funds. Vernet swung the conversation around to a friend of his, a Paris art dealer named Van Gogh, who had committed his brother to St. Paul, and spoke in glowing terms of his stay there. Did the doctor remember Vincent?

"Vincent van Gogh? The Dutch painter? Actually, he committed himself. It was against my better judgment to take him in at the time."

"You thought him dangerous?" asked Vernet.

Peyron considered the question for a moment. "I thought him sane. Subject to occasional fits of epilepsy, as I recall, but fundamentally sound."

"So when he was discharged—or discharged himself?—it was with your approval?"

Peyron shook his head emphatically. "By then, I thought him dangerous." He recognized the contradiction in his statements. "There were a number of . . . episodes. There was an attendant assigned to him, a country boy, strong as an ox. They always got along amicably. One day, the patient turned round and kicked him in the stomach. He claimed the police were after him."

"Were they?"

Peyron was arrested midthought; he weighed that possibility. "I suppose they could have been. I had made the mistake of letting him visit his friends in Arles the day before, and it had certainly upset him. But if the police really wanted him, they knew where to find him. Another time he complained he was being poisoned and demanded an emetic."

"Did you administer one?"

"Of course not. It was an obvious delusion. Next he attempted to eat his own paints."

"For which you gave him—"

"An emetic, I suppose. I'd have to check the records, of course."

"Pardon me, Doctor," I broke in, letting my impatience jump the fence ahead of me. "The attendant's name?"

Peyron was anything but certain of the name. He directed us to his chief attendant, Trabuc—"He keeps track of all those details." Where his lieutenant might be at that time of day, or any other, seemed an absolute enigma to the director, but he was willing to accompany us as we wandered the halls in search of him.

My favorable opinion of the place was bolstered when Dr. Peyron showed us the room Vincent had been quartered in for over a year. Not a large room—it had once been a monk's cell—but it was on the ground floor, and gave on to a poetically overgrown garden, albeit seen through iron bars. The atmosphere in the echoing halls accorded well with that sense of something suspended in time, floating in the almost-visible currents that ebb and swell between this world and the next. The patients were a genteel bunch, mainly wayward but wealthy old souls who had been squirreled away here by their families for safekeeping. They went largely unsupervised. Whether their relative freedom was mandated by a liberal philosophy of treatment or a lack of funds to hire more attendants was unclear. Vincent had been granted use of the cell next door to his own as a studio. "You knew he was happy when he was painting," said Peyron. "The trouble only started when he laid down his brushes." That seemed to be the nub of the director's diagnosis.

We finally tracked the attendant Trabuc down in the baths, where he was standing sentry over two old greybeards in adjoining tubs, both up to their necks in cold water, both wrinkled as raisins, one shivering and the other singing an old Provençal tune, "Magali." Charles Trabuc was balding, with the face of a disappointed tortoise, and an Adam's apple that bounced up and down out of his celluloid collar whenever he spoke. Peyron made introductions, handed us over to Trabuc, then faded back into his own duties, whatever they entailed.

"So you're friends of Vincent?" asked Trabuc. "How is the old fellow? Still messing about with the paints?"

"Monsieur Van Gogh is dead, I'm afraid," answered Vernet.

The shiverer started splashing the singer: perhaps he was a music critic. The singer only sang louder, and splashed back.

"Damn shame," Trabuc muttered. Then to the patients—"Stop splashing!" He lit a cigarette. "Painted me once, you know? Said I had a marvelous face. Of course, he'd paint an empty chair if he couldn't get a sitter. And be just as happy."

"Was he ever dangerous?"

"Oh, no . . . not really. We don't take any dangerous ones here. Mostly it's rich old aunts and uncles, their heirs want to make sure they're not handing out the inheritance to beggars in the street. Vincent didn't quite fit in, but they liked to watch him paint. Sometimes looked like he was throwing darts at the canvas, the way he'd fling those paints."

I wondered if the singer was a rich old uncle, perhaps a former banker in Avignon with two dozen clerks racing to the snap of his fingers. Now he was nearly submerged, blowing bubbles in the water. The shiverer meanwhile was rubbing his hands together briskly as though trying to start a fire.

"There's an attendant here, I believe his name is Poulet?" asked Vernet.

"Poulet? Oh, there was a mooncalf! Used to look after Vincent. Made a real hash of it."

"How so?"

"Well, every time they went to Arles—three or four times they went to Arles, Vincent had some furniture there, I guess, and they had just the cart, they'd make a day of it, probably throw back a few." Trabuc winked. "Every time they came back, he'd be madder than before."

"Could we talk to the young man? To let him know of Vincent's passing?"

"Oh . . . long gone. Three or four months. They never stay long, the young ones. Work's too hard. Though he was a game one, I admit."

"Do you know where he went?"

"Couldn't say." He checked his pocket watch. "Five minutes, boys! You can be quiet for five more minutes, eh?"

They couldn't. The singer spurted up out of the water like a trout on a hook, singing some cabaret tune about Montmartre, belting it out to the back rows.

"Stop that, you!" Then something jogged his memory. "He may have, uh . . . gone back to Paris."

"Poulet? He was from Paris?" Vernet asked.

"No, no, from the Midi, but he'd lived in Paris, used to go on about mirlitons in Paris, playing the mirliton, something like that, with the count."

"The count?"

"Oh, yes, claimed he was employed by a count. And drank with the count, too. Used to spin all kinds of fables—you know what boys are like these days. Said he worked for a dwarf, at one time."

"Do you recall the count's name?"

Now the shiverer, jealous of the singer, up and started crowing like a rooster, "Coo-rroos, coo-rroos!" and flapping his toothpick arms like the cock of the walk. The singer, not to be outdone, joined in, singing, "Too-loos! Too-loos!"–turning it into a barnyard duet. Trabuc's face clenched with anger.

"No idea!" he snapped. "All right, you two, out of the tub! Now! Run around till you get dry."

The two old scarecrows helped each other climb out of their tubs, slipping and sliding. I turned away for modesty's sake. I could hear their wet feet slapping on the tile, the breath whistling in their lungs like teakettles. Vernet gave me a nod, and we were leaving.

"You tell old Vincent to come by and see me sometime! We still have some of his things here!" Trabuc's memory was obviously not to be trusted.

When we found Peyron again, he confirmed the asylum still had some of Vincent's clothes, some letters, and even a few of his paintings. "Nothing worth very much, I assure you. I was thinking to burn it all." Vernet insisted, however, that the paintings and any personal effects be sent on to Theo van Gogh in Paris; again he left money to pay for it. When Peyron produced another straw hat with candles on it, the twin of the one in Arles, Vernet asked for it for himself. I wondered if it held a clue of some kind; Vernet didn't seem the kind to form sentimental attachments. But when I asked, he said simply that he hoped it would be a lamp to guide him in the dark.

"I'm afraid we're in the dark now," I remarked, as we rode in the trap back to the railway station.

Vernet gave me an enigmatic look. "My friend, when you have trained your ears to hear as you have trained your eyes to see, you shall make a first-rate detective." I couldn't make heads or tails of the comment, whether it was praise or censure. Riddle after riddle with the man. Not that I wanted to be a detective of any kind. At least our destination was no mystery; we were returning to Paris.

On the train he was dreamy and distant. Paris meant we were looking for Poulet. Every other question would hang fire while he tracked down his old retainer's killer. How he planned to find the man, whom we knew nothing about beyond his name, in a city of two million souls I couldn't begin to think. If we were going to look for a needle in a haystack, I urged Vernet, why not go after Gauguin? He was a painter. If he was known well enough to come to the attention of Dupuis, he must have friends among the Impressionists, he must know dealers—why, he was an associate of Theo van Gogh, wasn't he? We'd run him to earth, force him to confess all his crimes, the forgeries, the smuggling, perhaps even Vincent's murder! He'd attempted it in Arles– most likely, he'd been on the scene in Auvers—and secretly at that! Who was a more likely suspect? Restitution would be made, the wheels of justice would be oiled, the murderer hanged, our endeavors crowned in glory. Well, I didn't mention the glory part to Vernet, but the heart of my argument was unassailable. True, I didn't know precisely how all the clues fit together to form a whole, the hows and whys and wherefores of it, but those were mere details.

Vernet bestowed a patronizing, infuriating smile upon me, as if I were the tabby cat who had just dropped a dead sparrow at his feet.

"Gauguin may be a piece of the puzzle, but he is not the whole puzzle."

It was exactly this sort of vatic utterance that drove me mad. "Once we have his confession, surely all the other pieces must fall into place!" I insisted.

"Gauguin is a rather cool customer. He does not seem a man inclined to confession. Especially for crimes he may not, in fact, have committed."

"But he was there in Auvers! And again on the train! And don't forget the sabers. What other explanation is there?"

He sat back, steepling his fingers together in his lap. "What I cannot yet comprehend is the mechanism of the lottery. It seems rococo in its complexity."

"What do you mean?"

"If you can steal a painting—or any item of great worth—so that no one even suspects it's missing, and you have a buyer, or bidders, ready to take it off your hands, and pay handsomely for it, why complicate matters? Why include these Impressionists' paintings no one seems to want?"

"Well, to fool the customs inspectors! No one is likely to look for something of value among trash." There I was certain I had scored a point.

"Perhaps. But then why require the buyers to display them publicly? When we can answer that, we shall be able to answer every other question." He settled back, wrapping himself in thought. I imagined the cogs and flywheels of his brain engaging, whirring at great speeds without sound or friction. As for the cogs of my own mind, they had sprung to a stop. I was exhausted. There was league upon league of France between us and Paris. With no sleeper cars on our train, we were obliged to sit up all night. I stared out at the moon silvering the fields and forests as it stumbled across the night sky, until I woke the next morning with a start. There was the taste of muddy boots in my mouth and a crick in my neck. We were pulling into the Gare de Lyon, wreathed in steam.

Vernet was still sitting across from me, serene as a Buddha, surrounded now by a welter of newspapers. He didn't look as if he had slept at all, or needed to. I yawned and tried to rub the sleep from my eyes. "So how do we begin our hunt?" I asked.

He stood and stretched and reached for his bag. "Sufficient unto the day is the evil thereof. Get some rest. Tonight we shall take in a cabaret."

We checked in again at our hotel in the Rue Cujas. I decided a little catnap could do me no harm. Of course, Vernet had been joking about the cabaret. As I unpacked, I looked out on the street below and saw him sitting at a café table across the way, ostensibly plowing his way through yet more newspapers. In fact, he was watching the students hurry past on their way to lectures at the Sorbonne. The bustle of youth appealed to him, I think. He was a man approaching forty, I deemed, but his blood was still as hot and his heart as restless as that of the rawest country lad come to the city to seek his fortune. Age would cool his bones soon enough. I kicked off my boots and lay down for a few minutes.

When I woke, someone was knocking on my door; I had the feeling they had been knocking for some time. I was bewildered to witness the sun disappearing below the horizon. I shuffled to the door, and opened it to Vernet.

"Ready for a spot of dinner?"

He appeared perfectly refreshed and entirely composed. Not a word about the fact that I had slept the day away, nor a word of how he had spent it. I washed the sleep from my face in the basin; he handed me a towel.

We spent an uneventful evening at Les Deux Magots. I believe it must be Vernet's favorite café in Paris. He knew the waiters all by name, and chose the food and wines for both of us. Generally abstemious, he revealed himself that night to be something of a gourmand when the mood struck him. I would not have thought to pair *blanquette de veau* with a Côte de Nuits, but someday I shall return to Paris for both. It's one thing to watch Vernet charm his suspects into telling him their secrets, and thinking what naïfs they were, and another when he trains his considerable powers upon oneself. I'm afraid that by the end of the meal he knew things about my history and my inner landscape that even my wife does not suspect. Of course, he never said a word of what he had been doing all day.

"And now, the cabaret," he said, as the last sip of armagnac radiated warmth throughout my being.

So he had *not* been joking about the cabaret. Had I misjudged him? Did the hound turn aside from his quarry? Had he abandoned the urgency of his purpose?

We found a cab. Vernet directed the driver to take us to the Boulevard Rochechouart. We crossed the Pont Neuf onto the Right Bank.

"The Boulevard Rochechouart? Is that Montmartre?" I asked.

Vernet merely nodded, lolling in his seat. Did ever a man love a mystery more than he? I would have to drag it out of him. "I begrudge no man his evening's diversions, but must we risk our lives for it?" I asked. Montmartre's name for squalid entertainments was matched by its reputation for violent enterprise.

"If I've led you to believe we're visiting the cabaret for entertainment, I humbly apologize. While you were resting, I called on a friend here in Paris. A man who knows every nook and cranny of the city. He confirmed what Trabuc told us, about a cabaret in Montmartre, frequented by the lower classes and bohemians. Tonight we visit Le Mirliton."

I remembered Trabuc saying something offhand about Poulet and mirlitons. I had assumed, as anyone would, that he was talking about one of those little mouth flutes, what the Americans call a kazoo; it all sounded like nonsense. Vernet had heard something entirely different. The detective could expound upon the virtues of logic from morning till midnight, but it was his uncanny intuition that set him apart. Logic was the cladding of his thought, not the edifice.

"You hope to find Poulet there?" I asked.

"I hope at least to find the count."

"Was your knowledgeable friend able to tell you the name of the count?"

"The old duffers in the baths told us. Did you not hear them plain as day?"

"Indeed! I heard gibberish."

"You heard the fellow with the cast in his left eye sing about Montmartre. Which made Trabuc think of Paris. And when I asked the count's name—"

"He crowed like a rooster. No, the shiverer with the mole on his nose crowed like a rooster, then the singer joined in. As I said, gibberish."

"How many languages do you speak, Doctor?"

"Fluently? Five."

"Gibberish is a difficult tongue to master, even with years of study. When your interlocutor's mind is unbalanced, it is harder still. And while one man may sing it, two will never sing a duet. Those old fellows weren't crowing 'cock-a-doodle-doo.' They were singing 'Toulouse! Toulouse!'"

"Wait. You're saying Poulet is in Toulouse?"

"Set Poulet aside for a moment. Cast your mind back to the mezzanine gallery at Boussod et Valadon. Surely you recall the paintings we saw there."

"I cannot expunge them from my thoughts, try though I might."

"Then have you forgotten the painters' signatures?"

"Signatures are little use in making attributions. They are the one thing a good forger will execute flawlessly."

"Well, then, you remember Trabuc saying that Poulet had worked for a count?"

"Yes, of course."

"But he also said that he had worked for a dwarf."

I had dismissed the absurdity of the contradiction from my mind.

"In a very few minutes, I believe you shall meet count and dwarf both."

"The count and the dwarf at the Mirliton. It sounds like something out of Lewis Carroll. Shall we find them eating oysters?"

"We shall know shortly. I believe we have arrived."

# Chapter Ten

Our cab had drawn to a standstill outside an undistinguished facade. The name of the proprietor, Aristide Bruant, was emblazoned over the door and in the posters that nearly obscured the windows with his likeness, costumed somewhere between a Viennese count and an Argentine gaucho, with a red scarf thrown over his shoulder to signal his solidarity with the proletariat. I realized at once that this Bruant was the model for Vernet's own bohemian costume.

This then was the Cabaret Le Mirliton, just one of several down-at-the-heels establishments pocking the Boulevard Rochechouart that promised song and dance and bonhomie, or alternately enough noxious drink to make the first three superfluous.

Le Mirliton was of the first kind. As soon as we were inside the door, we were greeted by smoke and noise and the booming voice of the proprietor himself. "My God, look at these two! Have the sewers backed up all the way to Montmartre?"

There was Bruant, striding up and down the top of the bar in the same costume we'd seen in the posters, a gamekeeper's outfit with a scarlet shirt and scarf, an opera cape and wide-brimmed black hat. He pointed a rattan cane at us and said, "See how they gawk? Like sheep about to be sheared! Muttonheads!"

The crowd laughed. "What are *you* laughing at?" said Bruant, picking out a balding little pickle of a man in front of him, "You've already been sheared to your pink-and-white hide. And the rest of you smell of sheep dip!"

The crowd roared at every word. These were hardly the denizens of the underworld I'd expected to see. They were stock clerks and assistant managers, wine merchants and lace manufacturers, the shank of the bourgeoisie, along with their mistresses and perhaps a few daring wives. They had climbed the butte of Montmartre to come and be scandalized and insulted by the three-penny poet of the *bateaux*. Bruant gave them good value for their money. A piano player in the corner by the bar banged on the keys, and Bruant tore into a song.

Vernet drew a waitress aside, pushed a few francs into her palm, and whispered in her ear. She pointed to the back room. Then, noticing how much the gentleman had given her, she piloted us to the inner temple herself, the "Institute," as she called it. This was the half-world where beer steins gave way to glasses of absinthe, where the painters, poets, drug addicts, and dreamers were immured, safe from the bald curiosity of the shopkeepers, their faces picked out only by flickering candlelight. This was where we found him, the monarch of Montmartre at his corner table, a sketchpad on the table in front of him, a girl on either side.

He had seen us, and was waving us over as if we were expected. "Gentlemen! Do join us!" he called.

We approached his table. "Count Toulouse-Lautrec?" Vernet asked.

The gentleman so addressed nodded vigorously, rapping his knuckles on the table. If ever an aristo had spawned a black sheep, here he was. He had the look of a broken-nosed satyr, bested by a centaur after a few rounds of bare-hooved brawling. He wore a kind of rust-colored velveteen jacket that looked more suited to a butcher than a gentleman. The dwarf sitting next to him was better attired.

Yes, I said dwarf, though I didn't notice him till we were almost on top of them, his eyes opaque behind foggy pince-nez, and yes, it was the very same dwarf we had last seen regaling the customers with brothel humor that morning in Tanguy's shop that seemed a lifetime ago, though it had barely been a week. Not only that, one of the girls at the table was Mademoiselle Valadon, with her dark flowing hair, her intelligent eyes, her defiant mouth. The Paris art world, or at least this run-down, rat-infested corner of it, was evidently quite small.

"You're the foxy detective everyone has told me to watch out for," said the satyr.

"Why should you be worried, Count?" asked Vernet.

"Maybe I robbed the Bank of England!"

Vernet's eyes appraised him, a long slow weighing, then dismissed him and shifted to the dwarf. A look of recognition came into his eyes.

"It's more of a nickname," admitted the dwarf. "My father has arranged things with his lawyers so that he will never die, so I'll never accede to the title. Call me Henri. It lets the air out of my pretentions."

I was surprised to find that I was unsurprised. The count and the dwarf were not two men, but one and the same. Had Vernet known? Almost certainly.

"And you're a painter as well?" Vernet nodded toward the sketchbook.

"So you see. Brittle legs. Bad habits. I expected you to look me up sooner, Monsieur Vernet. You're looking for bad men, I hear."

"Success!" the satyr chimed in. The two men clinked their glasses together and drained them. The count, or Henri, waved the girls away. They slipped from their seats without a word and disappeared into the crowd. The king's courtiers knew their place. "This is my friend Monsieur Louis Anquetin, also a painter," he said, introducing the satyr.

"Also a bad man!" Anquetin winked at us.

Henri gestured to the vacant seats. Vernet and I settled into them.

"We're not the only villains, either. You're in Ali Baba's cave. See there?" Anquetin pointed to a nearby table. "Coiners. From England. You're probably carrying a few of their francs. And there? The gentlemen who tried to corner the market on copper and nearly brought down the nation. At that table, monarchists plotting to bring General Boulanger back, and right behind them, a table full of anarchists, pockets full of bombs, ready to bring down any government you have in mind. Safecrackers, footpads, and second-story men meet every second Thursday. For horse-nobbling and cardsharping, you'll have to apply at Le Moulin Rouge."

"Murderers?" I asked, half-facetiously.

"Oh, murderers? You'll have to be more specific. Gunmen, garrotters, stabbers, poisoners? Fratricides, patricides, matricides, paid assassins, or those who kill for sport? If they're not here, they'll drop by after work." The man apparently felt a need to fill the air with mindless prattle—perhaps to hide a guilty conscience?—and had no compunction about stretching the truth to its breaking point.

"I believe they're looking for forgers, Louis," said Henri.

"Oh, well, we're all forgers here," Anquetin answered.

"Speak for yourself," the little man said sourly.

The two girls returned to the table. Mademoiselle Valadon brandished a bottle of absinthe and glasses as if she were Eve with a basket of apples. The other girl, a fleshy blonde with her hair piled in a bouffant, was dragging a couple of chairs behind her. They squeezed in, Mademoiselle Valadon between the two painters, the blonde between myself and Vernet. Mademoiselle Valadon attended to the ritual of louching, a needlessly complicated procedure of diluting absinthe by pouring water over a lump of sugar that sits on a kind of sieve atop the glass. The water trickles through, turning the absinthe cloudy. The blonde passed the glasses around as if they were promises of further, more libidinous favors. I had sampled the concoction before. I prefer beer.

Vernet ignored the women and the drink both. "There are many bad men in the world," he said, dismissing Anquetin's buffoonery. "It takes no particular acuity to find them. Presently I'm searching for a man in your employ, Count. Jean-Francois Poulet."

"Poulet!" The name escaped from the blonde before she could stop herself.

Vernet nodded. "Mademoiselle, at least, knows the name."

Henri was unruffled. "As do I. A toast, gentlemen, to Poulet." He lifted his glass. Vernet eyed the cloudy green liquid in his own glass dubiously.

"Absinthe. Some say it clouds the mind. I say it clears the heart." Henri brought his glass to his lips. "How is old Poulet?"

"You're no longer his master?" Vernet asked.

"He began as one of my father's stable hands. No dab hand at grooming horses, so my father sent him up here to groom me. No good at that, either. I dispatched him to keep an eye on Vincent."

"Did you send Vincent to Arles?"

Henri seemed to consider the answer less straightforward than the question. He stared at his glass as if waiting for it to supply an answer. Finally, he drank it off and set it down neatly. "Vincent and I used to go to the Louvre in the afternoons to study the masters. He was particularly fond of Millet's big-shouldered peasant women. We knew them like old friends."

Anquetin lifted his glass to make another toast. No one paid him the least attention. Vernet waited stonily for Henri to continue.

Henri had absinthe dribbling down his chin. Mademoiselle Valadon pulled the silk handkerchief from his coat pocket and wiped it away. He nodded his thanks. "Vincent wanted to create a studio, a group of like-minded artists living and working together in camaraderie," he said. "I suggested Provence. The light is better, the air is healthier, the people are simpler. Paris is a cesspool, in every way."

"Yet you remained here."

"Yes. Well, it's *my* cesspool."

"And then you sent Poulet to spy on him?"

"To protect him!" Mademoiselle Valadon cried.

"Suzanne!" Anquetin's graveled warning was too late.

Vernet swiveled toward the girl. "To protect him from what, mademoiselle?"

She realized she had said too much. "Vincent was an innocent," she said, retreating. "People treated him cruelly."

"Suzanne hasn't learned how to be cruel. Terrible shortcoming in a woman." The mischief in the satyr's eyes was tinged with menace.

But Mademoiselle Valadon could not be silenced so easily. "Perhaps you don't know, Henri nearly fought a duel to protect Vincent's honor," she said.

Vernet looked askance at the little man.

"It was nothing," said Henri, uncomfortable. "A squabble between artists."

"Nothing!" cried Anquetin. "They had to pull you off the bastard! Henri cut the air with his swordstick like D'Artagnan against de Rochefort."

"He was a dwarf," Henri said, dismissing the subject. "A Belgian dwarf, at that," he added, to put the matter to rest entirely.

Vernet accommodated his modesty, returning to his original line of questioning. "Did you send Gauguin to Arles?"

Now Henri's back was well and truly up. "I have nothing to do with Monsieur Gauguin. There's a fellow I'd flog if I could reach up further than his navel. Don't talk to me about that jackal."

"Yet he and Poulet were together in Auvers after Vincent's death."

"I am not Poulet's keeper, monsieur! After Vincent's—accident— in Arles, I discharged the buffoon. Haven't seen him since. Don't know whose nits he picks now."

"Did you know Poulet followed Vincent to the asylum?"

A look passed between the two painters. No, they hadn't known, and they were disquieted by the news, though it could make no difference now.

"Do you know if he came to Paris?" Vernet continued, relentless.

"I know he has a knack for landing on his feet." Henri looked about, uncomfortable.

"You'd hardly expect it in such a blockhead," said Anquetin, snatching the baton. "What's all this worry about poor Vincent and that dunderhead Poulet, anyway? Word on the grapevine was that you were sleuthing out forgeries in the Louvre."

Suzanne colored. No need to look further for the source of Anquetin's intelligence.

"Does the grapevine whisper the names of the forgers?" Vernet asked him.

"What difference does it make? You're so wrought up about copies, copies, copies, which you defame by calling them forgeries. But if you visit the Salon, what are all those paintings of Greek gods and martyred saints and moth-eaten monarchs but copies of each other? What are they but copies of Ingres or Velazquez or Rubens, our esteemed forbearers? And what are those but copies of Titian and Tiepolo and Raphael? What's every painting since the fourteenth century but a copy of Giotto? And the judges nod their heads, right, yes, marvelous, yes, masterpiece, yes, let's give 'em a prize!

"Then along comes a fellow like old Manet and he rubs it in their faces, the bourgeois pigs, he drops one of those Rubens nudes in the middle of a picnic in the park, and the whole gang of forgers that vote in the Salon squawks like a bunch of innkeeper's wives because they've been affronted by an original."

"Monsieur Anquetin, your passion recommends you. I have no quarrel with forgers, though my philosophical friend here may differ." Vernet nodded toward me; I hoped every line in my face indicated that I did indeed differ. But he went on: "Forgery's not a crime in France. But theft is, and every forgery in the Louvre means a stolen painting in the hands of thieves and receivers. It means clandestine transactions, criminal conspiracy, the risk of exposure, desperation, and at the end of it all, murder. You cannot dismiss murder as a joke."

I doubt whether Anquetin was chastised, but at least he was silenced, trying to get his breath back.

Then Henri played another card. I say it was his play, because I'm certain the women were entirely under his direction, though I never caught the subtle signals that must have passed between them. The blonde brought her hand to Vernet's cheek, caressing it with the back of one long nail. It was a bold move, and he flinched as if he'd been struck, but she persisted. "You seem anxious, monsieur," she coaxed. "Let Louise take your mind off your troubles." She marched a glass of absinthe under his nose.

It was an unsophisticated ploy, more suited to the provinces than Paris. I was certain it would have no effect on Vernet. So I was almost dumfounded when he took the glass she offered, his fingers pressed on hers for a fleeting moment, a lecherous grin twisting his face. He drained the glass at one swallow. Did Vernet have an Achilles' heel in the fair sex? He set the glass on the table, staring at it as if it had just picked his pocket. His eyes traveled the long journey from his glass to the count's face.

"You know everything that goes on in Montmartre, monsieur," he said, raising his hands in earnest supplication. "Why not help me?"

Henri Toulouse-Lautrec looked down at his own hands: large, but with thin, stunted fingers. Were they brittle like his legs, I wondered? Was every brushstroke across the canvas an agony? He turned toward Mademoiselle Valadon. "Did you know Theo van Gogh was ill, Suzanne? You should go round and visit him."

"His wife would appreciate that, I'm sure." Both girls laughed.

He spoke to Vernet, almost in a whisper, though his eyes remained on Mademoiselle Valadon's. "I've followed your exploits in the papers, monsieur, and cheered you on. I've even imagined myself as a comrade by your side, charging through pea-soup fog in a hansom cab to apprehend some murderous devil or other. Today, regrettably, I must be on the side of the devils."

Anquetin remained silent, his riotous spirit quenched.

There was some commotion on the far side of the room, laughter and shouts of greeting, where a young Adonis had entered in full flower through a door at the back, a girl hanging on either arm. It crossed my mind that all of France must be inhabited only by a handful of actors doubling and tripling roles, for the golden-maned, immaculately tailored newcomer was none other than Dupuis, transported by flying carpet from Montpellier. There was a rustle of silk, and before I could turn round, Mademoiselle Valadon was across the room and in his arms. Henri's eyes, dark and endlessly deep behind the pince-nez, reflected the scene. The rest of us were no longer present as far as he was concerned. I wished fervently that we were not present in fact. The man struggled with the treachery of his body every day. This kind of humiliation was wholly gratuitous.

"Speak of the devil," said Louise. She bestowed a pitying look on the count. Then she loped over to join the crowd around Dupuis.

Henri's eyes were fogged behind his lenses. "You won't get far trying to question people in Montmartre, Monsieur Vernet," he muttered in a queer, thin voice. "People show their hindquarters sooner than their true faces."

"I need only one face," rejoined Vernet.

"Good luck to you. Get us a cab, Louis." Anquetin nodded and went out, a vassal after all. Henri remained absorbed in the goings-on across the room. Dupuis had made some ribald joke and the women all laughed like convent girls. Henri leaned over and touched Vernet's sleeve. "Ask Olympia," he whispered.

The words sent a shock through me. Olympia, the same name Vincent had mentioned on his deathbed! I couldn't help but let my gaze wander round the room, searching for some Delphic female face. There were only the vapid, listless looks of the painters' grisettes. "Does she work here?" I asked.

My naiveté purchased a crooked smile from Henri. "Olympia spends all her time on her backside. Look sharp, boys, you'll meet her."

Then I realized Vernet had not reacted at all to Henri's words. Had he perhaps not heard? His attention was trained entirely on the circus surrounding Dupuis. Was he jealous of the attentions of blonde Louise? This was the worst moment possible to let his thoughts stray from our object.

Henri nodded toward Dupuis and Mademoiselle Valadon, heads together, tender glances. "As you see, messieurs, I'm *not* aware of everything that goes on in Montmartre."

He climbed down from his chair, took up a pair of canes that were leaning against the wall behind him. "Do go look in on Theo van Gogh," he said finally, and hobbled off toward the front room. Never before or since have I seen a man so dignified.

We tried to take our own leave as unobtrusively as possible, but our exit unfortunately took us past the table where Dupuis was holding court. He spied us and hailed us as bosom friends.

"Vernet! Still sleuthing? You're an absolute Trojan, old man."

"How goes your business in Montpellier, monsieur?"

"Is there anywhere in the world so dull as Languedoc? I left your cousin and the general debating the merits of the Madrid Protocol. I was off on the next train after yours. Here, have a drink with me, gentlemen. I insist."

There were glasses of absinthe already poured on the table, glowing like votive candles. Dupuis put one in Vernet's hand.

"Doctor, would you find us a cab?" Vernet asked. I was only too happy to comply. As I went out through the front room, Bruant broke off his song to call me several kinds of swine; I dodged between his barbs to make the safety of the street.

I hadn't realized how drowsy the air of the cabaret had made me until I stepped into the bracing night air. The foot traffic had thinned to a few amorous couples pawing each other in doorways, and one or two discouraged footpads. A few private carriages were ranged along the street, their drivers drowsing. Yet there was the tinny echo of crowds emanating from the half-dozen clubs along the street.

At the top of the street a four-wheeler turned the corner toward me. I hallooed him as he came on, one slow hoofbeat at a time, the horse a chestnut with a white star above his eye. I could make out the driver's stocky form upon the box, his face a pumpkin in the gaslight as he neared, his left arm bound in a sling, his right arm with the reins lashed tight. He came alongside me but did not stop, nor even look down at me calling him as he passed. I would have run to seize the traces, but my attention was diverted by the sound of a familiar voice.

"Monsieur the Russian! Delighted to see you!"

I had imbibed no more than a thimbleful of absinthe—I was certain of that. Yet here I was, fallen prey to the worst sort of hallucination. From the green kid gloves to the grey homburg, there he stood, peering from side to side, as if he had just popped out of his burrow, last seen lecturing me on modern French painters and Rosicrucian ritual—Grunewald? Brunewald? Brunelle!—that was the name. He pumped my hand as I made a last doomed attempt to get the cabman's attention.

Brunelle took no notice of my distraction. He turned his attention to a poster in the window that advertised the attractions of a blonde dancing girl called "La Goulue" who vaguely resembled the girl Louise. In fact, I realized, it *was* Louise.

"Decadent, isn't it? But Sar Peladan conducts the secret rites of the Rosy Cross here every Tuesday at midnight, if you can believe it, in the upstairs room. I'm hoping he can persuade Charles Maurin to paint my wife and me as Osiris and Isis on a winged barge, with our dog as Anubis. It could go just behind the piano in the conservatory. There's a Corot there now, but it's only a lithograph. An angel of the Tetragrammaton appeared at last week's ritual. Wish me luck!"

Of course! If the leads in the play kept on reappearing, why not the clowns? Why shouldn't this silly Belgian tradesman appear out of nowhere in the middle of Montmartre at midnight, simply to keep me from catching my cab, blast him! And where was Vernet?

"Monsieur Brunelle, please excuse me—" I began, in far too civil a tone, but he cut me off.

"I'd love to catch up with you, my friend, but latecomers are subject to the Discipline of the Rule. Let's have supper sometime soon, eh?" With that, he darted inside the cabaret, leaving me breathless. The cab had turned the corner out of sight. The night air was still. Where in God's name was Vernet?

I wavered between the curb and the cabaret, growing more anxious by the minute. Vernet had no need of a nursemaid. Yet he was one man only, with an invisible enemy arrayed against him. Perhaps I should go into the next street to look for a cab? Perhaps not.

Bruant greeted me again by baaing like a sheep. I shouldered my way through the crowd at the front back to the Institute. Dupuis and the girl were still at the same table, alone now and tête-à-tête. I had no wish to bandy words with them. The room seemed an endless cavern of shadows and smoke, but that was the mirrors—it wasn't really big at all. Unless he was crouching under a table or hiding in a corner, Vernet should be in plain sight. I had made a terrible mistake leaving him alone in this place.

A patch of red on the floor. A bright red scarf that could only belong either to Vernet or Bruant himself, on the floor, lying just inside the tradesman's entrance. I picked up the scarf and pushed through the door, out into an alley littered with crates and bins. The rank smell of moldy beer and rotting cabbage rose up to assault my nostrils.

When I try to recall what happened next, it all plays out in my mind with the turbid weightlessness of a dream. The stars high overhead trembled like sunbeams skimming off the surface of a pond. There was Vernet, in the middle of the alley, listing like a boat in a storm, ready to go under at the first wave. There at the end of the alley the cab, the chestnut with the white star over his eye, pulling against the current. Then the crack of the gunshot, the horse rears and plunges, races up the street toward us, the carriage bouncing behind, the hapless one-armed driver, face white with terror. I'm calling to Vernet, who stands like a statue, his eyes two marble ovals; I can't even hear myself over the violence of hooves. Here is the cab, one wheel sparking a stone and shooting away on its own journey, the cab toppling upon us, the driver thrown into the air, still lashed to the reins. The horse, in a fury of terror, blacking out the night sky, and I too am flying, hurling myself across the alley, slamming Vernet's body to the ground, hooves spraying stones against my scalp, the carriage plowing through bins, smashing against the wall of the building, the driver's battered body juddering across the cobblestones, Vernet unconscious in my arms as I listen to the hoofbeats recede in the distance.

A crowd comes misting out of the cabaret. I'm distantly aware of questions, shouts, faces in my face, hot breath infused with absinthe.

Someone says we are dead, then takes it back, someone says the driver is dead; no one takes it back.

Vernet groans as he struggles toward consciousness. I roll away from him. I lie there staring at the heavens, remembering the driver's face as he sloughed past, his skull bouncing like a crushed melon against the paving stones. I had seen that face before, another actor in our stock company, standing surprised in the train passage with my Gladstone in his arms; he'd turned and fled and been flung from the train, cheating Death, then only to meet Him a few days later here in Samarra.

# Chapter Eleven

"I tell you, Doctor, I'm quite capable! Ivan Ivanovich, where are my boots?"

Vernet tried to stand. A stab of pain in his ankle forced him to drop back heavily upon the bed. He gave forth with a couple of choice epithets in English. The doctor, summoned from his bed when we came hobbling in off the street, resumed his examination unperturbed.

"Would you please leave off, Doctor? We've established that there's a tear in the ligament of the talocrural joint. You'll drive me out of my wits with your incessant prodding."

Vernet's frustration was patent. His temperament was wholly unsuited to inaction. In the moments after the attack, when he realized he couldn't stand on his own, he had browbeat me into half-carrying, half-dragging him over to examine the body of the carriage driver, so as to ascertain the cause of death. I could have told him (and indeed I tried) that the force of his skull hitting the stones was enough to kill a man, let alone being dragged for another thirty yards by the panicked horse before it came up lame. The face was so spattered with blood and brains as to be unidentifiable. But he must see for himself, even though his faculties were still deranged by the effects of the absinthe. Hadn't he heard a gunshot? Yes, it had sounded like a gunshot, I agreed, but I was no expert. There had been no gunshot wounds visible on the driver's body—we made sure of that. An operation that caused me to lose my excellent dinner.

The doctor began wrapping Vernet's ankle in new linen. "If you stay off your ankle, the swelling will go down in a few days, monsieur. Of your wits, I have my doubts."

"Yes, yes, everyone is mad but the doctors who make the diagnoses."

"Being dragged out of bed at three in the morning to tend to drunken roisterers can drive a man mad, I assure you." We had told the doctor that Vernet had turned his ankle getting out of a hansom cab. The alcohol on his breath had supplied the doctor with the rest of his diagnosis.

A tap at the door. I opened it to a stranger. And yet—not a stranger. Of course not.

Vernet beamed up at him. "You heard!"

"You created more stir at Le Mirliton than Buffalo Bill at the Exposition," returned the other.

The moustache had shrunk to manageable human proportions, carefully waxed, he had traded the glasses for a pince-nez, but surely this was the same copyist we had met at the Musée Fabre? There were the same robin's-egg eyes, at any rate.

The doctor closed up his bag. He jabbed the newcomer in the sternum with his finger. "Nothing but bed rest, three days!" he said. The other fellow nodded meekly. The doctor went out.

Vernet witnessed my confusion, and was delighted. "Dr. Lermolieff, may I present Inspector Goron of the Sûreté? You'll remember him from Montpellier, where he helped us extract the Vernet painting. He's been aiding in our inquiries from the beginning—in an unofficial capacity, of course."

Looked at strictly logically, it all made sense. There were men on one side trying to hide the criminal acts they'd committed, and men on the other side trying to bring them to light. On both sides, they would assume various guises to gain advantage and achieve their ends. Was I not "Ivan Lermolieff" after all, another actor in the masquerade? Yet I could not escape a certain lightheadedness, even nausea, when the people around me assumed the arbitrary fluidity of characters in a dream.

"What have you discovered?" Vernet asked.

"Not much, I'm afraid," Goron answered. "Shots were certainly fired. We found two bullet holes in the door of the cab. Which means someone was either a very bad shot or was intent on frighting and stampeding the horse, which is certainly what occurred. But no one admits seeing the gunman. No one would, in that neighborhood. We did, however, find one person you'd been looking for."

Vernet looked hopeful. "Who is that?"

"I'm afraid I must disappoint you further. The cab driver was identified by his employers as one Jean-Francois Poulet."

Vernet shut his eyes and set his jaw. His hands clutched reflexively at the bed linens.

"We can't determine, of course, whether the gunman's object was to kill Poulet or yourself, or, if we may entertain the notion, both. But it might be wise to take precautions in any case."

Vernet winced again as he tried to shift his leg. "So Poulet is permanently unavailable for questioning." He sat dully, rearranging the puzzle pieces in his mind. Was justice satisfied, by his lights? Or had he been cheated by Poulet's death?

"What about Gauguin?" he asked dully.

"No trace yet. He seems to be a vagrant of sorts. No fixed abode. Not in France, at least."

"Have you anything for me of a more medicinal nature?"

"These might help to ease the pain." Goron handed him a sheaf of papers. "The customs records you asked for."

Vernet leafed through them. "All duly signed by Leon Boussod."

"Except those last few," Goron pointed out.

Vernet read the signatures. One eyebrow shot up. "So we come full circle, back to Theo van Gogh."

"Him, at least, we know where to find," said Goron.

"I shall call on him tomorrow."

"No, no, my friend, tomorrow you will rest, and stay off that ankle, or I shall face the wrath of Dr. Monier. I don't like to upset a man who works with poisons. Van Gogh isn't going anywhere. He's taken ill." He looked to me. "Don't let this fellow out of your sight, Doctor. My men will arrest him if he tries to hobble away." He tipped his hat and gave me a wink.

"But stay: one more thing, my friend," begged Vernet. "You know Montmartre intimately. Have you come across a woman named Olympia?"

So he *had* been listening.

Goron laughed heartily, till he realized the question was serious. "Well, you are foreigners, no question. But everyone knows half the prostitutes in Paris call themselves Olympia. It's like hanging out a shingle."

There it was: the clue Toulouse-Lautrec had offered in whispered confidence was no more than a crass joke. That was apparently his idea of noblesse oblige.

Vernet, as you might suspect, was a trying patient. He was a man of perpetual motion, both mentally and physically. Goron got hold of a bath chair for him. Every morning I dutifully wheeled him down to the café and left him in the care of a group of street Arabs who seemed to gather round him like pilot fish round a shark. He had them running errands constantly as he sat reading newspapers, drinking endless cups of coffee, writing reams of letters, and sending cables to every destination from Arles to Zanzibar. He had whispered conversations with men who appeared to be the absolute dregs of the earth, but were in actuality top agents of the Sûreté (or so he told me, one of the few bits of information I dragged out of him during that three-day sabbatical). Between him and Goron, every clue was sifted, every alibi checked, every story scrutinized for its veracity. For my part, I declared that I would return to the museums to reproduce the studies the unfortunate Poulet had pilfered from me on the train. It might not prove particularly helpful, I knew, but at least it was a means of dodging Vernet's volatile moods.

But I didn't go to the museums. Instead my feet found their way back to the little shop in the Rue Clauzel where the old termagant Tanguy ground his paints and spouted treason. To this day I can't explain my reasons for the expedition. He was alone in the shop that day, sitting on a high stool at the counter, clucking over his account books.

I cleared my throat. "I understand you have some paintings here by Vincent van Gogh."

He did not look up from his book. "I remember you. You were in here a fortnight ago."

I nodded, guilty as charged.

"With that fellow . . . Delaroche?" He licked his thumb to turn a page.

"Vernet."

His nostrils flared. It were better not to have corrected him.

"I don't really know him," I protested. "We were—"

"And at the funeral."

"I was . . . taken with the paintings I saw there."

I had seen them surrounding coffin that afternoon that had left their mark upon me, but that first encounter with them in the attic room where Vincent lay dying, when they whirled about my head like fireworks ripping the sky into shreds.

He gazed at me from under frosty brows. There was something uncanny in his stare, as if I were begging entrance to the hall of the mountain king, and he was the goblin gatekeeper, divining the hidden secrets of my heart.

He clapped his hands together. "Come."

He slammed the ledger shut and jumped down from the stool. He led me back to his workroom, where he ground his paints. The smells of turpentine and linseed oil stood forth like sentries. We stopped at a side door. He searched through a ring of keys and tried a few till he found the right one and turned the key. We peered into the darkness of a storeroom.

He struck a match; the flame of a kerosene lamp hanging on the wall welled up, lighting Vincent's paintings. Once more that sense of vertigo seized me, nausea mixed with exhilaration. But it was different this time, too. The wild, whirling brushstrokes I remembered from the Auvers paintings had been reduced to mere stipples of color in laboriously plotted juxtapositions of complementaries, colors that seemed to dissolve in one another. Whenever I tried to look straight at any painting, the colors seemed to scatter to the corners of my eyes. It was still Impressionism, but taken to its logical, frightening extreme.

"These aren't like the ones I saw in Auvers."

Tanguy looked over my shoulder. "Oh, yes. The little dots. Seurat came up with that; for a while they were all doing it, even old Pissarro. Vincent's attack was constantly evolving. When he first came to me, he was as great a reactionary as you are. Millet and Delacroix, those were his gods."

"Reactionary! Those men were revolutionaries!"

"In their time, yes, but no longer. Every revolution deserves another revolution. Who would you call the greatest master of all time?"

"Leonardo, of course."

He nodded as if expecting just that answer. "The greatest revolutionary of his time. So hungry for novelty that he could hardly be bothered to finish one painting before he started the next."

"But he painted as men see."

"No, no, no, he taught men to see as he painted! What's Impressionism but Leonardo's techniques of chiaroscuro and sfumato pushed to their limit? One day men will see as the Impressionists paint."

"And you teach the Impressionists how to see?"

"Oh, no, monsieur, not me! These!" He dug into his pocket and came up with a couple of tubes of paint. There was nothing extraordinary about them; they were the same paints every artist uses. "Monsieur knows the Renaissance masters, eh? He knows they worked in studios, surrounded by assistants, grinding their own paints, sacrificing hand and eye to achieve eternity. But these, these little tubes of paint, they liberate the artist from the studio, from the assistants even, he's able to pitch his easel anywhere in the great world, in sun and fog and wind, even in the rain if he is brave enough."

I was reminded of Vincent painting under the stars over the Rhône, the candles in his hat threatening to set his hair on fire.

"And what does he find?" Tanguy continued eagerly. "Not eternity, but change, ceaseless change. All is movement, all is flux, not to be contemplated but only apprehended as it passes. The sun rides across the sky in a chariot of fire, the rain whispers or shouts, slapping him in the face. There are no saints of the church, no gods of Olympus, but city streets of living, breathing, moving humanity. All because of these tubes of paint. He can capture all that movement only if he hurries, but he can capture it in a score of pigments, thanks to aniline pigments in tin tubes."

He went on and on in this vein. I didn't bother to contradict him. Real painters were still working in their studios, studying the Old Masters, choosing elevated subjects to make art worthy of the name. Whether they ground their own paints or squirted them from tubes was of little consequence.

The storeroom was full to brimming with Vincent's paintings and drawings, half of them still rolled up and stuffed in crates. I came across a portrait of Tanguy himself, the style heavily indebted to the current craze for *Japonisme*. "How much is this?" I asked, thinking to flatter him.

"Not the slightest idea. None of these are for sale. Not yet, anyway."

"How much does Vincent's work generally go for?"

"Eh . . . the price of the canvas? Vincent never sold a painting in his life."

There were a few of Vincent's paintings in the shop that had actually been priced, so we returned there. Tanguy's walls were plastered with unsold and unsellable artists.

My eyes had been traveling over the canvases along the wall, and now my attention was arrested. "Wait, who's that?" I asked.

It was a bearded satyr with a broken nose, a spray of berries in the band of his top hat, a long clay pipe clenched between his teeth. The eyes were manic; the whole portrait seemed to swagger. Someone knew their subject well.

"Good eye. Louis Anquetin. For my money, the finest of the young artists. You'll be hearing his name for years to come."

"No, but who *painted* it?"

"Self-portrait."

Well, there was an eye-opener, no question about it. He pointed out a few more of Anquetin's works in a different style: portraits of Montmartre women, composed mostly of flat fields of color outlined in black, like the posters on the walls at Le Mirliton. He showed me a few paintings in the same style by Toulouse-Lautrec. Everyone was doing it, he assured me. I could have assured him that in Berlin and Prague, Rome and Vienna, no one was doing it. But I kept coming back again and again to the Anquetin self-portrait. There was an unsettling familiarity to it, and not merely because I had met the subject.

None of Vincent's paintings in the shop impressed me particularly. "No," said Tanguy, "these are pictures by Vincent the student. He was trying on everyone around him, Monet, Pissarro, Seurat, all those different disguises. Those pictures that were hung around the bier at his funeral, now *those* were Vincent van Gogh and no one else. He came into his own at the end. His brother is mounting a show soon, I believe. You'll want to wait for that."

I nodded, tendered my thanks, and left the shop. Did I really mean to spend money on one of Vincent's paintings? Hang it in my drawing room where my guests could view it and wonder whether I had lost my senses? Perhaps his pictures haunted me, but did I want to be haunted? Not likely. But the day had not been a waste. Perhaps I had no more appreciation of the achievements of Vincent and his coterie, but I had a better understanding of their aims, even if I still considered them failures.

And I came away with the unshakeable impression that the portrait of Alfred Bruyas that had started Vincent on his road to madness had been painted by Louis Anquetin.

# Chapter Twelve

After three days, Vernet rose again. He was given a clean bill of health by a grudging Dr. Monier. He showed no sign of even the slightest discomfort in walking. As soon as the doctor was out the door, however, he collapsed in his chair clutching his ankle, gritting his teeth in silent agony.

"Shall I get the doctor back?"

He shook his head furiously. In a few minutes he was up again, leaning on a stick, ready to take on the world, or at least Theo van Gogh.

It was hard to believe that Van Gogh had once again fallen under suspicion. In the hours we had spent with him, he seemed one of those buttoned-down Dutch burghers who tread the narrow Calvinist path to heaven every day, honest and even-handed in business, devoted to family and friends, if always a bit detached from them. If he were a trafficker in stolen treasures, he would have a good, solid rationale for what would be considered nefarious deeds in any other man. The only peculiarity about him was his association with the ne'er-do-well

Impressionists and his championing of their paintings, which might be explained by familial loyalty to his brother.

But there was his signature on a handful of cargo manifests where his signature had no business to be, and the nature of the items being shipped seemed willfully obscured. Theo van Gogh had questions to answer.

Van Gogh and his nascent family had recently installed themselves in a modest flat in a cul-de-sac off the Boulevard Rochefoucauld, within walking distance of Boussod et Valadon. Goron had a police spy watching the place, and Vernet had at least one of his street Arabs, his "Montmartre irregulars" as he dubbed them, watching it night and day. They had little enough to report, only that young Madame Van Gogh had made several trips to the chemist's in the last few days. Her husband had appeared under the weather at his brother's funeral. Now he was undeniably ill, having missed several days of work together, and her face as she passed down the street was said to be stricken with worry.

We were greeted by the lady herself at the door of their flat, cradling the baby in her arms. She was a no-nonsense little Dutch wife in a blue pinafore, with chestnut hair pinned up behind. She did her best to send us away, and her flat dismissals would have discouraged any tradesman or bill collector to the point of suicide. Vernet, having climbed four flights of stairs on his bad ankle, was not to be denied. He shouldered his way into the foyer, raising his voice.

"Tell him it's about his brother."

"My husband has no brother," she answered, wary.

"My condolences, madame. We were with him the night his brother died."

She had no answer to that. Still, she was unwilling to give way. Finally, we heard Theo's own voice, "Let them in, Johanna!"

She opened the door to the drawing room. The place exploded before our eyes like confetti at Carnival. Every inch of wall space, every stick of furniture, sofa, chairs, tables, piano, cabinets, and most of the floor were covered with paintings—nearly all, I guessed, the work of his brother. I felt as if I stood at the edge of a precipice, and the merest push might send me falling forever into one of those fantastic landscapes.

"Most impressive," was all I could say.

Theo van Gogh was kneeling on the floor in shirtsleeves and carpet slippers, a painting in either hand, three more leaning against the wall in front of him. His face was pale as ivory, his collar open. His shirt was damp with sweat. He eyed me narrowly, perhaps gauging the sincerity of my utterance. I hardly knew myself. His wife started clearing a couple of chairs so we might sit, while juggling the baby in her arms. When I tried to come to her aid, she thrust the baby into my arms. It had been a while since I had held an infant, but I am happy to report that my skills at chucking babies under chins have not diminished over the years.

"Monsieur Vernet, isn't it? What about my brother? Careful where you step, gentlemen," he warned.

Vernet folded himself painfully into the first chair that was cleared. He stared around him at the paintings. It seemed to me that he, too, must be struggling with the hallucinatory pull of Vincent's handiwork. "When I first saw your brother's work, I was convinced he was mad," he said.

Perhaps not the most tactful opening. But Van Gogh took it as a compliment. "You see now what he was attempting?"

"I confess I don't. But I've met some of the demons he was battling." He pointed to a charcoal sketch of Vincent lying on the piano stool. "Not one of his, I think?"

"No, it was a gift to him from a friend, Henri Toulouse-Lautrec."

"Vincent really did have a great many friends." Vernet said it as a fact.

"And fought with them all, at one time or another," said Van Gogh with some chagrin. "But always with affection."

"Yes. Not a mean-spirited man, I deem. But a truth-seeker will have his quarrels with the world." He stated it as if from personal experience. Was that how he saw himself? He had said something along those lines before. How had he put it? *Only an instrument of the truth.* I had looked upon the man as a kind of automaton, a carnival attraction that took in clues and spat out solutions. Perhaps he meant to be more. Perhaps he aspired to art. Or perhaps I was letting my fancy run away with me.

Madame Van Gogh offered me a space she had cleared on the sofa, relieving me of the child. She carried him into another room, singing softly to him.

"Please let me apologize again for my ill-timed remarks in Auvers," Vernet said to Van Gogh.

"Have you changed your opinion about my brother's death?"

"An opinion I could change. A fact, I cannot."

"It must be wonderful to be so certain of your facts," Van Gogh said caustically.

Vernet must have understood he was treading on dangerous ground. He rested his chin on the head of his walking stick, which I noticed was of ebony, carved in the shape of a falcon. "Often it is a curse," he said at length.

The weight of the statement, stripped of arrogance or bravado, seemed to carry to Van Gogh's heart. At any rate, he didn't challenge it. He fixed his eyes on the painting in front of him: the town hall at Auvers, garlanded by Bastille Day banners. I had been in Paris the day Vincent must have painted that, watching the fireworks over the Seine from my hotel room balcony, missing my wife like the devil. I wondered what the picture might bring to Vernet's mind. Our first glimpse of Mademoiselle Gachet, alone in the moonlight in the porch of the same building? At that moment I felt an ache of longing rattle through my whole frame.

Van Gogh set the painting down. "Are you here about the Bruyas portrait, then?"

This was news. Vernet hadn't informed me he had corresponded with Van Gogh about the Bruyas portrait. He sat forward now, all eagerness. "You said you had no memory of the incident."

"That's so. But my brother was a prodigious letter writer. Your wire prompted me to look through some of Vincent's old letters. Johanna?" he called.

Madame Van Gogh appeared. "Would you bring me those letters from the bedside table?"

She went out again, returning with a bundle of letters done up in a black ribbon, as though in mourning. Vernet scanned them, then handed them over to me. There were five or six letters, all mentioning the Bruyas portrait, or the man himself. The first was dated December 18, 1888. These words stood out for me at once:

*The portrait of Bruyas resembles you and me like a brother.*

The third letter remarked again on the uncanny likeness between himself and the portrait, which he seemed to take as an omen that he was on the right track with his "studio of the south."

So Vincent had indeed seen what we had seen—in the company of Gauguin, five days before his first attack—and it had affected him profoundly. How had he reconciled himself to it? Had he actually taken it as a sign from heaven? Wild coincidence? Macabre jest? Had Gauguin seen the painting? Had he pretended that any likeness was all in Vincent's mind? Or did he relent and let Vincent into the plot, only to find out the honest Dutchman wouldn't stand for it? Had they quarreled, the quarrel become violent, swords crossed?

As if in answer to my thoughts, Vernet reached out with his stick and tapped a long box of dark wood lying on top of the piano. "The sabers have arrived!"

"We have you to thank for those? I wondered why they appeared just now. I wish you'd sent them straight to Gauguin himself," said Van Gogh.

"Is Gauguin truly a skilled fencer?" asked Vernet.

Van Gogh shrugged. "I've never seen him in a fight. He's a bully, I know that."

"Did he bully your brother?"

Van Gogh grimaced. "Vincent let it happen."

"I would have taken Vincent for a fighter."

Van Gogh nodded. "But not that kind. He had enough to do conquering thirty centimeters of canvas every day without looking for others to bring low."

"Gauguin was not at the funeral, I think. Did he stop by to pay his respects?"

"He sent a note," said Madame Van Gogh.

"Might I see it?" asked Vernet, affecting nonchalance.

Van Gogh's temper flared. "Is it your habit simply to rampage through a man's private correspondence, monsieur?" The strain of his illness was telling on him.

"I've offended you again." There was actually a hint of contrition in his voice. "I'm afraid it's your correspondence that brings us here today. I revealed to you before that I'm working for a consortium with interests in the art world. What I did not mention is that Dr. Lermolieff and I have been engaged to investigate the theft of some quite valuable Old Master paintings."

Van Gogh darted a questioning look at me.

"He's the connoisseur. I'm the bloodhound," Vernet explained.

Van Gogh persisted. "What's that got to do with me or my private affairs?"

Vernet nodded in my direction. Goron had entrusted the customs documents to me. I took them from my pocket and handed them to Van Gogh. He leafed through them with growing incredulity.

"This isn't my signature! This isn't even part of my duties. Where did you get these?"

"Did Boussod et Valadon send these paintings to your New York agent?"

"We don't send Impressionists to America. There's no market for them."

"Your rival Durand-Ruel has opened a gallery in New York," I rejoined.

"And he's losing his shirt on it. Who's responsible for this?"

"You are Paul Gauguin's sole agent?" asked Vernet.

"No one vies with me for the honor," Van Gogh answered drily.

"Would you have a sample of his handwriting?" I asked.

Madame Van Gogh moved to a small escritoire by the window and handed me a letter that was lying there. It was from Gauguin, demanding an advance on his sales. I examined it side by side with the customs documents.

"If you'll indulge me, monsieur, your own signature—for comparison," I said.

Theo's brow knotted in suspicion.

"Dr. Lermolieff is a specialist in all matters of authentication, including signatures," Vernet hastened to say.

Madame Van Gogh appealed to her husband with her eyes. She furnished him with pen and paper. Grudgingly, he scribbled his signature and handed it to me. The letters were a bit shaky, but that hardly mattered. I gestured for Vernet's magnifying glass. He produced it. I studied the signatures from all three documents in juxtaposition. Certain discrepancies stood out immediately. I took the papers over to Vernet.

"You see? He barely even tries to mask it. Look you how the *v*'s slant to the left—and the open loop on the *g*. The unconscious mind will rise to the surface, every time."

Vernet nodded. I think he was eager as I to exonerate Van Gogh.

"Are you saying Gauguin forged my signature?" Van Gogh was incensed.

"Your client has involved you in some unsavory activities," Vernet replied.

Van Gogh shuddered to his feet. "Where's my stick, Jo?"

"Theo, no!" She threw her arms around him.

Vernet and I were both on our feet. "What are you thinking, monsieur?" Vernet scolded.

"I'm going to thrash Paul Gauguin to within an inch of his life." Vincent van Gogh may not have been a fighter. His younger brother was obviously cut from a different cloth.

But the flesh is weak. Theo swayed and stumbled, nearly fainting. I took his arm and guided him to the sofa. His flesh was on fire. He dropped his head into his hands. His wife hurried from the room.

We sat waiting for Van Gogh to come to himself. His flesh had the brittle look of an empty husk from which the spirit had fled: for a moment, for an eternity. What star would light his way home? His wife returned with a cold compress and a glass of water. The touch of her fingers seemed to spark him to life. He sipped the water while she put the compress to his forehead and laid his head against her bosom.

When Vernet finally spoke, he was gentle as a nursemaid. "Can you tell us where we might find Monsieur Gauguin?" he asked.

"He sent that letter yesterday," Madame Van Gogh volunteered.

Vernet took up the letter again, studying the text this time. "He proposes a voyage to Madagascar?"

She nodded wearily. "He's wanted to return to the tropics for some while. West Indies, East Indies, it's different every time. He told us he'd found a backer, but that must have fallen through."

"So he appeals unashamedly to his dealer for funds. Utterly devoid of scruple. You are too ill to confront him, Monsieur Van Gogh. Please allow me to convey your sentiments." He tapped the sword box again. "And return his toys."

I checked the address on the letter. "The Rue Boulard?"

"Emile Schuffenecker's address," said Madame Van Gogh.

Vernet nearly slapped himself. "Of course! Even Paul Gauguin could not have invented such a name. You know this fellow Schuffenecker, madame?"

"Gauguin's bosom friend. Another stockbroker caught up in the Panama Canal scandal, I think. Followed in his footsteps and became a painter. He asked my husband to take on some of his work, but—" She was too delicate to say it.

"The man has no vision," Theo croaked. He was not shy when it came to critical judgment.

His verdict seemed to satisfy the detective, aligning with whatever theories he had already constructed. At his nod, I took up the sword box and we made our farewells, assuring Van Gogh we would keep him apprised of the outcome of our interview with Gauguin.

As we reached the door, a final thought occurred to Vernet. He turned back to Van Gogh.

"Did your brother have a lady friend, monsieur?"

Van Gogh seemed taken aback. "I—I'm not sure. I think perhaps—"

"Someone named Olympia?"

I would have thought Goron had dissuaded Vernet from that line of inquiry. Van Gogh seemed fully aware of the connotation of the name. "Olympia? No, certainly not."

Soon we had packed ourselves into another hansom. Vernet directed the driver to take us to the nearest telegraph office, and he ducked inside hurriedly. By then I knew better than to question him on his errand. He would either volunteer the information or fob me off.

Nothing was forthcoming.

I studied Vernet's face as we crossed the Seine en route to Montparnasse, where the Rue Boulard lay. He sat forward, wholly engaged with the scenery as we passed, but not in the way of a tourist. He seemed to be cataloging every sight and sound of Paris, every boulevard and back alley glimpsed in passing. Even his olfactory senses came into play, as he drew the morning air into his nostrils.

"You do go about like a bloodhound," I remarked.

Vernet took it in good humor. "I'm not an armchair detective, if that's what you mean. Deduction without observation is mere conjecture."

I nodded. "Dr. Morelli preaches the same catechism."

"Morelli is a man after my own heart, a man of system and method. Europe has but a few such men. You are fortunate to know him so intimately."

Those who find romance in the steep shoulders of Montmartre will find none in Montparnasse. The hills that gave the area its name had long since been leveled by Baron Haussmann in his campaign to eliminate the narrow bottleneck streets so beloved of insurrectionists. The avenues are wide and characterless, incised by empty, treeless lots. The area would never be a haunt of the avant-garde.

Schuffenecker's house was a pinched two-story construction, with shelf-like balconies and a mansard roof pitched as steep as the Matterhorn. There was a pot of wilted petunias by the door. I shifted the saber box to my left arm and rang the bell while Vernet labored up the porch steps behind me.

The door was opened by a frowzy servant girl in a dirty apron. The sight of us sparked panic in her eyes. She asked us to wait for her mistress before even asking our business. Then she fled up the stairs as if we were behind her with cudgels. We heard voices calling back and forth upstairs.

Her mistress came gliding down the stairs, a little out of breath, a little hastily thrown together. She was a woman of slender figure, with dark hair cropped short around features sharp as a cut diamond. At first, she appeared nervous, but once she sized us up, she put on a bold face.

"My husband is away on business, messieurs. Perhaps you'll return next week?"

"You are Madame Schuffenecker? We're not here to see your husband, madame," said Vernet.

"The girl said you were bill collectors."

"The girl did not ask. You're entertaining a houseguest, I believe?"

Disconcerted, she took a second reading of our faces, trying to decide whether we were mere factors who could be dismissed, or principals who must be suffered. She rang the bell and the girl came running, almost tumbling down the stairs. "Tell Monsieur Gauguin he has visitors," she instructed.

The girl nodded and scampered back up.

"If you'll step into the garden, messieurs?"

We followed Madame Schuffenecker through the back of the house to what she called the garden: a sparse strip of faded grass, nearly sunless, where a table and a pair of cane-back chairs were wedged in a corner between walls clawed by ivy. I set the saber box upon the table.

"Please make yourselves at home," she said icily, and streamed away.

He came in his shirttails, his hair matted from the pillow. As soon as he laid eyes upon us, a smile blossomed upon his lips. "Monsieur, you keep turning up! Who is there to protect the populace of London from the criminal element?" We had discovered his true identity; it seemed he knew Vernet's.

"Monsieur—Gauguin, is it not?" returned Vernet. "Theo van

Gogh sends his regards."

"And my sabers!" He flipped back the catches, plunged his hands into the box, and drew them both forth. "Good God, I've missed them." He whipped the air with both blades, brazening out his discomfiture.

"There's a stain along the edge of one of the blades," Vernet pointed out.

"Is there?" Gauguin examined them, pretending surprise. "Ah! The Ginouxs have been slicing up stew beef, no doubt. Do you indulge, Monsieur Vernet?"

He tossed a saber to Vernet, who caught it neatly by the hilt and reflexively swept it round to short guard, the point quivering at Gauguin's breastbone.

Gauguin stepped back. "I can see you're no stranger to the noble art. Care to try a few passes?"

"Without masks?"

"I think we've left the masks behind, don't you?" Gauguin winked roguishly.

I appealed to Vernet with my eyes not to rise to the bait, but after a moment's thought, he put on a grim smile. He rose slowly to his feet, masking the lamed ankle. The two men took up their stances and touched swords. Vernet winced: an angry message as he put weight on his back foot. I wished fervently to put a halt to this dangerous exercise, but I could see the detective would give me little thanks for interfering. Pride goeth before a fall.

"What brings you to my door, monsieur?" Gauguin asked. "You and the silent partner, I mean." He tossed a look in my direction, meaning to provoke me.

I repeated innocently, "*Your* door, monsieur?" and watched the blood rise in his cheeks.

The sword-work began with the trading of perfunctory thrusts and parries, the two swordsmen getting the length of each other.

"I'd like your opinion on a matter relating to a friend of mine," said Vernet. "Not as a painter, but as a broker."

"I'm not as current in the market as I should be," returned the Frenchman. "Things change so quickly on the Bourse."

The pace of slash-and-parry was beginning to accelerate. Vernet had the stronger wrist, but, due to his injury, less mobility. He was virtually rooted to the spot, confined to defense. He parried every cut, but for his part offered no real assault. Gauguin was more experienced with the saber, but his were the moves of the practice floor, predictable and easily defended. He was given to elaborate *moulinettes* that were entirely ineffectual against a skilled opponent. I had been an indifferent swordsman at university, handier with a knife, my eye always more to be depended upon than my wrist. But I had witnessed a couple of mortal duels at Marburg. Desperation lends economy to a fencer's movements. This fellow had never had to fight for his life.

Vernet went on formulating his question, as though they were two old friends chatting in a café: "My friend has found it necessary to liquidate his enterprises. The market he supplies is collapsing. His creditors are dunning him."

"Creditors are obnoxious. But they must be paid." Gauguin lunged. Vernet swept him aside like a matador turning a bull. The Frenchman's lack of skill was fortunate, since his intentions seemed anything but sporting. Vernet continued:

"The contracts my friend has entered into are not entirely legitimate. He may not be held responsible for the debt."

Another thrust. Vernet caught it on his guard. Their blades locked together. Gauguin was beginning to grasp Vernet's insinuation, and not liking it at all. "There are debts—and debts of honor," he snarled. He threw his weight into the impasse, but Vernet was unyielding. Gauguin snarled and stomped on Vernet's foot. Vernet flew back against the wall and would have gone down had he not grabbed hold of the ivy for support. I leapt to my feet, but Vernet waved me back. His face was suffused with pain, but he assumed a mask of composure. "A man of honor, eh? Is that why you were discharged from Bertin's brokerage?"

"I've had little cause to regret it." Gaugin tore off his shirt, wiped his glistening face with it, and threw it to the ground. He took up his stance, determined as a bull. His breathing was ragged. The veins beat blue along his arm.

"What are a few creature comforts to a man of vision?" Vernet said, as if thinking out loud.

Gauguin made a grimace. "What the bourgeois call comfort, I call weakness."

Vernet hobbled forth, unable to fully mask his injury. The combatants engaged again, more cautious now, their blades gliding across each other with the tinny sound of summer rain. Gauguin took advantage of Vernet's weakness, shifting, shifting, shifting, forcing him to turn, turn, turn. Another lunge! Parried by a wrist of iron.

"Weakness?" mused Vernet. "Perhaps. But a warm coat, new boots—welcome on a winter day."

"In Panama the natives go sometimes without a stitch of clothing." Gauguin made a great roundhouse stroke that would have cut Vernet off at the knees, but Vernet beat him back with a furious flurry that put the Frenchman on his back foot.

"How picturesque!" said Vernet. "Have you considered returning?"

Gauguin grunted. "Been thinking of Madagascar."

"Madagascar! Nature, red in tooth and claw. Are you sure you're equal to it?"

Goaded, Gauguin redoubled his onslaught, substituting brute force for éclat. His cuts were wild and easily parried, but his recklessness forced the detective back, step by painful step. Vernet's back was against the wall again. Gauguin slashed at his scalp. Vernet was able to duck just under it, and Gauguin's blade stuck fast in the ivy. He yanked it out with a curse.

"At least you know how to clear brush," Vernet observed.

It was one joke too many. Gauguin made a wild lunge, leaving his feet. Vernet twisted; his ankle gave way. Gauguin bounced against the ivy and turned, slashing blindly even as Vernet collapsed. Blood flew from his sword. Vernet was on the ground, hand clapped to his neck below the ear, where blood was drawn. Another moment and Gauguin might gore him like an ox.

"Enough!" I cried, throwing my body between them.

It might *not* have been enough for the Frenchman, who seemed to have forgot himself entirely. There was a blood mist before his eyes, and I feared for my own life. But then Madame Schuffenecker came flying from the house, cried, "Paul, no!" Two small children, a boy and a girl, came running out behind her. Gauguin froze at the sight of them.

Vernet, on the ground, tossed his saber away. Gauguin skipped back as if bitten. His bare torso was drenched with sweat.

"A touch, monsieur!" Vernet favored me with a death's-head grin. "What say you, Dr. Lermolieff? Can you not tell the painter by the brushstroke?"

I helped him to his feet. His meaning was plain. Another inch and his ear would have been sliced in two, exactly the same as Vincent's. I took the handkerchief from my pocket and wrapped it around his throat where he was bleeding. It was only a scratch, thank God.

"Madame Schuffenecker! Thank you for your hospitality!" Vernet managed a gallant bow. "Please tell your husband how disappointed we were not to make his acquaintance."

She gave no sign of having heard him. She went to Gauguin, caressing his cheek as if it were he who had been wounded. Their eyes locked together. The children stood hugging each other like babes in the wood.

We were barely out the front door when I erupted in anger. "I knew you were a madman, but I hadn't taken you for a fool!"

He answered me with a look of puzzlement.

"You almost got yourself killed, and what profit? Did he confess his crimes? Did we learn anything at all? If this is your idea of gathering evidence, perhaps it's time we parted."

I had been gesturing forcefully with his cane, which he had forgotten. He took it from me tranquilly.

"My friend, I've misjudged you! You're like my Watson, cool marble on the surface, a fire raging beneath. Please accept my sincerest apology. I forget that you're unfamiliar with my methods. Let me assure you, I was never in any danger from Gauguin."

"Perhaps it was all a pantomime on your part," I answered gruffly, though I suspected he was merely engaging in a bit of bravado. "But you admit we accomplished nothing?"

Vernet brayed a laugh. He had regained his sangfroid, if indeed it had ever deserted him. "On the contrary. We could hardly have hoped for a fuller confession from Gauguin. But it was not a confession I sought. Not that cab, Doctor," he said, waving away the vehicle I had just hailed. "Let us take the next one. Which Monsieur Goron is driving."

If the old man with the white beard at the reins of the hansom Vernet whistled for was Goron, then he was a master of disguise. I followed Vernet inside the cab, but I still felt misused.

"Where to now, then?" I asked.

"Just round the corner."

We turned into a side street as he spoke. Goron reined the horse to a halt.

I peered out. Only another empty street. "Why have we stopped?"

"From his place on the box, Goron can see Schuffenecker's door. In a very few minutes, it will open. Gauguin will come out and get into another cab—driven, if all goes smoothly, by one of Goron's lieutenants. We shall follow at our leisure, and see where he goes."

With Vernet's strategy thus laid bare, I felt a fool. He had been goading the man into showing his hand! I was ashamed of my earlier harangue. But I had been frightened for my friend—when had I started thinking of him as my friend?—whom I had thought in deadly peril.

The next few minutes played out exactly as he predicted. Gauguin hurried out and got into the cab that the Sûreté had so thoughtfully provided. We followed them, crossing the river once again, into the tenth arrondissement, and the Rue du Faubourg-Saint-Denis, a street discreetly dotted with shops catering to the rich: jewelers and furriers, gowns, gloves, and hats for madame. Gauguin's cab stopped at No. 78, an anonymous door next to a brasserie. He got out, dismissing the cab, and went inside. Vernet's brow was knit in puzzlement, but his eyes stayed on the door. The other cab went around the corner, doubled back, and reined up behind us. Goron jumped down and went over to confer with his operative.

"Has something gone awry?" I asked.

Vernet held up a finger for pause. Goron came back and stuck his head in the cab.

"He cannot be here," said the inspector, his blue eyes full of puzzlement.

"Certainly not."

"Perhaps there is a cutout. As a precaution."

Vernet nodded. "There are no other exits?"

"Only through the brasserie," said Goron, who seemed to have the plan of every building in Paris at his fingertips.

"Then we'll wait for two men to come out. Tell your agent to be ready to follow the second man. We shall be responsible for Monsieur Gauguin."

By this point I was entirely mystified, of course, but Vernet begged patience. We settled in and waited, watching the morning traffic tick past, cabs on their way to the train station, carts rolling in from the country, carrying wide-eyed peasants drinking in their first quaffs of Paris, flaneurs strolling aimlessly from one moment wasted to the next, footpads eying the chance to separate them from their purses. Vernet never spoke, but stared at the offending door with the bunched energy of a tiger ready to pounce. It was a quarter of an hour before anything happened, and then we had a surprise. One man came out the door. That man was Dr. Paul Gachet.

# Chapter Thirteen

Goron's agent peered over at us from across the road, straining against uncertainty, trying to divine his chief's instructions. "Yes! Yes!" hissed Vernet. Goron waved urgently. By the time the fellow had his horse sorted out, Gachet had already turned the corner into the Rue des Petites-Écuries. The driver caught up with him halfway down the street, but the doctor paid him no mind. He seemed in a mood to walk. He waved the cab away. The driver dropped back discreetly into traffic.

"Your quarry has vanished, Vernet!" the inspector called from his perch. "What's happened to him?"

"Barring the supernatural, I think we can posit that he is either still inside the building or has found another means of egress," Vernet returned.

"This is why you are so admired for your deductive powers, my friend!" And then a most amazing thing occurred: the chief of the Sûreté and the great detective laughed like schoolfellows.

Gauguin, however, was no longer inside. The nameplate on the street door informed us that Gachet had a surgery on the top floor.

We charged up five sets of stairs and down a long hall till we came to Gachet's door (gasping, for my part), which was locked. It took no time at all for Goron to pick the lock ("Let me do it, monsieur. When I do it, it is legal, or nearly so.") We entered a vacant reception room with a few uncomfortable-looking chairs and a wall full of paintings by Gachet's Impressionist friends, and went through into the surgery, which was also empty.

Perhaps I should say *uninhabited*, rather than empty. Goron had moved to examine Gachet's desk, Vernet to the windows. But my attention was arrested by the monstrosity standing before me. Instead of a normal examining table, it was a chair, or bed, a kind of chaise longue supported by a steel frame, with leather straps up and down its length. What looked like electrical cables ran from rails on either side of the couch to an ominous black metal box, and from thence to two copper coils, each near as tall as a man. On the wall beside it was a panel displaying banks of dials and numbered gauges. "What on earth is this thing?" I asked.

The others looked my way. "Ah! Your Dr. Gachet is a visionary!" cried Goron. "Or a quack, depending on who you listen to. That, my good sir, is an Oudin coil."

"I've seen something like it at Bart's in London," Vernet agreed. "The patient reclines on the condensing bed, holding on to the electrodes. The current flows from Leyden jars to the induction coil, and thence the resonator coil—"

"The current? Electrical current, you mean?" I asked, amazed. "What the devil would you want to electrocute your patients for?"

"Cures nearly everything, its adherents claim. Especially a bad brain, eh?" said Goron, making a joke of what seemed a medieval horror.

"It certainly has a nightmarish aspect, but in the hands of a competent physician, the current acts only as a stimulant," said Vernet, trying to reassure me. He left unvoiced the question of whether Dr. Gachet qualified as a competent physician.

"I hope he doesn't have another one of these infernal machines back home in Auvers," was all I could say.

"Perhaps that's what makes the daughter so skittish," joked Vernet. I failed to see any humor in the remark.

Goron was rifling through the drawers of Gachet's desk. The scope of the Sûreté's authority must be vast indeed, I surmised—either that, or I was up to my neck in criminal conspiracy. "What's this?" he asked, holding up a notebook he had found in one of the drawers.

"An appointment book?" I guessed.

"Then what's that?" He pointed to an appointment book already sitting open on the desk. I made a gesture of surrender.

He opened the book and leafed through the pages. "Here we have something of importance," he intoned.

"What is it?" asked Vernet, who was on the floor with a magnifying glass, searching no doubt for footprints in the dust.

"I have no idea. But it's in code. No one bothers with code unless it's something important."

"Decode it," said Vernet, as if it were the simplest thing in the world.

"It's no cypher I've seen before."

Vernet let out a grunt of exasperation. "Take the book. I'll examine it in due time."

I glanced at the writing, and felt a thrill go through me. "I can read it," I said quietly.

Vernet and Goron both stared at me in surprise. "It's mirror writing," I explained. "Da Vinci invented it for his notebooks."

"How did you guess that?" asked Goron.

"He didn't guess," Vernet answered matter-of-factly. "In everyday life, Dr. Lermolieff is the world's foremost authority on Leonardo da Vinci."

I blushed. How much did Vernet know about me, about my reputation, I wondered?

"You do keep interesting company, Monsieur English," Goron said, with a sideways grin at me. "Is Dr. Gachet also an authority on Da Vinci?"

"More likely he has read Lermolieff's book," was Vernet's retort.

Goron shrugged and handed me the book. "I deliver the doctor into your custody." I put the book in my breast pocket.

"Ah, here is Gauguin's exit," Vernet exulted. We joined him at the north window. He pointed out what was unquestionably a boot print in the dust of the sill. He swung the casement window wide. The window opened onto the mansard roof. He stepped up onto the sill.

"What are you doing?" I asked.

"Following Gauguin. You see there where the copper is dented when he slipped and put his foot in the rain-gutter. The trail is as clear as breadcrumbs."

"And if your ankle plays you false again?" I asked.

"Bury me in Sussex." He stepped out onto the ledge, which was only a few inches wide, with tiles crumbling like pastry. A fit of vertigo nearly overcame me just watching him.

"Do you expect us to follow you?" asked Goron. With his stout figure and soft hands he looked no more of a rooftop mountaineer than I.

"As you please. At some point our quarry must light to earth, and so shall I! You may join me there if you like."

That option suited both the chief and me. We locked up the office and decamped to the alley behind the building, where we looked up to find Vernet slipping and sliding along the roof above us, following some invisible trail.

"He'll break his neck!" I cried.

"Steady on, monsieur," said Goron. "There are a hundred deaths that man could die every day, but he'll never perish in a fall. His mother was a cat and his father a mountain goat."

Vernet had already made his way sidling like a crab to the end of the roof and was looking about himself, trying to raise the scent, while we stood in the alley beneath him, craning our necks and shading our eyes against the sun.

Then he jumped.

My heart leapt in my throat. It was only a few feet, I would guess, a hop and a skip, but if you were standing in the street below, it seemed an unbreachable chasm. He hit the roof across the alley spread-eagled like an insect, scrabbling at the terra cotta tiles that went rattling past him down the roof, exploding into powder as they hit the pavement below. He grabbed hold of a chimney pot and was able ride out the avalanche.

This second roof was pitched less steeply than the first. He was able to crawl to the peak and straddle the apex. He had apparently deduced that Gauguin had done the same before him. His eyes swept the view from Port St. Denis to the Gare du Nord.

"Stay where you are!" he called down to us. "I'll come back to you."

And so we stood there in the alley, this French policeman and I, as Vernet danced and hopped and scuttled and squirmed his way across the rooftops in pursuit of his prey. Goron lit a cigarette and offered me one; I demurred. He tore off pieces from his false beard, and pulled out stuffing from under his waistcoat, losing thirty years and thirty pounds in five minutes. We might have been two strangers waiting for a train, unable to strike up a conversation, avoiding each other's eyes. This was the chief of the Sûreté, I told myself, a man with eyes in every street and salon in France. Surely Vernet had confided in him, or he had divined himself, many of the mysteries of the case that plagued my mind. If I asked him, perhaps he could unravel the whole tangled skein. Or perhaps he knew even less than I, and it would be betraying Vernet's confidence to mention a single detail to him. It might behoove us that some unofficial matters did not become official. The endless uncertainty preyed upon my mind.

"You and Vernet must be old comrades in arms," I ventured at length.

"He once called me a miserable bungler. In a book."

I made a gesture of commiseration.

"Someday I shall write my own book." He laughed.

That was the death of that conversation. I had no wish to be immortalized in Goron's book. Perhaps I should write my own book, in self-defense, I mused.

As the dreary minutes ticked by, I became restless and fretful, certain some ghastly accident had befallen Vernet. What if Gauguin had guessed he was being followed, and had lured him into some devilish ambush? Four stories above the street, the slightest push might be fatal. I pictured him lying broken and bloody in some dark alley.

When I voiced my concerns, however, Goron replied, "The Englishman has asked us to wait. I do not take his instructions lightly. I have no doubt he is perfectly safe."

In the end, it was more than half an hour before we spied Vernet once more. When we did, he had a look of chagrin slapped across his face, and was firmly in the grip of a uniformed policeman approaching us down the alley.

"Your pardon, monsieur, this man claims you are Inspector Goron of the Sûreté?" the policeman asked, trying to find the right mix of respect and suspicion with which to address his superior. Goron, I would learn, was so accustomed to going about in disguise that few in his own force were familiar with his real features.

"That's correct. What has occurred?"

"May I see your card, monsieur?"

A police chief is not accustomed to being questioned by an inferior. Nevertheless, Goron reached into his pocket and dug out his police card.

The policeman scrutinized it as if it were the Rosetta stone. Finally, he said, "Thank you, Monsieur Chief. This fellow claims you will vouch for him."

Goron pinned Vernet with a gimlet eye. "What has he done?"

"He was attempting to assault a young woman in the privacy of her boudoir."

Vernet had stood quietly by up until this point, but the charge drew a quick rebuff from him. "I was knocking on the skylight, hoping to be let in! There was no other way down from that infernal roof. The fact should have been abundantly clear, but mademoiselle refused to listen to reason. The roofs of Paris are not like those of London."

"Nor is rooftop etiquette, apparently. Did you ask her if Monsieur Gauguin had come through that way?" asked Goron, chuckling.

"Gauguin took the rain pipe, I presume, because it had been pulled away from the wall entirely. Else I would have availed myself of it."

Goron whistled. "Gauguin is more courageous than I gave him credit for."

"Or more desperate." Vernet shook off the officer's grip. The man attempted to lay hands on him again, but Goron intervened.

"Thank you, officer. I'll be responsible for this man."

The officer dipped his head, but he wasn't quite ready to surrender such an egregious villain. "I should mention, sir, that he could show me no papers."

"No papers, Vernet?" Goron put on a pained expression.

"You know as well as I that there are few things more liberating than leaving one's identity behind."

"Perhaps, but there are ingenious craftsmen all over Paris who will gladly provide you a new one for a modest fee. We encourage visitors to spend money here."

Their offhand remarks must have scandalized the officer. He cracked a smart salute and marched away double-time, washing his hands of the whole affair.

"You've lost the trail, then?" Goron asked, still needling Vernet.

"I have no doubt I could pick it up again if only I had the use of Toby. My resources in Paris are inadequate to the situation. But I've no doubt we can make Gauguin reappear when we need him. Our business now is with Dr. Gachet."

"Then we must return to my office in the Quai des Orfevres. That's where we'll find my agent, or at least a message from him."

We repaired thence to the Palais de Justice. As soon as Goron lit from the box, tossing the reins to a groom, he was issuing orders to subordinates who flocked to him from every nook and cranny. By the time we reached the sanctuary of his office, we knew that his agent had not yet checked in. Once more seated at the center of the mighty hive that was the Sûreté, Goron was no longer a detective, but the head of a vast bureaucracy whose wheels could not turn unless it was fed by a hundred forms a day, every one signed or stamped by the chief.

"Gentlemen, you are free to remain," he said, looking up briefly from a stack of papers. "Or you may find a more comfortable setting in which to wait. The instant our agent returns, I shall send for you."

We elected to remove ourselves to a sidewalk café on the Parvis Notre-Dame that Goron recommended, just across from the cathedral. Sitting in the shade of the chestnut trees, drinking café au lait, listening to the doves' contralto, and nibbling on a brioche, I could almost pretend that I had come to Paris for nothing more than the restoration of my good humor, that the man across from me was no more than a stranger who had kindly offered to share his table with me. He sat reading his paper while I watched the world stroll past. It was more than I could stand.

"Shouldn't we be doing something?" I burst out. Peace and serenity were all well and good, but weren't we hounds on the scent? Since the day Vincent had been murdered, our invisible adversaries had been running for the antipodes. By the time we were ready to apprehend them, they might all be safely beyond our grasp.

"This is the heart of detective work," said Vernet, gazing at me placidly over the top of his newspaper.

"This? What is this? What are we doing?" I felt like pounding on the table.

"Waiting."

I took a deep breath. I had become so accustomed to running, from Paris to Auvers, Auvers to Arles, Arles to Montpellier, Montpellier to Paris—oh, yes, and I was forgetting our stopover in St. Remy—that I could hardly credit Vernet's words. "You've handed off the matter to the police. The police, in every case of yours I've read about, excel only at laziness and incompetence!"

"Literary license. Watson has never got along with Inspector Lestrade. If you are feeling anxious, you might read."

"I don't care for the Parisian papers. They're nothing but sensationalism."

"Read a book."

"I haven't got a book."

"Nonsense. There's one in your pocket."

I felt my coat pocket. The notebook of Dr. Gachet! I had forgotten it entirely. I asked our waiter for pencil and paper, and was deep into deciphering it when the messenger arrived from Goron, asking him to join us in his office. We hurried back to the Palais de Justice to find the chief of the Sûreté waiting for us alone.

"Has he not returned?" asked Vernet with some surprise.

"I've just received a wire. Have a look."

Vernet read it, then handed it to me. It was from Goron's agent.

2.13 PM  FOLLOWED SUBJECT TO 59 RUE ST LAZARE
         STOP
2.47 PM  SUBJECT LEFT ST LAZARE TOOK CAB GARE
         DU NORD STOP
3.05 PM  BOARDED TRAIN WITH SUBJECT STOP
3.58 PM  SUBJECT LEFT TRAIN AUVERS-SUR-OISE
         STOP
4.10 PM  SUBJECT ARRIVED DOMICILE STOP
4.19 PM  DISPUTE BETWEEN SUBJECT AND YOUNG
         WOMAN IN GARDEN STOP
4.44 PM  FOUND BOY TO SEND AS MESSENGER STOP
AWAIT INSTRUCTIONS FLORIAN END

"A most thorough accounting," I commented. "Does it mean anything?"

Goron rang the bell for a clerk. "Find out who lives at 59 Rue St. Lazare." The clerk nodded. "Oh, and send a wire to the police at Auvers to collect Sergeant Florian from this Dr. Gachet's. Tell him well done."

The clerk went out, then returned in a few minutes with a name on a slip of paper. Goron read it, then shook his head, chagrined. He smiled up at Vernet. "Monsieur, I congratulate you on your perspicacity. You were indeed correct." He passed the paper over to us. Vernet did not even bother to look at it, but I most certainly did, my curiosity burning.

The name on the paper was that of Eugene Dupuis.

I stared dumfounded at Vernet. "You knew?"

He allowed himself the ghost of a smile. "There were certain indications. Why do you think I let him slip laudanum in my absinthe? I had to force his hand."

"But you could have been killed!"

"I put my faith in you."

An awful thrill went through me. All this time we had been in the dark, standing at the edge of an abyss, and now the lights were blazing. We were ready to take the leap.

"So you'll arrest him?" I asked. "Can I be there?"

Goron laughed out loud, then tried to cover it with a judicious cough. Vernet could barely contain his delight.

"We have arrived at the truth, Ivan Ivanovich, or the greater part of it. But the truth is of little importance to men like Monsieur Goron here. He must have proof. He must have evidence. Reflect on what evidence we have collected."

It was but a moment's reflection. "It's all a house of cards," I whispered.

"But a house of cards is not nothing," said Goron.

"Now we know where the mortar must be applied," Vernet agreed.

"Then how to proceed?" I asked.

"I, for one, would adore to see the contents of that notebook deciphered," said Goron.

Dueling in the morning, rooftop hunting in the afternoon, a return to scholarship in the evening. Vernet went out, saying he had business to attend to that would not require my presence. I didn't know whether he truly had work to do, or whether his restless nature simply would not allow him to stand still, especially there on the edge of the denouement of our investigation. But I welcomed the chance for solitary work and contemplation.

Even with Gachet's mirror-script reversed, it was difficult to make out the details of his transactions. There were a jumble of abbreviations and several columns of figures. Were the abbreviations the names of the paintings, or the painters, or the forgers, or the smugglers, or the receivers? Were the figures payments to the forgers, or prices paid for the forgeries? Or perhaps the notebook had nothing to do with forgeries at all. It could have been a record of Gachet's own art collection, or even a list of patients who were undergoing Oudin coil therapy, meant to be confidential. There seemed to be no system to the notes at all, or perhaps different systems had been applied as the idea struck. I was dealing, after all, with the less-than-methodical Dr. Gachet.

Of course, I wasn't starting at square one. There were some names I knew already, from General Normand's intelligence, or that I had gleaned from our investigation, and those I could match to their initials. Surely AW must be Antoine Watteau, as JHF must be Jean-Honore Fragonard. But if all the entries in that column were painters whose works had been stolen, then there were painters we hadn't accounted for. Did the notation "CL" mean that I should return to the Louvre to examine the works of Claude Lorrain? Or did the list include works not yet plundered, but planned for? Who were the forgers? "PG" was listed nowhere—perhaps he simply had not the talent for the work?—but there was an "LD" and an "LA"— Dumoulin and Anquetin? But then who was "BD"? Was the five thousand, for instance, a payment to "ES"—Emile Schuffenecker, or to "ES"—Earl Shinn, the fellow Normand had mentioned who authenticated the Master paintings for the Americans? Was the denomination francs or dollars? I worked long into the night, trying to make some sense of it all.

It seemed I had only just shut my eyes when I was wakened by a pounding on the door. I opened it, bleary-eyed, to Vernet.

"Goron needs us."

I glanced at the clock. It was not yet six. "Have we time for breakfast?"

"You have time to put on your trousers. Carry your boots." He, of course, had already made an impeccable toilet and was fully dressed. I cursed him under my breath.

There was a carriage waiting for us in the street, the horses fairly dancing to be off. I was still knotting my cravat as we flew through the streets to the Quai des Orfevres. We were shot into Goron's presence as soon as we arrived.

The chief of the Sûreté was sitting at his desk in his shirtsleeves, chafing under the ministrations of his barber giving him a shave. He looked as if he hadn't closed his eyes all night.

"Your pieces are all on the move. Schuffenecker has disappeared from Pont-Aven in Normandy. Mademoiselle Derousse left Auvers last night. There are one or two others we have under our eye who seem to be arranging their departures."

A clerk entered with a tray of coffee. I fell to gratefully. Vernet followed suit with less enthusiasm, no doubt missing his morning tea.

"What about Dupuis?" Vernet asked.

"Still abed. But his mistress did not stay the night."

"So the satellites move, but the sun remains."

"Unless we can get hold of the horses that drive his chariot, the sun remains inviolate." Goron pushed the barber away, wiping the lather from his chin and gulping his own coffee greedily, burning his lips. "Ow, ow ow! . . . and your cousin has left Montpellier for Paris."

I had thought it nigh impossible to surprise Vernet, but he was thunderstruck by this news. "Impossible! Lecomte never travels."

"Nevertheless."

Vernet paced the floor, pondering the implications. "We must take the kettle off the fire before it starts to sing. Where is Dr. Gachet?"

"I thought we were finished with Gachet!" Goron groused.

The reproach in Vernet's eyes was a spur to Goron. "Get me Despres," the chief told his clerk. "Now!"

The clerk hurried out.

Vernet looked at me. "You brought the notebook?"

"I've got it here, but I'm still working out the details."

The clerk returned with another agent, a gawky young man with spectacles so thick he might have been blind.

"Despres, I need you to place a telephone call."

Despres nodded, went to a cabinet on the wall, and unlocked it. Inside was a telephone.

"We need the police station in Auvers-sur-Oise," Goron told him.

"The sergeant's name is Rigaumon," volunteered Vernet. "A rather prickly customer."

Despres nodded and cranked the phone to life. He began shouting into it.

"The Auvers police are on the telephone?" I asked.

"The post office. But they're just next door," Goron answered.

Our family had been on the telephone in London, but there was spotty service yet in Tuscany. My wife mourned as though she had lost a family member, but I secretly rejoiced. A more insidious imposition on a man's privacy could hardly be imagined. It was a useful tool for the police, certainly, but then so was a truncheon. Goron's discomfort with the instrument was apparently so extreme that he employed this fellow Despres simply to handle his calls. I envied him.

Despres navigated his way through the exchanges and made his connection. He began yelling down the wire for Sergeant Rigaumon.

"Ask them about the movements of one Dr. Paul Gachet. Find out if he's stirred from his house," Goron instructed.

Rigaumon must have answered. Despres started repeating Goron's questions rapid-fire.

"Yes, sergeant . . . yes . . . yes?" He put a hand to the speaking horn. "Should they stop him?" he asked his chief.

Goron shook his head vigorously.

"No, no, thanks," Despres said into the phone. "We'll manage him at this end."

Despres rang off. "He's gotten on the train for Paris." He began locking up the phone cabinet again.

"Doctor, we must return Gachet's notebook immediately," said Vernet.

I nodded, patting my coat pocket where our treasure lay.

"We could provide a diversion when he gets off the train," Goron offered.

"No, that might rouse his suspicion. If you'll lend us the driver we had coming here, he has a healthy disregard for safety. We'll get there ahead of Gachet, if your man doesn't break our necks."

And before we knew it, we were once more whirling through the streets of Paris.

"I haven't finished deciphering the notebook," I said, trying to focus on the pages as the cab tossed us about.

"You have the ten minutes it will take us to arrive. Gachet was panicked by Gauguin's visit yesterday, but he's had time to calm down. He's remembered that he left the record of his crimes in that notebook. He races back to retrieve it. If he doesn't find it, all his suspicions will turn to certainty. Then will our rabbits truly run."

I snapped the lead off three pencil points and was reduced to writing on the lining of my jacket with a piece of chalk before we arrived, but I got most of what I needed. We went tearing up the stairs at 78 Rue du Faubourg Saint-Denis. I stood panting like a hound while Vernet picked the lock on Gachet's door. He couldn't match Goron's easy facility with lockpicks (nor his immunity from prosecution, thought I), but eventually we were inside the office once again, running through the waiting room to the surgery. I handed the notebook over to Vernet with a pang of regret, only to find out that the desk drawer had somehow gotten locked. Vernet went to work on it.

"How much time have we?" he asked.

I consulted my watch. "That depends on how quickly you think he can get here from the Gare du Nord. Let us hope he elects to walk again."

"Desperation gives a man wings. Go into the hall and stand sentry."

It was good counsel, for I was only out in the hall a minute or so when I heard footsteps on the stair. I pulled the office door shut behind me.

"Doctor Gachet!' I boomed out as he came into view. "How fortunate! I was afraid I had missed you. Could you spare me a minute, my friend?"

He stopped at the top of the stair, wary. "Have I made your acquaintance, monsieur?" He ran his hands through his coppery scalp.

"The name is . . . Lermolieff! We met in Auvers." Let me keep a cool head here, I told myself. Mustn't forget my own name.

The memory flickered feebly in his mind. "You're an associate of Theo van Gogh."

"I was at his brother's funeral. Your eulogy was moving." As I hoped Vernet was, right now.

He had placed me. "You and that detective!"

"Monsieur Vernet? Oh, no, monsieur, not a detective exactly, he's a—a journalist, a reporter. Always asking questions, you know how they are."

"A busybody."

"Perhaps you're right," I said, trying to appease him.

"I'm very busy this morning, monsieur. Is this an official visit?"

"I seek your advice. Not for myself. A friend." It was weak, but my mind was in a whirl.

"The busybody? Send him for a rest cure. The Swiss Alps. Pardon me, please."

I had been feinting left and right, trying to block the door, but now I was obliged to stand aside. He set the key in the lock. At first he had trouble turning it—he was trying to unlock a door already unlocked—but eventually he got the door open.

I laid a hand on his arm. "I've grown close to Theo van Gogh these last few days. His condition grieves me."

"Theo is a man of delicate constitution. The stress he underwent with his brother's death has no doubt laid him low." Gachet opened the door. I slipped into the outer room ahead of him, looking about wildly for a sign of the detective. I whirled round and interposed myself between the doctor and his surgery door.

"It's far worse than that!" I cried. "I fear he may be following his brother into madness."

Gachet could hardly be less concerned. "If he wants to consult with me, I should be glad to examine him," he said, pushing past me into the surgery.

"Oh, but I'm afraid he won't be willing! Van Gogh's faith in the doctors was shaken by his brother's death." The surgery was empty. There was no one at the desk, no one near the couch, no one anywhere at all.

Then I saw it. The north window stood slightly ajar. Vernet, madman that he was, must have decided to repeat his roof-walking trick of the day before. But had Gachet seen it, too? It was imperative I keep him distracted long enough for Vernet to get away. He might be a master of disguise, but he was too large to impersonate a pigeon.

There were some rather awful etchings on the wall behind the doctor's desk, which I hadn't noticed the day before. I squinted up at the signature. "Who is this Van Ryssel? Another Dutchman?"

"You like those?"

"They're remarkable," I said, skirting a lie.

"My own work. Amateur stuff." But even as he said it, he beamed with pride.

"Amateur! So modest. Your use of line smacks of Ingres." If he were as vain as every painter I had ever met, I knew I could play upon those strings forever.

Gachet sighed like a girl. "Sometimes I wonder what I might do if I devoted myself solely to painting."

"But a nerve specialist and a painter both? *Extraordinaire!*"

"I find art a relief from the mundane cares of medicine. The great Leonardo da Vinci was also a renowned anatomist, you know."

Would he dare to lecture me on Da Vinci? I turned around, looking for another diversion. "And that? That must be a Monet!" It was a picture of a haystack, hanging above the couch. I was taking a reasonable chance.

"It's a copy, actually. I'm sure you could tell."

He was sure? How could I possibly tell? How does one tell a copy of a haystack from the original when every stalk is painted a different color? How does one even begin? I stared at it, witless.

"My student, Mademoiselle Derousse, made that. She's remarkably talented, for a young woman."

Blast, he'd noticed the open window! He was moving toward it.

What now? Thinking furiously, I turned to the Oudin coil, running a hand over the shining copper tubing.

"You use this apparatus to treat your patients?"

He turned from the window without looking out. "Electrotherapy can be effective in treating cases of melancholia. Also, it is beneficial for those who suffer from syphilis. I'm something of a pioneer in this field."

I breathed a sigh of relief. The man's vanity was a lever that could move the world.

"Perhaps we could convince Monsieur Van Gogh he has syphilis. He keeps going on about an assignation with some woman named Olympia."

I hadn't meant to mention the name; it had simply slipped out. But there was no question of its effect on Gachet. He stared at me, the blood draining from his face, his lips working, but not a whisper emerged.

"How does this thing work?" I asked, patting the condensing couch.

I had gone too far. A look kindled in his eyes that may have been professional enthusiasm but struck me more as sadist's delight.

"Here, let me show you. Give me your coat. Sit there. No, no, sit, you'll find this fascinating." I did my best to beg off, but now he had the bit between his teeth, he was going to run with it. "Lie back and grasp the electrodes—there and there."

I found myself on my back, staring up at the ceiling, remembering prayers from my childhood—*dein Reich komme; dein Wille geschehe, wie im Himmel so auf Erden.* To say I didn't trust the man was wildly understating the case. I was putting my life in the hands of a charlatan who might also be a murderer. I wanted to run howling from the room, but I knew I must give Vernet time to make good his escape.

"Ready, then?" He clapped his hands. I nearly jumped to the ceiling. "Oh! The lotion! Mustn't forget the lotion!" He squirted some kind of lotion on my palms, then wrapped my hands round the electrodes again. I braced myself for the shock.

A switch was thrown. There was the hum of the transformer, and the crackle of voltage. Violet sparks crackled from one coil to the other in a danse macabre. I felt a jolt, or imagined one, and then a warm thrill pervading my entire being.

"Are you comfortable?"

I tried to nod. My muscles were numb, or at least too far distant to call upon. I may have shivered. A bird may have passed. Gachet's eyes were drawn to the open window. I was sunk in a torpor. I couldn't speak, couldn't lift a finger; I had no means of distracting him. He went to the window. He would shut it, that would be an end of it—no, he looked out! To his left, to his right, he must have seen Vernet inching across the tiles! He shut the window, secured the catch, and turned toward me. He shot a piercing glance at me. The game was up! My palms were sweating, even with the lotion, but I was unable let go. He glided over to the control panel, his back to me. Would I be electrocuted? The hum of the transformer soared to its highest pitch. My ears popped. The noise stopped. Silence.

"Was there anything else?"

"Eh?" I found my hands sliding off the electrodes. I drew myself up to a sitting position.

"Was there anything else? I'm very busy today, Monsieur Lermolieff. If there's nothing else?"

And now I was back from the medieval torture chamber of my imagination, in the quotidian world of a doctor's office in Paris on a summer morning, wiping the lotion from my hands with my handkerchief. I could hear pigeons cooing outside the window. I put on my coat, bade the doctor good morning, and left—fairly flying down the stair.

I stood out in front of the building, shivering in the morning sun, not knowing whether to mount a search for Vernet or find a cab and simply return to the hotel to wait, when a four-wheeler actually stopped in front of me. I was attempting to wave it on when Vernet leaned out and invited me to join him inside. I climbed in. Vernet called to the driver and we were once again in motion. Always in motion with Vernet.

"How was your stroll?" I asked.

"I'm afraid the diamond-cutter down the hall from Gachet will discover he's had a break-in. He'll be relieved to find nothing missing, however, and may take this as a warning to have bars installed in his skylight. How did you find Dr. Gachet this morning?"

"Nervous as a cat." I relayed the gist of my interview with the doctor, including his fraught reaction to the name "Olympia."

Vernet beamed. "We'll make a detective of you yet, Lermolieff. And now we must take steps to smoke out our friend Gauguin."

"How do we accomplish that?"

"We'll offer him something he can't refuse."

# Chapter Fourteen

With this object in mind, once we had breakfasted we made our way again to see Theo van Gogh. Theo's exertions of the day before had taken their toll on his fragile health. Today he was confined to an armchair, generaling Madame Van Gogh and her brother, Monsieur Bonger, in the never-ending inventory and cataloging of Vincent's canvases.

"Messieurs, forgive me if I don't get up," he said as we entered the drawing room. "Do you come with greetings from Gauguin?"

Gauguin had not returned to Schuffenecker's, nor had he been spotted in any of the familiar haunts of his crowd. "Your client has managed to make himself scarce." Vernet said nothing about the duel.

"One of his talents. I should have warned you. We're quite busy here, however—"

"Theo, this isn't one of Vincent's, is it?" asked Bonger, holding up a canvas for his inspection.

"No, of course not. It's a Cezanne. It should have been framed. I said so to—"

Vernet broke in. "Monsieur, I have a particular favor to beg. Could you send word to Gauguin that you'll advance him the necessary funds for his passage to Madagascar?"

Van Gogh turned his attention back to us, astonishment in his face. "I'm not in the habit of lying to clients, monsieur. I couldn't raise a sum like that if I wanted to."

"Lying is not a habit but an art. Monsieur Gauguin would tell you that if he were here. But he's gone to ground. It's imperative for his own safety that we find him quickly."

"When did you become concerned with Gauguin's safety?"

"Gauguin has cultivated some dangerous connections. Lately they have tired of him. They're clearing their ledgers of all red ink. Jean Poulet was murdered three nights ago outside of Le Mirliton. Gauguin may be next, if we cannot find him soon. I want him alive and well."

Van Gogh took a moment to consider this new intelligence, and weigh it in his own scales of morality. "What would you have me do?"

"A freighter leaves Calais for India tomorrow night. It stops in Madagascar. Tell him you've booked his passage, and you'll remit the rest of the money when he makes landfall. We'll be waiting for him at the train. Trust me—it's the only way to keep him safe."

"He won't be deceived. Unless"—an idea presented itself to Theo—"unless he has the money in hand. Nothing but bank notes will convince him."

"Gauguin's no fool. He'll wonder where you got the money from, Theo," said his brother-in-law.

"Tell him you sold a few of his paintings," Vernet suggested.

"Gauguin's prices are not such that a few paintings would do the job," said Bonger. This brother-in-law was a po-faced stick of a man whose only admirable quality seemed to be his solicitude for his sister and her husband.

"We shall trust to his vanity, Andries," Theo replied.

"How much, then?" asked Vernet.

"I think three thousand francs would be sufficient to bait the trap."

Vernet did not blink at the sum. "I'll wire my principal for the funds, and have a courier deliver them to you."

"That should satisfy Gauguin."

"But where will you send the money to, Theo? If Monsieur Gauguin has disappeared?" asked his wife.

Van Gogh's eyes appealed to Vernet.

"Send it to Schuffenecker's. I have no doubt his good lady wife can get a message to her friend," Vernet said acidly.

Bonger held up his canvas again. "Theo, this Cezanne, I think the paint's cracking."

"Cracking? Where?" He squinted at the painting. "Damn his eyes!" Van Gogh flew into a sudden fury. "I told him it must be framed!"

The sound of an infant crying broke from the bedroom.

"Theo! You've woken the baby!" Madame Van Gogh threw an accusing look at him and hurried into the bedroom.

"Blame Gachet! Blast him!"

The name turned the tumblers in Vernet's mind. He gestured imperiously for the painting in question. Bonger hesitated, then handed it to him. He studied it close up, even went so far as to sniff it. "Monsieur Van Gogh, you say this is not one of your brother's paintings?"

"No, of course not. It's a Cezanne. If Gachet had had it properly framed—"

"Would the sight of a cracked painting have angered your brother, too?"

"Vincent would have thrashed Gachet for this."

"A Cezanne, you say, not a . . . Guillaumin, perhaps?"

Vernet stared off into the distance. For once I could follow his exact train of thought. He was casting his mind back to that night at Ravoux's, the conversation with Gachet:

*"Vincent was fussing over a painting I'd acquired that hadn't yet been framed, he claimed the paint was cracking—"*

*"One of his paintings?"*

*"No, no, a friend of his—a Guillaumin, I think it was."*

Vernet put the painting in my hands. I knew at once what he was asking. But could I manage it? Had I seen enough of Paul Cezanne's paintings by now to make the necessary judgment? A swarm of images leapt to mind.

The painting was a mess, something dashed off in an hour, I'd guess. It seemed to depict a buxom nude, draped coquettishly across a bed, or perhaps it was a cloud. A servant girl has just stripped the bedclothes from her body, revealing her nakedness. In the foreground, a bearded, balding gentleman seated on a divan, surely her client, is seen turned away three-quarters from the viewer, drinking in her pink flesh. I searched my memory, reimagining the Cezannes I had seen before. His singular technique was hard to forget.

"I cannot be definitive, of course . . ."

"But you've arrived at a verdict," said Vernet, pleased with his trick pony.

"It's not Cezanne."

Van Gogh and Bonger exchanged skeptical looks.

"I caught the odor of beeswax. Is there any reason a painting should smell of beeswax?" asked Vernet.

Van Gogh thought for a moment. "It may have been relined."

"Relined? What does that mean?"

"It's a method of flattening the surface of a painting while strengthening its support. Sometimes the entire painting is transferred to a second canvas. The beeswax is used to attach the original primer to the new canvas."

"Is it possible you can show me?"

"If my wife will heat an iron . . . Johanna! Andries, we'll need a flour paste, enough to cover the canvas. Doctor, the canvas must be removed from the stretcher. Bring him some pliers, Andries. Monsieur Vernet, I believe there are some newspapers in the cupboard there."

We all sprang to work under Theo's direction. Bonger dragged a table into the center of the room and set the painting on it. He went to the kitchen and came back with a pair of pliers. I set to work separating canvas from stretcher.

"Where did this painting come from?" asked Vernet, spreading newspapers on the table.

"Gachet's collection. He and Cezanne are old friends. Gachet asked us for a painting of his garden that Vincent had made. He promised to send me a Guillaumin nude in return. He sent this instead. It's a rather notorious parody of Manet's *Olympia*, if you've seen that? Cezanne dashed it off on a bet. It's called—"

Vernet sucked in his breath. The name hung in the air.

"It's called *A Modern Olympia*."

Soon Bonger had the flour paste ready, and used it to stick the newspapers to the canvas. Madame Van Gogh brought in a hot iron, and Bonger began moving it across the back of the canvas according to Theo's instructions. The tension crackled like the lightning bolts from the Oudin coils. We could all smell the wax growing warm, melting. Then, unexpectedly, two canvases, one peeling away from the other.

"Now, Andries. Slowly." It was a whisper.

Bonger lifted the second canvas with infinite care. It peeled off, revealing another painting entirely. Madame Van Gogh dabbed away the liquefied wax with a cloth, revealing a painting whose copy I had uncovered in the Louvre only two weeks ago: Watteau's *The Judgement of Paris*—but this, this was the original!

"Not mad. Not mad, Doctor!"

Vernet laughed a long, hearty laugh, slapping my back. Somehow we found ourselves in a bear hug, laughing and pounding each other's backs, almost dancing with glee. We remembered our dignity and drew apart. Our staid Dutch friends were watching us, astonished. They were even more astonished when it was borne in on them that they had a Jean-Antoine Watteau original lying on a table in their modest family room.

"Monsieur Van Gogh, I'll arrange for the police to remove this painting as soon as humanly possible. Until then, I fear you and your wife may be in some danger. Please take this."

Vernet tugged a revolver from his coat pocket. The rest of us drew back at the sight of a firearm. It was as if children around a Ouija board had summoned an actual demon. He handed the gun to Van Gogh, who took it as if it scorched him.

"It's more intimidating if you point the muzzle away from yourself," Vernet cautioned.

"Why should we be in any danger?" asked Madame Van Gogh, her voice quavering.

"Vincent saw this same painting at Gachet's and berated him because it was cracked. Three days later he was dead."

We left the Van Goghs with admonishments on both sides. Vernet immediately fired off a cable to his brother in London, arranging for three thousand francs to be sent to Theo van Gogh without delay. It seemed a sizeable chunk of cheese, but I supposed it would be recovered when we trapped the rat. We then returned to the Palais de Justice to inform Goron of our discovery, and arrange for the Watteau to be returned to the Louvre. Goron congratulated us and promised to see to the painting's retrieval himself.

"That leaves us idle as tinkers until we spring the trap on Gauguin tomorrow night, Dr. Lermolieff," said Vernet. "How shall we occupy our time? Shall we take in a museum?" He was joking, or so I hoped.

"If I may make a suggestion? Sybil Sanderson is singing at the Palais Garnier tonight," said Goron.

"Good sir, you drop manna in the way of starvéd people," replied Vernet. Thus we were decided, without, of course, a yea or nay solicited from me. But I was not displeased.

# Chapter Fifteen

I t would be our fate to see only the first half of *Esclarmonde* that night. Even as the overture was being played, events were occurring that would demand our attention. This was how the police report laid out those events:

At 7:15, Chief Goron arrived at the Van Gogh apartment, accompanied by Monsieur Honore, one of the directors of the Louvre, whose name is a byword for discretion—only to find no one at home. At 7:28, Madame Van Gogh arrived home, having visited a nearby chemist to obtain medicines for her husband, who had taken a turn for the worse, and was too ill to leave his bed. On entering the apartment, however, they found it deserted. Monsieur Van Gogh had disappeared without leaving any note of explanation, leaving his infant son unattended. Madame Van Gogh became distraught, claiming that her husband's illness could put him in mortal danger. When Honore requested the painting he had come for, she stated that it had already been taken away by another policeman. She couldn't tell us the policeman's name, or describe him.

That was the report handed to us by the policeman who tracked us

down in the Salon de la Lune between acts. Goron had sent a swarm
of them to find us, but they had been barred from entering the audi-
torium during the performance, and had been too intimidated by the
grandeur of the attendants to assert their authority. Vernet had a few
choice words for both the officers and the attendants, but they were all
in English, so no one could claim to be offended. English is an extraor-
dinarily expressive language for such purposes.

When we arrived at the Van Gogh flat, we were greeted by a scene
of quiet despair. Andries Bonger had arrived to comfort his sister. He
stood by looking helpless as she walked the floor with the child in her
arms. Honore from the Louvre was sitting in the armchair, staring in
shock at Vincent's paintings, arrayed like heraldic shields along the
walls. Goron looked as if he had been trying to pull every hair from
his head. He tried to embrace Vernet in Gallic fashion, but the Englishman was having none of it. There were two large policemen at the
door, guarding what was already gone.

Vernet's tone in interviewing Madame Van Gogh was curt and
unsympathetic, which perhaps was the best tonic for her nerves.
Had her husband received the three thousand francs and sent it on
to Schuffenecker's? Yes, of course. Andries had taken the money and
delivered it himself into the hands of Madame Schuffenecker. Bonger
nodded vigorously. Had she read the letter before sending it? No, Theo
had written it in bed and sealed the envelope himself. Not that she
would read her husband's private correspondence, in any case. She
was not that kind of wife. Was everything the same in the house as
when she had left? No, her husband was gone! And what else? This was
important. She looked about the room. His coat and hat. His walking
stick.

And the gun!

No, there had been no sign of a struggle, Goron affirmed. Either
Van Gogh had been drugged or else he had left the house of his own
volition.

"Most certainly of his own volition," said Vernet. "The carpet slippers, arranged side by side next to the street door, tell us that."

He was too ill to even leave his bed, his wife insisted. Yet we had all heard of instances of fever that had given men false strength and the ability to accomplish superhuman feats—before it burned their insides to ashes.

What about the man who had taken the painting away, Goron asked. Was there nothing she remembered?

She had not seen him herself. Vernet's warnings had so disturbed her husband that he insisted on rising from his sickbed to meet the man alone. When the bell rang, he ordered her to take the baby into the bedroom and remain there until he called. Their visitor had only been there a minute or two. Long enough to leave her husband exhausted.

Vernet picked up a drawing from the top of the piano and studied it. "The gentleman was short, about five-foot-three, and stout, well dressed, well off. Nearsighted."

"Have you got a drawing of him there?" Goron asked, mystified.

"Sadly, no. I believe this is a drawing of the hospital garden in Arles. But it's been moved from the sideboard over there to the piano. That's correct, is it not, Madame Van Gogh?"

"All the drawings were on the sideboard."

"As our imposter enters the room, he turns to avoid the boxes of paintings here and there on the floor. The stack of drawings isn't flush with the edge of the sideboard, but he is short enough and his belly protrudes enough that he brushes against it and the top drawing is swept to the floor."

"He could have simply picked up the drawing to look at it, then set it down on the piano," suggested Goron.

"Look again at the drawing. You see that on the edge? The imprint of his boot. The left side of the right boot. A small boot, fashionably narrow. Yet the print is quite definite. A heavy man."

"But there's no dirt on the drawing from the sole of his boot," said Goron.

"No, the boots are new and kept immaculately clean. The owner takes cabs, or perhaps he owns a private carriage. As I said, a wealthy man, fashionably dressed."

"And how do you know he was nearsighted?" asked Andries Bonger.

"He's a very careful man, yet he's left us this clue. He did not notice the drawing lying on the floor."

"Then who did pick it up? My men have strict orders—"

Vernet merely nodded toward Honore, nearly forgotten in the armchair. Honore emerged from his reverie just long enough to say, "One can't have the works lying about on the floor, eh?"

Goron swore under his breath.

"You notice the thief took both canvases with him, Lermolieff?" said Vernet. "A tribute to your powers. They feared you might be able to identify the painter who forged the Cezanne."

I appreciated the compliment, though I had far less confidence in my abilities than he seemed to. The Cezanne had been a special case: his patchwork style was brutal, with slashing diagonal brushstrokes, like rain in the mountains, but it was also highly individual, his works immediately recognizable even to the untutored observer. There was none of the gauzy uncertainty that plagued his Impressionist compatriots. Whoever had forged *A Modern Olympia* had neither the skill nor daring to capture his style convincingly. The forger was a timid fellow; most of his kind are.

Vernet put his hand to the knob of the bedroom door. He turned. "Madame, I have no wish to intrude upon the sanctity of your boudoir, but I believe you said your husband wrote the letter to Gauguin from his bed?"

Madame Van Gogh nodded.

"A man as methodical as your husband would use a lap desk, I think? If you would afford me the opportunity to examine it?"

She nodded, then hurried into the bedroom, and brought forth the lap desk Vernet had anticipated, setting it before him on the table in the dining room. He ran his palm lightly across the blotter pad, nodding to himself with satisfaction.

"Excellent, madame. Lermolieff! Have you a pencil?"

By this point Vernet was well aware that I always carried about my person various pencil stubs, bits of chalk and charcoal, gum erasers, and a penknife. I dug in my pockets until I came up with something suitable.

We looked on eagerly as Vernet began shading the pencil across the surface of the blotter, the words of Theo van Gogh's last letter springing forth. Soon, enough was revealed to make his purpose clear:

> *ear Gauguin,*
> *he minions of the law are preparing to descend upon y*
> *ou must flee immediately, withou hesitation or delay. Mada*
> *rtinique, wherever the heart dictates, you must g NOW. Enc*
> *u will find the money necessary to fund you voyage. I*
> *carcely know what crimes you may be responsible fo*
> *e balance of your guilt r innocence, but I know what*
> *oes to a man of ur temperament to be locked away fr*
> *he world. I will not aband you to barred windows as*
> *id my brother.*
> *T.V G.*

"He's betrayed us," I said. It was a thoughtless remark; I was soon to regret it.

Madame Van Gogh pounced upon me immediately. "Who are you that my husband could betray you? Beggars off the street imploring his aid. My husband has only stayed true to his friends, even when he is betrayed by them."

"Indeed, madame, my admiration for your husband increases daily," Vernet countered smoothly. "I only hope that he has not put himself in peril of his life in helping an undeserving client."

Madame Van Gogh's defiance collapsed into a fit of shuddering terror. She was but a moment from fainting. Then we heard the child cry from the bedroom. Immediately her spine stiffened, and she ran to him.

"Tell me truly, monsieur, has Theo come to harm?" asked Andries Bonger.

Vernet dismissed the idea with a peremptory gesture. "If our foes wanted him dead, he'd be stretched on the bed in there with pennies on his eyes."

"But he's been kidnapped!" Bonger protested.

"I saw no evidence of abduction." Vernet looked to Goron for confirmation.

"We found no sign of violence whatsoever," agreed the chief.

"There lie your brother-in-law's carpet slippers neatly by the door, where he exchanged them for his boots. There is the shoehorn on the table. Our foes had already obtained the painting. What would they want Theo for? And if they did want him, they would hardly be foolish enough to let him bring a weapon along."

"The gun? Surely they took it to threaten him with," protested Bonger.

"I was thinking of his walking stick. A Penang lawyer, wasn't it? Not the kind of clout you'd want to leave in the hands of your victim. No, monsieur, your brother-in-law has risen from his sickbed of his own accord, fired by the determination to accomplish some all-consuming purpose—or by madness. Whatever peril he may face, he has chosen it of himself."

"At the risk of his life?"

"His brother Vincent risked his life every day in battle against the demons within; his only aim was to describe the world as he saw it." His gesture swept in the entire harum-scarum menagerie of Vincent's mind and hand. "Do you really think Theo is any less driven, any less reckless?"

"And what of his wife? Did he give no thought to her welfare?"

"Your sister is a woman of no less steel than her husband. Did you not know?"

Madame Van Gogh had just entered with her child in her arms. Just a girl in a little Dutch cap and blue apron. Yet she stared at us with eyes as cold as the North Sea.

# Chapter Sixteen

"This devil Gauguin has escaped you once again, my friend!" Goron chided as we stepped into the street. Andries Bonger had asked to accompany us, but Vernet had dissuaded him, telling him his sister needed his protection. Bonger seemed relieved by the suggestion. Surprisingly, Honore had stayed behind as well. Whether he was inspired by Van Gogh's paintings or appalled, I couldn't tell, but he wanted to see more. When we left, he and Madame Van Gogh were deep in conversation, comparing Dutch painters to their French contemporaries, perhaps the strangest sight in a day of strange sights.

"You'll be posting men at every train station?" Vernet asked.

"I already have." Goron opened the door of his carriage and made the sweeping bow of a footman.

"You can recall them." Vernet slid into the carriage and made himself comfortable. The police chief sighed and darted me a look. I shrugged. We clambered inside.

"We'll find Gauguin at the Gare du Nord. The train for Calais departs just before midnight." Vernet sounded as confident as if he had consulted Gauguin on his itinerary.

"That boat for Madagascar doesn't sail until tomorrow night," the inspector objected.

"He's an old ship rat. He'll slip aboard tonight and find somewhere to hide among the cargo. He'll feel safer among the bilge pumps than anywhere on dry land. Come now, we have scant time to prepare our little play."

A Paris train station is a different animal at midnight, as the sleeping lion is different from the daylight hunter. All the hunger which motivated its thousand restless starts and stops, its sudden explosions of energy, has been extinguished. The solitary traveler treads carefully, trying to muffle the cannon-blasts of his bootheels on the platform. He flits from one shadow to the next, walking in the belly of the beast.

A locomotive snorts like a sleepwalker at the platform. A few silent porters load baggage on the train. A conductor calls from far away, bidding passengers to board. A pair of lovers hold each other tight, sharing a yearning kiss, a tender farewell.

Vernet and I, crouched behind a stack of trunks, were close enough to hear their talk.

The lady's veil was lifted back over her hat, revealing her heart-shaped face. "What shall I tell Emile?" Madame Schuffenecker asked her paramour.

"Tell him to send money." Paul Gauguin's wary eyes swept the platform, seeking to penetrate every shadow.

She stepped back. The veil dropped over her face. "Is my husband in danger? Tell me the truth, Paul."

"Madame, the time for that question is long past. Your husband helped himself with both hands, then disappeared at the first whisper of trouble. Depend on no one but yourself."

"And you? You're running back to your wife?"

Vernet stepped out from his hiding place and doffed the porter's cap that had shadowed his face. He smiled ingratiatingly. "No need for recriminations, madame. Monsieur Gauguin will be with us yet a while."

Gauguin jerked away from the lady's embrace. He fixed a look of sheer exasperation upon Vernet.

"Have you no life of your own that you must constantly involve yourself in my private affairs?" He spoke as if the entire echoing train station were his private cabinet.

Vernet replied calmly, "Pardon the intrusion, monsieur. I'd like to consult with you about the theft of some paintings. And the murder of a man well known to you in spite of your denials—Vincent van Gogh."

"Yes, Vincent was a friend. That's none of your affair. If you think I killed him, you're not nearly so clever as they say."

"Was it as a friend that you traveled to Arles to spy on him? To confound him and make men think he was mad?"

"I went to Arles in good faith. I found myself nursemaid to a madman, for which I received only the most niggardly recompense. Had the filthy beggar attended to his own affairs, he might be alive and well today."

"You mean, had he not seen the portrait of Bruyas. Which you made certain he did see."

"An unfortunate joke. People should learn not to mix themselves up in my affairs."

He threw an arm around Madame Schuffenecker's waist, hugging her tight against his body, and whipped a knife against her bare throat. It was so swift and casual a move that we were taken entirely unawares. "This woman, for instance," he said.

"Paul!" the woman screamed.

I lunged forward, but Vernet threw an arm out to bar my way.

Gauguin's cheek was against the lady's. His voice was as calm as a bishop at prayer: "Steady on, old girl. The blade's honed to perdition. You won't feel a thing."

"You won't harm her, you know," said Vernet, matching his tone to Gauguin's. "You're not the savage you pretend to be, monsieur."

"Don't be so sure," Gauguin chuckled. "Human sacrifice might be just the thing to begin a trip to the tropics."

"Tickets!" cried the conductor. "Please have tickets ready, messieurs and mesdames!"

Gauguin eased back toward the train, dragging the woman, unresisting, with him. They ascended the first step of the carriage. It seemed we were beaten.

The conductor loomed up behind Gauguin. He tapped him on the shoulder.

"Monsieur and madame, your tickets, please!"

It was only a moment of confusion. Gauguin tried to twist around with the woman in his arms. The conductor brought a cudgel down upon his skull. He dropped like a stone. The knife flew from his hand, clattering on the platform. Madame Schuffenecker tore herself away. She took a step toward Vernet, then fainted dead away, collapsing into his arms.

I had not recognized Goron as the conductor, even though I knew he was near at hand. He dropped down on Gauguin where he lay prone, planting a knee in his back. Vernet tried to revive the woman. I collected the knife.

It was a pretty thing, I saw, as I turned it in my hands, a bright stiletto with an ivory handle carved in the shape of a tiger. I knew a little something of knives, and this one was expertly weighted. Gauguin's own handiwork, I guessed. He had threatened his lover's life with an objet d'art. Apropos, I suppose.

He was coming round now. He made a feeble struggle, but he had no hope of dislodging Goron.

"Monsieur Gauguin, may I introduce Chief Goron of the Sûreté," Vernet said pleasantly. "He will be your guide through the nine circles of French justice."

Goron cocked a pistol against Gauguin's ear. "I've heard so much about you, monsieur." Gauguin ceased his struggle and lay perfectly still.

Madame Schuffenecker's eyes fluttered open. She discovered herself in Vernet's arms.

"Is the woman alright?" Goron asked.

"Better than she deserves," said Vernet.

"Take your hands off me!" the woman demanded, all offended bourgeois propriety, as if she were a matron accosted by a beggar in the park. Vernet released her right willingly. She tottered away a few steps, swaying, still faint from her brush with death.

There the crisis should have ended. Another moment and Goron would have blown his whistle, bringing an army of police to our aid.

Where he came from, to this day I cannot guess. One moment the pool of lamplight around the column was unbroken. The next, Theo van Gogh was standing there, leaning on a stick, the muzzle of Vernet's gun in his hand gaping wide as a blunderbuss. His pulse must have been beating like a hummingbird's wings. "Let him go," he rasped. You could almost hear the bullets rattle in their chambers. Shock took us all.

"Monsieur Van Gogh, you're ill," said Vernet, recovering. "Let me help you." He took a step forward.

"Stay where you are, please. I can pull a trigger. Just as you showed me."

His stick clattered to the ground. Clasping the gun with both hands, his back against the column, he was able to hold it more or less steady, though his eyes were those of a drowning man. He jerked the muzzle toward Goron, directing him to move away. Goron released Gauguin, who rose triumphant as the phoenix, though a good deal dustier.

"I beg of you, monsieur, consider what you're doing," Vernet implored. "Would you be thought mad, like your brother?"

"Your words are nothing but cant. Paul will paint true pictures and be scorned by your like, just as Vincent was. Bailiffs will hound them to the four corners, but they will never be broken."

"I don't scorn them," said Vernet solicitously. "I fear for them, that they may be gulled and cheated, their reputations dragged through the gutter by men who would use them for their own profit, then cast them aside. Let your friend Paul tell you how he convinced your brother he was mad."

Van Gogh's eyes met Gauguin's, searching deep within them, seeing the truth laid bare. Still he stared, hoping, perhaps, to find some shared sympathy, some shred of human decency. I think even he could see there was none. "Vincent believed in you, Paul. I believe in you," he whispered. But the conviction had drained from his voice.

Gauguin tossed a disarming smile Vernet's way. He moved confidently to Van Gogh's side and laid a consoling arm on his shoulder. "I never meant to harm Vincent. Only to keep him out of our way. You know he was always something of a bull in a china shop." He eased the gun from Van Gogh's trembling hands, whispering assurances. He scanned his audience: Vernet, Goron, myself, even the bewildered Madame Schuffenecker, all frozen there before him. He hefted the gun in his hand, seemed ready to toss it away.

"But understand this!"—he jammed the gun against Van Gogh's temple—"I'll blow your brains out if you don't come with me now."

No fear flickered in Theo van Gogh's eyes, only resignation. Like a child, he let Gauguin take him by the wrist and guide him to the train. The engine was chuffing, building up steam.

I can hardly sort out what happened next, events collapsing in upon one another, all in a frozen moment. There was the gunshot, the bullet that whistled between Gauguin and Van Gogh, exploding against the side of the train, the glimpse of Jules Brunelle, the gun big in his little paw, as he stepped out between the carriages, deadly earnest in his eyes, poised to fire again. There he was, after the attack on the train to Auvers, before the attack in Montmartre. There he was, after he had destroyed the forgeries in Louis Dumoulin's fireplace, testing my abilities with the painting of the watercarrier. There he was in Van Gogh's apartment, taking the Watteau from Theo's hands. There I was, turning, slow as a sundial, the blood roaring in my ears, the knife leaping from my hand, rotating through space, blossoming in his chest, the surprise in his bright feral eyes as he dropped to the ground, the overwhelming feeling of terrible purpose pounding in my brain, as if every moment since I had arrived in Paris had led me to the Gare du Nord at midnight only to kill this horrid little man, this assassin, and consign him to hell.

Then the clock ticked again. Gauguin was hustling Van Gogh aboard as the train began pounding down the platform. Vernet swung aboard the carriage behind them. Madame Schuffenecker threw herself at Goron, her claws tearing at his face, keeping him from following. I found myself running, running, the lights of the train striking down shadow after shadow, catching up to the last carriage and hanging on for dear life by the handrail till I could pull myself up onto the steps of the observation car and lose my dinner in noisy chunks over the side. I heard another shot split the night.

I made my way into the first carriage, a sleeper. Curtains up and down the aisle had been thrust aside as heads poked out nervously. A woman screamed from the next carriage or the next, and the heads popped back in like turtles in their shells. I started down the carriage, in a fog of nausea and blind panic.

I opened the door to the saloon carriage and flung myself to the floor as another gunshot roared through the enclosed space. The woman recommenced screaming. Passengers were throwing themselves to the floor behind their seats, shouting, weeping, their everyday lives oysters cracked open by terror. Gauguin towered at the far end of the carriage, keeping Van Gogh in a choke hold with one arm, the gun's muzzle balanced on the Dutchman's shoulder. Would to God there were a Dr. Watson at hand, with his trusty service revolver.

Vernet's voice boomed out: "Monsieur! The police await you in Calais! Are you determined to be hanged?"

For answer Gauguin squeezed the trigger again. The gun misfired. He flung it from him with a snarl. It hit the floor and went off, the bullet shattering a window. Someone near me whimpered like a kitten.

Vernet rose up like a ghost unfettered, halfway down the aisle. "Give yourself up, Gauguin."

I made it to my knees. A few of the passengers had crept to their feet. Those closest to Gauguin, seeing him unarmed, edged toward him in a body. Thrusting Van Gogh behind him like a sack of meal, he snatched the stick out of the hands of the nearest of his assailants, brandishing it like a saber. The crowd scuttled backward.

Vernet cast about for some kind of weapon. A rheumatic old pensioner, huddled in his frock coat behind the seat, tapped him on the shin, offering his blackthorn. Vernet accepted it gratefully. The passengers parted like the Red Sea as he closed with Gauguin, the two men inscribing sigils upon the air with their sticks. I moved up warily behind, wishing I still had Gauguin's knife.

Vernet laid on, and a swift volley of cuts and parries followed, the drumbeat of sticks counterpoint to the stroke of pistons driving the train. If Vernet's ankle still bothered him, he showed no sign of it. This time he was not playing to provoke; lives were at stake. His new ferocity must have shocked his opponent; he forced Gauguin back, step by step, until the latter nearly stumbled over Van Gogh, who had been leaning against the connecting door all the time, like a package waiting to be claimed. Gauguin grabbed him by the shirtfront and slung him into Vernet's arms. He elbowed the door open, skipped nimbly across the gangway, and disappeared into the next carriage.

Vernet took a moment to hand Van Gogh into my arms. Sympathetic passengers crowded round to give aid. Vernet followed Gauguin. I watched him leap from our carriage to the gangway, and throw open the door into the darkness of the next car. There was a loud crack, and he went down like a brick.

What was I to do?

Van Gogh had been lowered onto a seat, and the woman who screamed was wiping his brow with a lace handkerchief soaked in eau de cologne. Someone produced a flask of brandy and put it to his lips. He was well tended to. Meanwhile, if Vernet were injured, who could help him but me? If he were dead, who but I could stop Gauguin?—though God alone knew how. I put my head out the door, felt the night wind whip at my face, and crossed the heaving chasm between cars.

Vernet had thankfully not stayed down long. The first thing I made out was his narrow back, black against the softer black surrounding him. Someone had smashed the lanterns in the carriage. I could hear glass crunching beneath my bootheels. The only light came from a curtain that had caught fire. The shadows of a few passengers drifted among the seats like revenants in a churchyard.

Blood ran down Vernet's cheek from a cut on his scalp; he seemed barely to notice. Gauguin faced him, but he kept shifting from side to side, readier to retire than advance. His guard was slack; he was tiring. I could do no more than bear witness to the struggle.

Vernet advanced in high tierce. Gauguin met him. They danced up and down the aisle in a blur of traded blows. Gauguin grunted like a cornered boar. He was obviously fagged, whereas the steel in Vernet's wrist seemed annealed by his own blood. He feinted to his left, then struck right, not at his opponent's body but down upon his exposed wrist. Gauguin howled in pain and dropped his stick. He lurched backward, reached up into the overhead rack with his left hand, and dragged a pile of luggage down on Vernet's head. He turned and ran.

I went to Vernet's aid. He emerged chagrined from beneath a steamer trunk, shaking himself like a dog. His face and head were bruised, but it was the cut in his temple that troubled me most. My attempts to minister to his wounds were met by a brusque dismissal.

"You need something to stanch the blood!" I warned, trying to press my handkerchief upon him. "Else you're liable to faint."

He took the scarf from his throat and wrapped it around his forehead, making a hasty knot at the side. He looked quite piratical as he stood, shedding his coat and handing it to me.

"How can I help?" I asked.

"Keep away."

It was sound counsel, I admit that now. But at the time I thought he only meant to protect me at his own peril, and that false sense of bravado that he stirred in me at such times would not hear of it. Once he had crossed the gangway to the next car, I was compelled to follow.

I pushed through the door to find myself in a deserted dining car, lit only by the moon hopscotching windows. The drawers of a sideboard had been rifled open, silver spilled across the floor. Vernet was limned in the center of the car, white tablecloths on either side fluttering like ghosts. He held up a hand to warn me, a finger to his lips to keep me silent. He moved through the car, turning and turning, tuning his senses to the flashing moonlight and the thunder of the engine.

A shadow lunged from the darkness. Vernet dodged, a heartbeat too late. A carving knife glinted in Gauguin's hand. A red gash jumped out on Vernet's shoulder. He dropped his stick. Gauguin turned and leapt again, aiming for Vernet's back. I cried out.

Vernet whirled, planting a boot in the Frenchman's ribs. He threw himself upon his adversary. They went crashing across tables, then hit the floor, locked in a desperate struggle for the knife.

Vernet reached up and swept a tablecloth over Gauguin's head, blinding him. He seized the knife arm with both hands, pounding Gauguin's wrist against the floor. Gauguin roared with pain, surrendering the knife. Vernet picked it up and sent it quivering into the wall at the other end of the carriage.

Gauguin untangled himself from the cloth and scraped to his feet. He eyed his opponent like a cornered fox. Both men were standing on the end of their nerves.

"Why continue this folly?" asked Vernet.

Gauguin gave him a sullen look. "I didn't kill Vincent."

"I know, I know." He waved me over. "Doctor, if you'll bring me one of those curtain sashes? We'll have to restrain you, Monsieur Gauguin, just to be certain."

Gauguin nodded, resigned. The fight was gone out of him.

But fate had one more wild trick to play.

"Monsieur Vernet? Is anyone there?"

Theo van Gogh stood with the door banging behind him. Whether he could be said to be conscious or was caught in the meshes of a walking dream I cannot say, but for a moment he sucked in all our attention. And Gauguin made his move. He tore past Vernet, moving like a bullet straight for Van Gogh. Whether he planned to get hold of him again or simply knock him down I'll never know, for Van Gogh collapsed in front of him like a pillar of salt. Gauguin hopped over his supine body and shot out the door.

Vernet was a hair's breadth behind him. I was treading on Vernet's heels. Still we were too late. There was no one on the gangway. "He's thrown himself from the train!" Vernet threw a leg over the guard-rail. I grabbed him roughly by shoulders. He flinched in pain. "You're wounded," I cried against the wind. "The fall likely killed him; it will certainly kill you. Even should you both survive, he's already miles away; you'll never find him in the dark." Indeed, it was pitch-black on the embankment rushing by below us.

"Without the painting, without his confession, we have nothing!"

There was only one answer I could make: "We'll have his confession."

A look of understanding passed between us. Vernet nodded and collapsed against me. We had surrendered the chase.

Theo van Gogh lay in fitful dreams abed. The doctor, that same aggrieved police functionary, was taking his pulse for the hundredth time. Madame Van Gogh was draped over him like the Madonna in a pietà, watching every rise and fall of his breast, oblivious of the outside world. I stood in the doorway, signaling the doctor to come into the parlor, where Goron wanted him. The doctor dismissed me with a backhand gesture. I went back into the drawing room, shrugging by way of apology.

Goron chuckled. He was helping Vernet put his shirt on. Vernet's shoulder and scalp were both swathed in bandages. "Dr. Monier spends too much time in healing, and not enough in filing reports in triplicate. A bad fit for our bureaucracy," said the chief mournfully.

"Any trace of our suspect?" Vernet asked, wincing as he navigated his arm through his sleeve.

"Harbor police searched the boat from stem to stern, with the captain cursing them every step of the way," answered Goron. "Since dawn we have men searching the railway embankment between Rouen and Calais. But I'm fairly certain he won't be found."

Vernet raised an enquiring eyebrow.

"We checked the passenger manifests for every ship departing

Calais since last night. There was an interesting entry for the *Northern Star*, which sailed at six thirty this morning for Copenhagen."

He handed Vernet a copy of the ship's passenger list. The detective scanned it as he fumbled with the buttons of his shirt. He read aloud:

"'John Watson, M.D.'" A slow smile of appreciation spread across his face. "Cheek!"

"Gauguin's wife and children live in Copenhagen. They're estranged, but I've no doubt he can worm his way back into her good graces."

"Then we have nothing." Vernet's face was stormy.

I could quell my curiosity no longer. "Did you learn anything about the Belgian, Jules Brunelle?" I asked.

"Ah, yes! Good eye, Lermolieff—and damned good knife work. Your talents are wasted at the Pitti Palace. He was Belgian, all right, but his name was de Groux, not Brunelle, and he was certainly not in the business of ladies' gloves. That little police lieutenant friend of yours in Brussels was a great help to us there, Vernet. Says he was an assassin with three certain kills and half a dozen more suspected. No convictions, of course."

Vernet cocked an eyebrow at me. "You knew?"

"There were indications," I replied, attempting modesty.

The doctor emerged from the bedroom, scratching his beard distractedly and staring at the floor. He seemed unaware of our presence.

"How's your patient?" Goron finally asked.

He looked up. "Which one?"

"This one's a horse," answered Goron. He slapped Vernet on the back. Vernet's face went white.

"Monsieur English, you have a positive talent for mayhem," said the doctor. "I see your ankle's swollen again. As for that poor fellow"—he cocked his head toward the bedroom—"it's never good for a man in the throes of brain fever to go for a midnight excursion on a train. He's safe for now, but I wouldn't give odds he'll dance at his son's wedding. He needs a nerve specialist."

"I'm sure Gachet would take him on in his chamber of horrors,"

Goron said.

"Won't Gachet be in prison?" I objected.

"No one is going to prison," said Vernet, visibly dejected at the thought.

"Without Gauguin we have no case against the doctor," Goron agreed. "We might have played them off one against the other under interrogation, but now he's safe enough."

"But if we had Gauguin's confession? In his own handwriting? Wouldn't that make your case, gentlemen?"

They both looked at me curiously. Eventually both nodded in agreement.

"Well, then." Before me on the table lay a bundle of correspondence that I had requested from Madame Van Gogh. The letters were tied up with a ribbon. "These are all the letters from Gauguin to Van Gogh." I untied the ribbon and took out one of the letters. I began reading.

"Pardon me, monsieur, do you expect to find a confession in those letters?" There was a note of mockery in Goron's voice.

"I do," I answered confidently.

The sky was smeared with vermillion dawn as we returned to our hotel. I had a long day ahead, and would be burning the midnight oil once again. It was agreed Vernet would call a final meeting of the consortium. They would require one more report from their authentication expert. The die was cast.

# Chapter Seventeen

Eugene Dupuis kept a suite of rooms in the Rue St. Lazare, with a terrace looking out on sidewalks lined with plane trees. He was sitting at breakfast in the cool of the morning, serenely stirring the cream in his coffee. He was expecting a visit from Monsieur Lecomte that morning, an occurrence rare enough to upset the equanimity of even the most sanguine, but the lark was on the wing, the snail on the thorn, and his affairs were in order. He was probably half-convinced Lecomte's wire was some sort of prank. Then his manservant came to the door, announcing that gentleman's arrival. Dupuis composed a smile upon his face.

"Monsieur Lecomte! The mountain comes to Mohammed."

Lecomte looked profoundly uncomfortable so far away from his own breakfast table, which made Dupuis smile all the more. His mask of bonhomie cracked for a moment when Vernet and I followed Lecomte out onto the terrace. "You've brought your retinue with you, I see," he said, recovering himself. He took note of Vernet's bandaged temple. "Bar-room brawl?"

"Midnight excursion," Vernet returned.

"I suppose civility is too much to ask of the Anglo-Saxon."

"I didn't come for badinage," snapped Lecomte, in undisguised ill humor. "Where's my coffee?"

"Octave, you mule!" Dupuis barked at his manservant. "Bring coffee. Bring champagne. Bring us the head of John the Baptist."

"Bring three more chairs," Vernet directed, more practically. The servant bowed woodenly and left to carry out his orders.

"Monsieur Vernet, are we to hear more tales to beguile? Has the Eiffel Tower been made away with? Does the Seine run backward?"

The servant returned with the chairs. We took our seats without a word. Dupuis seemed discomfited by the silence.

"Are you all struck dumb?"

Vernet nodded toward the empty chair the servant had left. "Merely waiting till we are all here."

The servant returned. "General Normand, sir."

"Normand?" Dupuis's eyes flashed fire at Vernet. "Well, show him in, damn you."

Octave ebbed, then flowed in again with Normand on his crest.

"General, what in the name of all that's holy brings you to my door at this hour?"

Normand snorted in disapprobation, standing on his dignity. "I'd hoped you could tell me. I came in response to your wire."

"I never sent a wire."

"I took the liberty of sending it in your name. Thank you for your punctuality, General," said Vernet.

Normand bowed stiffly.

"Have a seat, then, old fellow. Apparently, our every waking hour is hostage to this English detective's whim."

The offer was ungracious enough that the general seemed ready to decline, but after a moment's indecision he lowered himself into the chair. He made an interrogative gesture toward Vernet.

"I asked you here, General, because I can now provide a more complete answer to your questions about the stolen paintings you saw in America," Vernet began.

"I would be most interested to hear it, sir."

"To begin, we know now that at least twelve Old Masters were stolen and replaced with forgeries. Eight of them were from the Louvre, three from the Musée du Luxembourg, and one, interestingly enough, from the Musée Fabre in Montpellier. Three of them, a David, I believe, and . . ." He jerked his head toward me.

"A La Tour and a Boucher," I supplied.

"Thank you, Doctor. These three had yet to reach their final destinations, and were traced to a custom shed in New York City, from whence they were repatriated yesterday evening."

I fancied that Dupuis's brow darkened at the news.

"In Montpellier we demonstrated to you how these paintings might have been stolen and replaced with fakes. But the actual method of abstraction is a matter of academic interest only. As you reminded us, a gentleman of rank and fortune could walk out of the Louvre with a Poussin under his arm, and never be questioned."

"Are you impugning men of honor?" the general asked.

"On no account, General. But men like yourself, for whom France's artistic patrimony is a matter of honor, might consider in the future making it more difficult for men without honor to pillage it with reckless abandon."

"Your point is taken. Continue, if you please."

"You'll recall that James Stillman told you he'd won the Delacroix in a lottery. He meant that quite literally. A handful of wealthy American collectors had been approached, each individually and secretly, although they soon found each other out, since Americans thrive on self-confession. The most delicious secret is one that everyone knows. These great and good men were presented with a remarkable proposition, a chance to acquire a few truly great pieces of art from France's premiere collections, works that were simply unattainable by legal means. The Americans were instructed to bid on certain designated lots of paintings by Impressionist painters. They knew only that each lot contained at least one stolen masterwork. They had no idea which, and they had no idea why the deal was structured in such a byzantine fashion, but it was a gamble each was more than willing to take. Now I know why."

Normand looked at Vernet expectantly, but received only a smile.

"Well, why then, monsieur?"

"Well, and what would be the most obvious result of such a scheme?" Vernet returned.

It hadn't struck me till that moment. The pieces all fell into place.

"It would drive up the prices on Impressionists!" I said.

Lecomte seemed to have arrived at the same conclusion. "Which would be fortunate for anyone holding a number of Impressionist paintings," he added.

"But weren't the Impressionists being sold off cheap?" Dupuis objected. "What did the general call them? Lottery tickets?"

"Yes, that seemed a contradiction at first," I said. "Until, almost by accident, we discovered that the Impressionist paintings being sold to the Americans were forgeries. Simple enough to pass off—relatively unknown works, which the buyers did not even care about. The owner was keeping the originals for himself till he could sell them at a fat profit."

"Which dealer was it?" the general asked.

Vernet nodded. "Which dealer, yes? From the first, certain cards were forced on us. Paul Durand-Ruel, Julien Tanguy, Boussod et Valadon, Theo van Gogh, dealers large and small who championed the Impressionists, who had invested heavily in them, sometimes their entire fortunes. It's always the dealers in these stories, isn't it? The painters are pure, the collectors are virtuous, but the dealers are money-grubbers who will stop at nothing to recoup their investments. European collectors won't touch the Impressionists with a bargepole. But the American nouveau riche, desperate to prove themselves men of taste, wanted European culture; if they couldn't get Old Masters for love or money, perhaps they might be persuaded of the worth of the Young Turks. I was meant to look among the dealers for my suspects. Collectors— Parisian collectors—were our allies, after all. They opened their doors to Dr. Lermolieff, allowing him to compare the suspect Old Masters in the museums to their presumably authentic holdings. And they never questioned why the doctor needed to make such comparisons in the first place. Oh, perhaps they whispered among themselves. Perhaps their whispers even reached across the Atlantic and made their way into the salons of Philadelphia and New York. What harm in that? If it bolstered the Americans' faith that their ill-gotten goods were real coin of the realm, what harm?

"Surely then there would be whispers among the artists themselves? Forgers always talk. They want their friends to know they're in the chips, they want to be stroked and petted, complimented on their ability to fool the collectors. But no one was talking, no one among the Impressionists at least, because this play benefited them particularly.

"So all the suspicion was cast upon the dealers, and particularly one minor functionary at Boussod et Valadon: Theo van Gogh, an alien from Holland, a man who had little to recommend him beyond his zeal for Impressionists and his lack of worldliness. The ideal scapegoat.

"But Van Gogh had a brother.

"Vincent van Gogh was the wild card. Vincent was the chink in their armor. He was one of the Impressionists himself, more or less. He knew something or suspected something, it was in the air, but no one was sure how much he knew, how much he suspected, or what he might do if he knew all. There was the odor of sanctimony about the man. Oh, no one wanted to hurt him, but he had to be gotten out of the way. He had to be handled delicately. Accidents happen.

"But then Vincent was killed—"

"Pardon the interruption," said Normand, "but who the devil is Vincent van Gogh?"

"Theo van Gogh's older brother," I answered.

"A penniless painter. A madman," said Dupuis.

"A man of uncompromising integrity in a world of compromise," said Vernet. "Not unlike yourself, General."

"Ah. I understand. Carry on, then. Who killed the man?"

"That is the heart of the matter. The official story is that Vincent shot himself in a fit of madness. We knew he was mad, after all, because he shot himself. And we could be certain he had shot himself, because he was mad. A brilliant piece of circular logic. But if he were sane—what then?

"So I followed in Vincent's steps, to see what he had seen. I walked the streets of Arles, where an entire town conspired to drive him to madness. I stood where he stood in the Musée de Fabre, in front of the portrait of Bruyas by Delacroix, that one of the forgers, in a fit of perversity, had modeled after Vincent himself. That was when his suspicions were first inflamed. I saw Cezanne's *Olympia*. Vincent had seen it at Dr. Gachet's, and it reawakened his suspicions, which had slumbered for months in the asylum. Vincent loved his friends, he had no wish to see them come to harm, but he also had his integrity, his insatiable, inexecrable integrity, which was dangerous to his friends. Vincent led me to Dumoulin, to Schuffenecker, and Louis Anquetin—the men who forged the Old Masters—to Gachet and his student, Mademoiselle Derousse, who forged the Impressionists; to Paul Gauguin, who got the canvases smuggled aboard ships and out of France. Behind them in the shadows, pulling their strings, stood their master. He'd promised them all handsome recompense, which likely none of them has actually seen. He was ready to sacrifice them all, if need be, to the necessities of fortune."

"This éminence grise? Someone who'd made a fortune?" asked the general.

Vernet shook his head slowly. "Someone who'd lost one."

It began to dawn on the general. "The Panama Canal Company!"

"Entire fortunes were thrown away on that folly of madness. Thanks to Chief Goron of the Sûreté, I was able to gain access to a list of major stockholders. Even you lost money, General."

"A negligible sum. It was the damage to my good name that I regretted most."

"True. Your ambitions were never counted in coin. For some, however, it was a catastrophe. But let's pass on. There were other revealing documents."

"All these documents!" cried Dupuis. "I thought you detective fellows went about examining boot-prints in the rose beds, cigar ash on the carpet, silk threads caught upon the stair rail. This kind of detecting sounds like the work of an articled clerk."

"You're a romantic, Monsieur Dupuis—that much is obvious. Would you be happier if I told you I obtained these documents by means of some cunning subterfuge?"

"It would make for a snappier read in the scandal sheets."

"What are the documents you refer to?" asked Lecomte, trying to turn the conversation.

"Gallery sales. Art dealers are naturally reticent about their clients, but in each case we were allowed access to records going back more than a decade. The Impressionist paintings the Americans were bidding on, and hanging in their salons as a kind of inside joke—so they thought—were not in fact acquired from the dealers whose names were on the bills of sale. Those paintings had all been purchased over the course of several years by one man. Eugene Dupuis."

Dupuis set his cup down, and dabbed his lips with a napkin. "More coffee, messieurs?" he said, as innocently as if Vernet were referring to another Eugene Dupuis entirely.

"But this is absurd!" the general said, rallying to Dupuis's defense. "The mill in Montpellier, the laboratories. Synthetic indigo. Dupuis, tell the man!"

"All mortgaged to the hilt," said Vernet. "Our host here is a desperate man. His schemes were born of desperation, and such schemes often result not merely in fraud and theft, but in murder. So it was in this case," he concluded grimly.

Dupuis sat back lolling in his chair, as if he had just been entertained by a tall tale shared among friends. "It's a brilliant opus you've composed, Monsieur Vernet. I'd like to hear it at the opera house with a full orchestra. But it's only chin music. You have no evidence, no witnesses, only conjecture. All your running about and ferreting about have been in vain. Let me extend you my sympathies."

Vernet nodded to me. I took a paper from my breast pocket and unfolded it on the table, smoothing out the creases in deliberate fashion. Dupuis watched me with growing disquietude.

"What's that supposed to be?" he asked, making a bad show of indifference.

"We have acquired a document of a rather damning nature, Monsieur Dupuis," said I. "A confession, written and signed with Paul Gauguin's name, affirming the existence of the forgery ring operating under your direction. It further asserts that you employed the assassin Jules de Groux, who murdered the man Jean-Francois Poulet, an underling who was himself responsible for—"

Dupuis seized the confession and brought it up before his eyes. I doubt that he was actually able to read a word, so overwrought with emotion was he.

"It's all there, I assure you. Every crime you've undertaken," Vernet said solemnly.

"This isn't real! This is a forgery!"

"I have examined this document myself," I said calmly, taking the paper from his nerveless hands. "If it's a forgery, it is the work of a master forger."

"No one will believe it!"

Vernet pointed across the road, where Goron was standing in the shade, smoking his pipe tranquilly, flanked by uniformed policemen.

"Perhaps you recognize Monsieur Marie-François Goron of the Sûreté? He's eager to arrest you on the strength of this document. Indeed, he is here for that express purpose. He granted me the indulgence of a quarter of an hour for this meeting, but he champs at the bit."

"Original or forgery, the effect is the same, isn't it?" I said.

Dupuis made a stab at the letter. I swept it away.

"Copies of the letter are already in the hands of an examining magistrate," Vernet assured him.

The smiling Adonis face had become a battleground for rage and fear. "It was all Gauguin's scheme! He was the one who invested my funds in the Canal. He ruined me. I wanted to have him prosecuted. But he came to me with this mad scheme to restore my fortune. What was I to do?"

"A gentleman's fortune is in his honor," said the general.

"Pah! Tell me that again when you're down to your last sou!"

Lecomte, who had been mostly silent, sat forward with the penetrating gaze of a prosecutor. "Those Old Masters will have to be recovered from the Americans, you know."

"As if they'd ever give them up," Dupuis returned. "Do you have any idea how much they paid merely for the chance to acquire them?"

Lecomte was implacable. "They're welcome to exchange their worthless Impressionist copies for your worthless Impressionist originals, if they've a mind."

"Perhaps they'll even find worth in them now, considering what they paid," I mused.

"And of course you'll make restitution," said Lecomte.

"For twelve masterworks? You can't be serious. I'd be ruined!"

"You were ruined from the beginning, monsieur. You simply refused to admit it," Lecomte replied.

At the same moment, the manservant opened the door behind us to announce another visitor. Goron brushed him aside, impatient of ceremony.

"Monsieur Eugene Dupuis, I arrest you on charges of murder, grand theft, and fraud. Will you please accompany me to the Palais de Justice?"

Dupuis rose from his seat and bowed gravely to Goron. His face was pale as death, but his hand was steady as he drank the last of his coffee and set the cup back on the table. "Monsieur, if you'll allow me a moment to dress myself, I shall be at your disposal," he said quietly. "Bring me my morocco case, Octave."

Goron nodded his assent. Dupuis went into his cabinet. The servant soon followed after, carrying a small leather case.

Vernet rapped on the table twice. "Well, cousin, are you satisfied?"

Lecomte drew himself up portentously. "With your results, I suppose. Your methods, I fear, were hardly those of gentlemen. But what can one expect from a pair of professionals?"

Vernet ignored the slight. "You agree that the theory I proposed explains the facts completely?"

"Strictly speaking—"

"And that no other theory could serve so admirably?"

"Enough! Admit it. You manufactured evidence!"

Vernet chuckled. "I'm not a barrister. I'm not out to sway the opinions of judge and jury. You hired me to find the truth. Evidence is not truth. Truth is absolute, evidence merely an artifact. Anyone can manufacture an artifact, and paint it every color of the rainbow. Few can arrive at truth. Vincent did, after years of wandering in the wilderness. He erected fingerposts to guide me all along the way." There was a wistful note in his speech, as though Vincent had literally been at his side through the entire ordeal. Well, perhaps he had.

The servant came out of the bedroom and bowed ironically to us, if such a thing be possible. It struck me that his life was about to be thrown into turmoil, but he floated away as if it were simply another Wednesday.

"I'm curious, Vernet. When did you first suspect the truth?" Normand asked.

"The evening we arrived at Auvers-sur-Oise. You remember, Dr. Lermolieff, the wire from Lecomte, those words, 'particularly urgent.'"

"I wielded those words against you like a cudgel," I said ruefully.

"My cousin has never in his life considered anything 'urgent.' But it was urgent for Dupuis to lure me away from Auvers. Vincent was dead, and Dumoulin's forgeries had been cast upon the fire. But Gachet was still there, and the girl, both nervous as cats. They might talk. He sent that wire in your name, cousin."

Lecomte gave a little shrug. "It was an effective ruse."

"But you *didn't* come at once," the general said. "You made us wait for days."

"Forgive me, General—I had to lay a trap of my own. You see, there was yet another card being forced on me, so insistently I couldn't possibly ignore it—Dupuis himself. Were he not a part of the consortium, he would never have fallen under my suspicion. Of course, he wanted to be part of the inner circle, so he could anticipate my every move and counter it. But he did not choose himself for the role. If he was the card, whose hand was the dealer's? General Normand, who gave you the letters of introduction into American society? How is it that everyone you met was a member of the lottery?"

My eyes met Normand's across the table. Then we both turned toward the fat man with the bulldog dewlaps whose fingers were drumming nervously upon the table.

"You see, Monsieur Dupuis didn't merely make one foolish wager. He compounded it by making another. His liquid capital had vanished. His one desperate hope was that Dupuis et Cie might bring synthetic indigo to market before his competitors. He told anyone who would listen that he was on the verge of a breakthrough. Perhaps he was. But he was racing against time, and against far better funded competitors in Germany. He could only find one backer, and that backer required him to mortgage his remaining Montpellier properties in exchange for the funding. That backer expected him to default on the loan in short order, but somehow Dupuis kept paying his premiums. The backer was a man of some perspicacity. He soon discovered Dupuis's new stream of income, and he devised a means to dam the stream. Then this appeared in the papers two days ago."

He drew a sheet of newspaper from his coat pocket and dropped it in front of Lecomte. "You must have seen this, too, cousin," he said to Lecomte. "Nothing else could have brought you to Paris."

The paper was the *Neue Zürcher Zeitung*, a daily out of Zurich. The article circled was laughably small, a mere mention of a patent awarded to a Dr. Heumann, professor at the Swiss Federal Polytechnic, for the manufacture of synthetic indigo on an industrial scale.

Vernet leveled a look at Lecomte as though drawing a bow. The older man met his eyes for a moment, but could not hold them. "Bravo, cousin! Dupuis mortgaged his Montpellier factory to me to finance his interest in the Canal. When that went belly up, he had nothing left but his worthless collection of Impressionists. He wagered me their value would increase one thousand per cent in three years' time. A fool's bet—till he tried to put his thumb on the scale. So I called you in to even the playing field."

"You expressly asked me to leave John Watson in England."

"Your friend brings his publisher with him wherever he goes. This was a family matter."

"Then you led me round France like a dog on a leash."

"I let you run free as soon as you had the scent. I knew you'd bring your quarry home."

"And now you've left Al Hambra for the first time in twenty years."

"I confess, I wanted to be in at the kill."

"You had done far better to stay home. Dupuis was desperate. I can almost forgive a man what he does in desperation. But you were merely greedy."

"I only wanted my birthright. Our birthright, cousin. Chateau Vernet restored to its former glory. What could be wrong with that? Those soot stacks will come down now. Your brother would applaud me."

"Yes, you'd be right at home in the Diogenes Club, searching for an honest man to deceive."

Goron interjected himself into the conversation. "I'm sure you'll have a speech ready for the Montpellier gendarmerie by the time you return home, Monsieur Lecomte. They searched your home this morning on my recommendation. At this moment, my friend Inspector Michelet is wondering why you have a Horace Vernet in your library that rightly belongs to the Musée Fabre."

Unease crept into Lecomte's eyes. He turned to Vernet. "That's the painting you took from the museum. You and your accomplice! Chief Goron! You must believe me."

"Can you produce this accomplice?" asked Goron. There was not a hint of duplicity in his face.

Lecomte became agitated. "General, you remember him! The copyist at his easel."

"There were any number of copyists, I remember," said the general coldly. "I did not take names."

"I'd recommend you reserve your defense for the examining magistrate," said Goron.

"You see, cousin, the official police *can* be discreet when they wish," said Vernet.

Lecomte's alarm had turned to outrage. "How dare you treat me in this fashion? We're flesh and blood!"

"Your game of cat and mouse resulted in the deaths of three men."

"They were inconsequential!"

"You might get away with talking that way about a cutthroat like Poulet, though he'd be better off hanged. As for Vincent, some might argue that it was a kindness to help him cease upon the midnight hour, though hardly without pain. But Père Tireauclair, who served our family faithfully his entire life?" His voice had risen to a shout.

"Regrettable. But he was an old man near death, of use to no one. Who will mourn him?"

"I will. Though the world waltzes on in ignorance, I will. But"— Vernet struggled to keep the emotion from stopping his speech—"but no one will mourn you."

Lecomte rose ponderously to his feet. "I shall not be insulted. Do you intend to try to hold me, Inspector Goron?"

"I'll leave you to the mercy of the gendarmerie in Montpellier, monsieur. But one of my men will accompany you on the train home. For your own safety."

"Then I shall take my leave." He turned resolutely toward the door. Then a gunshot shattered the air.

By that time I should have become accustomed to the sound of gunfire, but to hear it there on that quiet summer morning at a gentleman's breakfast table, among the silver and porcelain, was particularly horrifying. We all rose, but Goron warned us off.

"This is police business, gentlemen," he said somberly. He went into

Dupuis's cabinet and shut the door behind him. A moment later, the two policemen who had been waiting in the street joined him in there.

"I was wrong. In the end he acted the part of the gentleman," said Normand brusquely.

Vernet said nothing, but looked at him with a kind of loathing. Or perhaps it was self-loathing. I could not think this was the denouement he had expected.

We all sank into our chairs once more, staring at each other wordlessly. Octave came round with a tray of glasses and a bottle of brandy. A gentleman's gentleman to the last.

After a few minutes, Goron opened the door a crack. "Dr. Lermolieff?" he said, beckoning to me. Why he would summon me rather than Vernet seemed incomprehensible, yet it became clear as soon as I entered the room.

I won't describe the appearance of the body, except to say that Dupuis lay on the bed, the pistol in his right hand. I noticed that he actually had dressed himself as for a public event. Vain to the last. The morocco case lay open next to him. I saw this only in the flash of a moment, for I was stricken with horror, and turned away as soon as I saw him.

Next to the bed was a chair of the type young gentlemen usually toss their clothes on to annoy their valets. It must have been directly before his eyes as he was sitting there loading the gun. Propped up on the chair was a painting, the last thing Dupuis looked upon in his life. It was Delacroix's *Shipwreck of Don Juan*, the same painting General Normand had seen three thousand miles away in New York. Byron's lines on the subject forced themselves upon my memory:

*And if Pedrillo's fate should shocking be,*
*Remember Ugolino condescends*
*To eat the head of his arch-enemy*
*The moment after he politely ends*
*His tale: if foes be food in hell, at sea*
*'Tis surely fair to dine upon our friends*

Dupuis had found himself lost at sea, and had dined upon his friends for as long as he might.

"What does it mean, Doctor? Why would he have a copy of this painting? And why would he . . . ?"

Goron let the question hang in the air.

Even as I took out my handkerchief and dabbed the flecks of blood from the canvas, I had my suspicions. It would take me two more days to confirm my intuition, but I warned Goron then and there. "I believe this to be the original," I told him.

# Chapter Eighteen

The death of Dupuis and discovery of the Delacroix threw Goron's well-laid plans into chaos. The forged Gauguin confession had been meant as an instrument to pry a real confession from Dupuis. With Gauguin's disappearance and Dupuis's suicide, we had scant evidence to convict the remaining members of the ring. There was serious doubt that any of them had been recompensed for their illicit efforts.

Nor could he go forward with the effort to restore the originals to France. "We were ready if necessary to drop down the chimneys of these upstanding sons of America to retrieve the originals," said Goron. "Now we have the Delacroix and the Watteau (which we found shoved in the bottom of Dupuis's armoire), we can't be sure that the paintings in their possession actually *are* the originals. We can hardly ask the American government for their cooperation. There are no laws against owning copies."

The suicide of Eugene Dupuis could not be kept entirely out of the press, but the reason was attributed to his losses in the Panama Canal, a common enough complaint. Goron is determined the public shall never know about the Old Masters lottery. Whether he can indeed keep such a conspiracy secret only time will tell. None of the conspirators who remain in France will be arrested, although their every move will be scrutinized by the Sûreté for years to come. Gachet has already claimed that his notebook contains nothing more than the names of paintings he has seen and liked, and the dates he first saw them. Poulet's death has been declared misadventure, and Van Gogh's a suicide. Dupuis's properties were searched from attic to cellar, but no more of the stolen paintings were found. Our entire enterprise had been a failure, just as Dupuis had predicted. A puppet show, with Lecomte as Mangiafuoco.

Lecomte himself was promptly arrested when he returned to Montpellier, but he was only detained in prison for two days—although one may well believe that another two days away from his beloved manor was dire torture for him. There is to be a trial, which will certainly mean a great deal of trouble for him, and a great deal of money out of pocket, but a conviction is unlikely. It is far more likely that his ambition of restoring his great-grandfather's estate will be achieved.

My own work was accomplished, my family awaiting my return. But of course, there was a blizzard of paperwork to be got through. The Paris police force is largely comprised of clerks insisting upon signatures and seals upon pain of death. No one had been arrested, no one accused, the death of Dupuis self-inflicted, yet Vernet and I were treated by the examining magistrate as something akin to suspects in a dark conspiracy to bring down the French bureaucracy. Even with Goron as our champion, we endured several days of this abuse.

It was during those days that Vernet and I sealed our friendship. We spent our free hours walking the streets of the Latin Quarter, sitting in cafés, listening to the scrapings of street musicians. We did not visit a single museum or gallery. Vernet seemed melancholy.

At first I attributed his mood to the failure of his investigation. No, he assured me, in spite of Dr. Watson's encomiums, he had

experienced as many failures in his career as triumphs. He kept referring back to Montpellier, and the little gamekeeper's lodge at the
boundary between Al Hambra and the Dupuis laboratories. "It seems
a mad place for Dupuis to conceal Poulet," he said. "And then to meet
with him there, with Lecomte and myself both on guard."

He said these things with a kind of banked rage. He was still
grieving for the loss of the estimable old servant Père Tireauclair. I
think he felt cheated of the chance to bring his murderer to justice. I
would have showered condolences on another man, but with this bot-
tled-up Englishman it seemed the worst kind of intrusion. I merely sat
with him in silence. As for me, I was missing Louise and my daughters
painfully, chafing to be away.

Suddenly he jumped up from his seat, nearly overturning the
table. "Excuse me, Doctor, I have an urgent errand." Before I could
even open my mouth, he slapped a handful of coins on the café table
and ran into the street, hailing a cab. I was utterly nonplussed.

It was the strangest farewell I had ever been subject to. But farewell it was. We had only just come from the Palais de Justice that day,
where we had been informed that the Dupuis affair was officially
closed. They would not be requiring our further assistance. I paid
the waiter and went back to the hotel to pack. Vernet was a man of
outlandish manners and wild tangents. I did not expect to see him
again.

But of course, the only thing certain with Vernet is uncertainty.
A few hours later, my luggage was loaded in the cab. I was just about
to step in myself, when he came running up the street toward me,
shouting for me to stop.

"Where are you going?" Vernet asked, once he had caught his
breath.

"Home."

"No. You're coming with me to Montpellier."

I was shaking my head. He was nodding. I tried to tell him all the
reasons I could not possibly accede to his request, how I had just purchased presents for my daughters, Irma and little Gisela, but he raised

a hand. "I need you." He seemed to think that was all the argument necessary.

"My luggage is in the cab," I said, faltering.

"Excellent. We'll take it with us." He called up to the driver. "Drive like the wind, old fellow!"

"No hurry, monsieur. Your train does not leave Gare de l'Est till seven!"

"No, our train leaves Gare de Lyon at twenty after six!"

"Pardon me, monsieur the second, but monsieur the first made clear his wish to go to Gare de l'Est. Is that not so, monsieur the first?"

What could I say? "No," I answered flatly. "Gare de Lyon."

The driver seemed wounded by my betrayal of his allegiance, but the promise of having his fare doubled by Vernet put sunshine once more upon his countenance. We rattled away at such a pace that it was all we could do to keep our teeth in our heads. We didn't attempt conversation until we were settled on the train to the south.

"Poulet was hired by the cab company on the third of August," said Vernet.

It sounded like an offhand comment at first. Then I started counting over the days on my fingers. "But he was hiding out at the gamekeeper's lodge until the fifth!"

"No. He was already gone. By the time Père Alphonse became suspicious enough to make the trek out to the hunting lodge, Poulet was in Paris."

"If Poulet wasn't there, who met the old man at the lodge that night? Or was his death an accident after all?"

"Remember Dupuis's appearance after dinner that night? The muddied boots, blackened sleeves?"

"But that was before Père Tireauclair met his death."

"Yes, but then Père Alphonse tells them he thinks someone is hiding at the lodge. Perhaps he even mentions that he is going out there to have a look around."

"Well, and what difference would that make?"

"What if Dupuis doesn't want anyone nosing about the place?

What if he's hidden not someone but *something* out there? He might have gone to visit his treasure, to add to it, or take something away, like your Delacroix. What if he thinks Père Alphonse may have glimpsed him out there?"

"The originals! You think they're hidden at the lodge?"

"That is what we shall learn, you and I."

I tried to reorder my thoughts in light of this new theory. "Then it wasn't Poulet who killed Père Tireauclair."

Vernet shook his head. "Dupuis must have followed him to the lodge."

"So when you told Dupuis we knew all . . ."

"He thought I was putting the noose round his neck."

"And that was the reason for the morocco case."

It takes one's breath away, the twists and turns of fate.

We arrived at Montpellier the following morning. Rather than take a cab, and depend upon the discretion of the driver, we hired horses for the ride out. We avoided Al Hambra altogether, coming round from the east, where the Lez river snakes its way toward the Mediterranean. Vernet was obliged to break the lock on the gate at Dupuis et Cie; the plant had been closed. There was not a soul on the grounds, not even a caretaker. This suited our purpose admirably. We rode between the shadows of the chimneys, and rounded a small lake that lay between the plant and Lecomte's property. We were making for a distant line of cypress trees.

The gamekeeper's lodge sat green and somnolent in the morning sun. Dust had settled once again upon the floorboards, erasing the palimpsest of footprints from the day we had discovered the body. I had it in my mind that Vernet had, by some mystic means, already divined the exact location of the hidden paintings. I was soon disabused of that notion. Vernet stared into one room. He stared into the second room. He stared into the hall.

"What are we looking for?" I finally ventured to ask, growing impatient.

"A cellar door."

But there was no cellar door, nor a cellar. We banged upon every plank in the floor with our sticks, hoping for the echo of some hollow place. There were no hidden panels behind the walls, no hidden space between the ceiling and the roof. The rooms were bare. The lodge would not give up its secrets; it had no secrets to confide. The paintings were hidden somewhere else, or were in the hands of the Americans, as we had once thought.

We walked out blinking into the noonday sun. I don't know which of us was the more disconsolate: Vernet, whose self-confidence had seemed unshakeable, or I, who had placed such faith in his powers.

We slid back into the saddle and sat upon our mounts, unable to turn away from the sight of the lodge. What had actually happened there that night? Could it simply have been an old man, half out of his senses, wandering the grounds and taking a terrible fall in the dark? That was the story that satisfied the police. If there were another man there, as the evidence suggested, was it Dupuis, or perhaps merely a tramp surprised in the act of seeking a night's shelter?

A pair of rooks that were perched upon the stack of firewood under the window began cawing, eager for us to be off. We turned back toward the cypress alley with our backs to the past. We neither of us spoke, each mired in his own thoughts, lulled by the slow roll of the horses beneath our seats, and the whispering breeze from the sea.

We passed by the still lake and the shuttered laboratories and arrived back at the gate. I dismounted to open it. Vernet merely sat his saddle, staring out to the horizon. I swung the gate wide, hoping the banshee shriek of the hinges would bring him back to earth.

"The axe," he whispered.

He whipped his horse around, dug his heels in its flanks, and galloped back the way we had come. I stared, a shout dying on my lips. The axe? Was he planning to chop down the lodge? I climbed into the saddle and rode after him, leaving the gate standing open. I'm no equestrian; he soon disappeared into the distance. I slowed my horse to a canter. What was the hurry? I knew where I would find him.

He had flung his coat off and rolled up his sleeves. The sweat had already broken out on his forehead. He was rooting through the wood-pile, heaving logs to either side of him, watching them as they hit the turf. I had a hazy notion that he suspected a pit beneath the woodpile. I started to help him clear the logs, but he waved me away. I stepped back as he pitched a log at my feet. "Split it," he commanded.

I looked at him questioning. There was the rusty old axe I have mentioned, leaning against the wall now. Except the axe wasn't rusty at all. The handle was green with moss, but the blade shone as if recently oiled.

If I am no equestrian, I am less of a woodsman. But he was nodding urgently. I lifted the axe and brought it down awkwardly on the log, just missing my own toe.

Half the log sheared off and flew twenty feet, shying one of the horses. I was a prodigy!

Or I was not. Each half of the split log revealed a long cylindrical hollow hacked out of the middle. An empty hollow. I was splitting a log that had been split once before; the two halves had been fitted back together. Why?

"Nothing," I said, dumfounded.

"Not nothing, Lermolieff. Now we know what we're looking for."

The log under his hand was beechwood; most of those in the pile were. But the log I had split was something much softer—cedar, I think. He scrabbled and scratched through the pile till he reached another cedar log, and tossed it my way. I took a hack at it.

Not nothing, not this time. The log split open. In the hollow, wrapped in oilcloth, a long metal canister. I unwrapped it carefully. I took out my penknife and prized the lid off the canister. I fished the tightly rolled canvas out of its container and unrolled it, just far enough to make sure.

"It's the Cabanel," I confirmed, rolling it up and easing it back into the canister. Authentication could wait till we were out of the midday sun.

Vernet was grinning. I found that I was grinning, too, a wide, foolish grin I couldn't wipe off my face. We attacked the woodpile like wild men, two hours without stop, till we were both black with grime and drenched in sweat. We had twelve canisters collected, and the woodpile was down around our ankles. I leaned back against the wall and mopped my face with my handkerchief.

Three of the canisters held paintings we hadn't even known were stolen. We would learn that copies of those three paintings—a Fouquet, a Le Nain, and a Chardin—were not actually hanging in the Louvre, not in the public galleries at least. The authenticity of all three had been questioned by the museum staff itself. They had been quietly removed from the floor while they were being analyzed. Now fourteen original masterworks have been returned to their accustomed places. Whether the public derive any more pleasure from the originals than they did the fakes is a question for the philosophers.

The American collectors know by now that their Old Masters are nothing of the kind; the whispers will have steamed their way across the Atlantic. They all knew they were taking a gamble; they were all rich enough that they could afford to lose. Having become acclimated to ersatz Impressionists, they've apparently decided to embrace the real item. Not Old Masters, perhaps, but still very French, and therefore desirable. Durand-Ruel's Impressionist gallery in New York is doing gangbuster business, as the Americans say.

One of our originals never resurfaced. It was of course the portrait of Bruyas from the Musée Fabre. If I could ask Dupuis one question, it would be: why that painting? It could hardly be numbered among Delacroix's great works, and could hardly arouse the cupidity of a collector. I have my own idea, of course. We saw Dupuis as a fraud, murderer, and thief. But perhaps he saw himself as another Bruyas: a benefactor, a patron of the arts. What man sees himself as anything but noble? I think he meant it for his personal collection. Of course, Louis Anquetin had other plans. The satyr was the kind of man to take collateral in lieu of payment. My guess is, he's still holding on to the original.

We visited the Van Gogh family one last time before the end. Theo had recovered from his illness, at least temporarily, and felt nothing but gratitude for our efforts. He couldn't possibly repay us, he said, even had he been as wealthy as Alfred Pope. But his brother had often paid his friends, and even his debtors at times, with his own paintings. He hoped that we would each take something of Vincent's to remember them by. I sympathized with the tradesmen Vincent had seen fit to favor so, but took the offer in the spirit it was meant. I chose a drawing of an Arlesienne with an enigmatic smile; it might have been Rachel. Vincent's drawings display a gift for draftsmanship that is lacking in most of his paintings. Vernet found a portrait of Mademoiselle Gachet at the piano that he liked: not wisely chosen, perhaps, but I forbore to express an opinion. If he was happy with it, who was I to interfere?

It was September, and the autumn rains punishing the roses, before my work was done and I finally left for home. Vernet had returned to his beloved London a few days before. We had parted with warm protestations of friendship and promises to work together again, which neither of us believed. I returned to my beloved wife, my beloved daughters, and my beloved work. And I found myself restless and dissatisfied. For a month in the summer of 1890, my life had been a chapter out of a *roman policier*. The cloistered world of the art connoisseur seemed thin gruel after all the excitement. I found myself rereading my diary entries from those weeks. I even made a clandestine raid upon my wife's private papers so I could read the letters I had sent her. But the poverty of my prose was no substitute for the richness of my experience. In the back of my mind I had a yen to write something resembling the stories I had seen penned in *The Strand* by Dr. John Watson. Nothing so sensationalized, of course. Not a yellow-back novel meant to goose the general public, but a serious work of scholarship, to be published and circulated privately, something to be shared with my family, and of course Dr. Morelli. Perhaps I could send a copy to the Van Goghs.

Fate has intervened. Having spent months trying to beat dross into gold, I have no clue what to do with the finished work. Winter was cruel: Theo van Gogh died in January, five months since we said our farewells. Dr. Morelli quit this world a month later; my grief is still fresh.

Before I began this enterprise, I would have called Dr. Watson's accounts mere feuilletons that could be tossed off in an easy hour. I am since humbled. I will put the manuscript away. Perhaps one day I'll take it out again and try to set it to rights. Or I might toss it in a box and ship it off to Vernet. Let him decide how to dispose of it. It is his story more than mine.

"J.P.R."

# Epilogue: John H. Watson, M.D.

There ended the manuscript of "Dr. Ivan Lermolieff," as I will continue to call him. On first reading I judged it an extremely serviceable narrative, subject to emendation. But I had no more idea what to do with it than Lermolieff himself had. I put it away in my desk, hoping that would put it out of my mind. But it nagged at me. As I went about my daily business, tending to the few patients that remain in my practice, my thoughts kept circling back to it again and again until I could think of little else. I brought the manuscript out and read it again carefully, and yet again, line by line, certain the fault must be mine alone. But in the end there could be no question: with all his explications and unveilings, Lermolieff had somehow failed to identify the murderer of Vincent van Gogh! What could possibly account for such an egregious oversight? It was utterly preposterous to think that Holmes would have concluded his investigation without unraveling the great riddle that had plagued him throughout. Had Lermolieff deemed the murder a mere sidelight to his summer adventure in Paris, not worth the mention? Far more important to catalogue the meals missed and concerts interrupted due to the importunities of justice! True, murder had been more than he'd bargained for, true, true, and as it happened, his assistance had been essential to whatever degree of success could be claimed in this case. One might even argue that he had saved the life of Sherlock Holmes. Who was Vincent to him? If Holmes had divulged the tale to me when he first returned from France, who would Vincent have been to me? A manic meddler whose fate was incidental to the matter at hand, whose death—while tragic—was inessential to the story.

And yet I gathered from Lermolieff's account that Vincent (everyone seemed to call the man by his Christian name)—though they had only met him on his deathbed, and only spoken to him in the disjointed ramblings of his mortal delirium—had almost from the first become an object not only of the writer's curiosity but his affection. I refused to believe the identity of his murderer could be thought of so little consequence. Was Lermolieff's prose style so oblique that he had managed to indicate the murderer without actually naming him, or that the murderer's identity was so self-evident, at least in Lermolieff's mind, that it was superfluous to mention? Was the killer obviously Brunelle, or obviously Gauguin, or obviously Gachet? Gauguin had insisted he did not kill Vincent, and Holmes had agreed. Gachet had wept bitter tears at Vincent's funeral. He might be melodramatic, but he was no Edmund Kean. Brunelle was the obvious choice. But if he had shot Vincent on Sunday and escaped detection, why return to Auvers on Monday? And why would Vincent protect an assassin he had never laid eyes on before by refusing to speak?

I've never claimed the analytic powers of Sherlock Holmes, but I don't think myself such a dullard that I can't see beyond the nose on my face. I turned the question over and over in my mind for days, till I could hardly think of anything else. I kept picturing Holmes as he was in our youth, stretched out before the fire at Baker Street, working his way through one of those famous three-pipe problems. I remembered how the light of epiphany would flash in his eyes, and we would be up, throwing on our wraps, rattling down the stair to the fogbound street. I was ready to risk life and limb, knowing that Holmes had the answers in hand, and would presently reveal all. Now Holmes was gone, and all was black mystery.

It was a week before I decided I must search out the true identity of this man Lermolieff and communicate with him. A visit to the catalogues of the British Museum Library revealed the most salient fact about Dr. Ivan Lermolieff: he did not exist. Lermolieff was only the nom de plume of this Italian, Dr. Giovanni Morelli, the connoisseur whom "Lermolieff" names repeatedly as his mentor, the genius behind the Morelli method. Why an Italian chose to masquerade as a Russian in his writing was a mystery. Had he also chosen to masquerade as a German masquerading as a Russian? Was Morelli in fact Lermolieff?

But Morelli had been seventy-five years old when these events occurred. I could hardly see him throwing himself in front of runaway carriages and chasing after fleeing trains at such an advanced age. And six months later he had died.

In fact, "Lermolieff" makes repeated claims that he is not Morelli himself but one of his adherents. Very well then. I would take him at his word. Armed with the names Morelli and Lermolieff, I went to see my friend Dudley Toth at his Mayfair gallery. Was the name Morelli known to him? Without a doubt it was; he had but one word for the man: Philistine. Art was to be appreciated, not analyzed to death, and anyway Morelli was no more of a scientist than Madame Blavatsky. Suffice it to say that Toth was no admirer of the Morelli method. I wondered aloud whether Morelli had any followers in the art world. Followers! Apostles! The most celebrated of them, Toth said, full of indignation, was this American, this Bernard Berenson, who handed down his pronouncements from some cloistered villa in Tuscany, where he no doubt sat at the right hand of his heavenly father, Morelli.

It sounded a promising lead. Lermolieff lived in Tuscany, or had in 1890, if the manuscript was to be credited. Perhaps Berenson was Lermolieff? But he in turn seemed too young to fill the role. Besides, my impression was that Lermolieff was a German from Saxony. Where there any Germans among Morelli's apostles?

Not exactly, Toth said. Well, perhaps. There was an Englishman, not a real Englishman, of course, one of those bloody cosmopolitans, but he'd done a great deal of work with the National Gallery, and lived in London. Wife was a Turk. Or an American. She'd translated Morelli into English. Oh, yes, she was an art historian, too. So were the daughters. One Italian, one American, both art historians. Out of all this muddle I got that the man was at the least born in Germany. And I got a name.

Then I went to the National Gallery. They were less forthcoming, but more coherent. Yes, of course, they knew the man in question. He was a British citizen, originally a German, had divided his time between London and Florence. Retired a few years ago to Lugano, Switzerland. An address? Who was asking? Dr. John Watson? *The* Dr. John Watson? Yes, of course they could give me his address. Was there anything else they could do to help *the* Dr. John Watson? (I am eternally grateful for the small privileges afforded me due to my association with Sherlock Holmes. People always think I'm working on a case with him. Many of those who remember that he's dead *still* think we are working together. And so we are.)

I wrote to Lermolieff, explaining how I had come into possession of his manuscript. I complimented him on the quality of his prose. Perhaps I resorted to a bit of flattery. Then I begged him for the solution to the crime. Demanded a name. Ended with more flattery. And once having posted the letter, I wished fervently that I had cabled him, or even gone to the extravagance of telephoning. Then I climbed the walls as I waited a full six weeks before the arrival of a reply.

In his letter, Lermolieff apologized for the delay. He had been traveling. In fact, he had spent some days in London, and had thought of calling upon me to express his condolences on the death of Holmes, but, as we were unknown to one another, he didn't like to take the liberty. (I spilled an entire pot of tea and scalded my knuckles on reading those words.) He thanked me for my kind words regarding the manuscript; memoir was not his forte, and praise from a master was encouragement indeed. Lermolieff was not averse to resorting to flattery, either, I saw.

He would be happy to see the manuscript published at last. His only request was that his true identity remain secret; "Lermolieff" was the name I should use for him.

I have acceded to his request throughout, though scholars in the art world may certainly see through the threadbare ruse, as he is well aware. But this is the fig leaf he requires. Since our first exchange we have become frequent correspondents. Though we have only met once in the flesh, I now count him as a friend.

As for revealing the identity of Vincent's murderer, taking that last step had troubled him and Vernet both. While his account was originally meant as a private record, he had been acutely aware of the possibility that it might someday become public. Accusations of murder made without proof might have subjected him to legal action. Events were remote enough now that he no longer feared such a possibility. Nor were he and Vernet (he could not help calling Holmes by that name) entirely unsympathetic toward the person who had committed the crime. Indeed, the crime itself had inflicted a terrible punishment upon the killer. So even now, almost forty years later, he hesitated to reveal the answer. But finally, he elected to put his faith in me, as Vernet had put his faith in him. Did I still have the portrait of Mademoiselle Gachet? Examine it closely, he said. There I would find the final clue I needed to unlock the mystery.

I will readily declare that I cursed Lermolieff's discretion. I suspected he was toying with me to bolster his own vanity. The portrait of Mademoiselle Gachet had been stashed away behind a cabinet in my consulting room for months. I carried it into the sitting room and set it on a chair in front of me. I sat staring at it for hours, uncomfortably aware that I was, in a sense, replaying the last moments of Eugene Dupuis's life as he sat before the *Don Juan*.

I turned the canvas around and stared at the back for nearly as long as I had stared at the front. Finally, I lost my temper and took a pry bar to the blasted thing, wrenching the painting out of its frame so I could make a thorough examination of the sides. At last my appetite overcame my obsession, and I walked down to the corner pub for curried chicken and a pint of bitter. I exchanged a few pleasant words with the landlord and tried to clear my mind. The regulars were debating Tich Freeman's latest triumphs on the cricket pitch. I may have had a second pint.

When I returned, the painting was still waiting, staring at me. I tried to ignore it, pulling a copy of Somerset Maugham down from the shelf and settling in to read. But I got no peace; I knew Mademoiselle Gachet was watching me read. I believe I dozed for an hour. When I woke, the Maugham had tumbled from my lap, and the answer was staring me in the face.

I went to the lav and bathed my face in cold water. I came back and pulled down a Bradshaw to look for the Calais trains. I packed a valise with a change of clothes and a few necessities, wrapped the painting securely in brown paper and twine, and stepped out into the night to hail a taxi for Victoria.

There was no express train to Dover; we would have to stop at every farm and village along the way. Far better I had waited till morning. But I wouldn't have slept in any case; my thoughts were a jumble. Instead I watched the fields and forests of the south of England judder past under the moon as I sat up, almost solitary, on the night train. It had been seven years since I had last come south. Then I had traveled with Holmes and Mrs. Roberts to Dover, and we had gone on all the way to Luxor. That had been our final case together. There would be no reunion this time.

Crossing the channel was the same. I stood at the taffrail, watching our wake cream in the moonlight, with the voices of Holmes and Dupuis, Van Gogh and Goron all whispering in my ear. I breakfasted at the station canteen in Calais, standing hollow-eyed, and was in Paris by noon. I had not really seen the city since before the war. I promised myself I would tour the sights on my return leg. I knew I was lying to myself. At my age men do not tour. Either need drives them, or they live from nap to nap.

I stepped off the train in Auvers-sur-Oise before one. I asked directions from the railway clerk. He had them by heart, and recited them with weary contempt. I was to learn that certain places in the town had become stations of the cross for those who admired the penniless Dutch painter who had drawn his last breath there. I bought an apple from a stall and stepped into the road. It was a cool autumn day with the leaves scudding across the path as I walked out west of the village, but in my imagination it was a roiling July day with the scent of gunpowder lingering in the air. When the Gachet house came into view, the red tile roof and chimney stack just visible beyond the drystone wall, I could hardly repress a shudder of familiarity. The gate shrieked with rust when I opened it. I walked up to the door and knocked.

I could hear someone moving around inside. Could it be old Gachet himself? I had no idea if the man were alive or dead. I had not rehearsed a speech for him. Or the son? What was his name? Surely he had moved away to make his fortune long ago. She would be alone.

No one came to the door. I knocked again. There was no sound from within, and yet I felt a presence. It was as if whoever was on the other side of the door was standing absolutely still, holding her breath, hoping I would become discouraged and go away.

But I had come too far. I rapped on the door till my knuckles ached. Eventually my efforts were rewarded with the sound of the latch being drawn.

"Yes?" One bright eye stared out from the crack in the door.

"Mademoiselle Gachet?" The railway clerk had informed me that she was still a mademoiselle, though she must be nearing sixty.

"I have nothing to say to you." She had heard my foreign accent, and divined my purpose, at least so far as she understood it. I was just another pilgrim on the Van Gogh highway, come to disturb her lonely peace. She tried to shut the door, but I wedged my foot in it to stop her.

"Mademoiselle, I come from Monsieur Vernet! You remember Monsieur Vernet?" It was the only calling card I had, and not a good one at that. I was counting on her to remember a man she had met only once, nearly forty years ago. But at least I had made no mention of Vincent van Gogh. That alone should give her pause.

She tried to grind the door shut on my foot. "I bring a gift from Monsieur Vernet!" I called desperately.

Her curiosity took hold, or perhaps it was her cupidity. She opened the door just wide enough to admit me. She backed away next to the piano. The same piano. It was her safe harbor, I judged.

She stood rubbing her hands together nervously. Her powers of hospitality had not been tested for a long time. She offered me a glass of wine. I accepted with reluctance, as the decanter was furred with dust.

"Vernet wasn't his real name, you know," she informed me as she poured the wine. "He was an Englishman like yourself, a detective. The greatest detective in the world." There was a note of pride in her voice. She handed me the wine, looking at me slyly. "Everyone here knows that. He was the great Holmes. He was most kind to me, he and his friend, Dr. Watson."

I caught myself staring at her rather rudely. It took me a moment to realize who it was she referred to as "Dr. Watson." It was a reasonable enough mistake. Where there was Holmes, there must be Watson: the world knew that. She supplied her own explanation for my puzzlement. "You thought I'd be younger. You expected a beautiful twenty-year-old girl."

"No, mademoiselle, I assure you . . ." I could make no satisfactory reply. The sylph-like beauty of Lermolieff's manuscript had indeed been turned to an aging spinster in the blink of an eye. Any attempt at gallantry would surely be recognized for what it was.

"May I know your name?" she asked.

How was I to answer? "My name is Mycroft Holmes," I stuttered. "Sherlock was my brother."

It seemed to satisfy her. "Have you come to ask me questions? Your brother said people might come to ask me questions."

"And did they?"

"Over and over. But never the right ones."

"I'm not here to ask anything of you. You love your father, mademoiselle."

"My father died twenty years ago."

"My sympathies. But he was dear to you."

"I hope I have feelings, the same as anyone else."

"You would have done anything to keep him from harm."

She nodded warily.

"And Vincent?"

"Vincent, Monsieur Van Gogh, was amiable, he was persistent, he was endearing . . . but he was *old*, everyone said so. He was . . . unsuitable. And there was another to think of."

What was it Theo van Gogh had said? That his brother was a well-loved man? And Holmes, too, had remarked that Vincent's death had more to do with love than anything else. I could imagine her as a young woman, golden hair streaming down her back, tears streaming down her face, standing at the crossroads in front of Vincent's easel, watching him work, frightened and conflicted, torn between her father and the only man she would ever love. She would see the Colt revolver, hanging perhaps on the side of his easel. She might become faint, extinguished almost by the awfulness of her own resolve. I could hear the sound of thunder, and the beat of black wings filling the sky.

"I've come to return this painting, mademoiselle. I think it rightly belongs to you."

She took the painting from my hands. She untied the twine with stiff fingers and tore away the paper. She gazed long and lingering at the painting, without saying a word. She must have been too affected to speak.

"Ah!" she said finally. "But you know, monsieur, I already have this painting."

My French is anything but flawless; I required her to repeat what she had said, several times, until she became almost angry. "Of course I'm certain, monsieur! The painting has hung in my father's study for forty years. Please, come see!"

She led me back through the house to what must have been at one time her father's study. It was clean and well dusted; for all that, there was a disused air about it. The walls swarmed with her father's Impressionist trophies, several different painters whose names are unfamiliar to me, though I fancied I could pick out the Cezannes and the Van Goghs from the crowd, just from reading the Lermolieff manuscript. There were a number of empty squares also, where paintings had been plucked from their spots on the wall and never replaced. I guessed they had gone out into the world to pay for mademoiselle's keep. Whatever kind of fraud he was, one couldn't fault Dr. Gachet's instincts as a collector.

And there it was, just above her father's chair, the twin to the painting in my hands, Mademoiselle Gachet at the little piano, her long hands—they *were* long, I could see that now, with the model standing before me—poised above the keys nervously. She was uncomfortable sitting for her portrait, I could see that, just as she was uncomfortable with me staring up at the results.

"He painted two copies, then?" I asked. I had read this was something of a habit with Van Gogh. He would give one copy to his subject, and keep the other for himself.

"Oh, no, I wouldn't hear of it. To be hung in a gallery somewhere for people to gawk at? How vulgar."

"Then where does this come from?" I held up the copy in my hands.

She gestured for the painting. I handed it to her.

"Open the drapes, please, Monsieur Holmes."

I obeyed her. Sunlight invaded the room, hungry. It swiped the side of her face. She studied the painting, unfazed.

The tiniest of smiles played upon her lips; perhaps there was even the specter of dimples. She enjoyed out-detecting the great detective, even by proxy. When she spoke, it was to herself, as if she were alone. "Blanche. I had forgotten."

"Mademoiselle," I asked softly, "who is Blanche?"

She seemed startled by my presence. She recovered herself. "Mademoiselle Derousse, I mean."

The name struck a chord. Lermolieff had mentioned the name, I knew. But I could not summon it forth. "Who is Mademoiselle Derousse, please?"

"Little Blanche. The housekeeper's daughter. Of course, her mother was dead by then, or she never would have run so wild."

"Your housekeeper's daughter painted this?" I couldn't hide my incredulity.

"Even as a little girl, from the first day she came to us, she'd steal my brother's pencils, she'd ruin sheets and sheets of paper, she copied everything she saw, Pissarro, Cezanne, all of my father's friends. They were all fond of her, they encouraged her, probably too much, a lady doesn't copy paintings, a lady can't be a painter."

It came back to me. "Your father's student! She lived nearby, I believe?"

"She lived right here. She crept into my bed at night when we were small. Father called her a student, but she was more talented than he was, more talented than my brother, even. She could copy anything so you couldn't tell the difference. Look, here, on the back of the canvas, her mark."

I had stared at the back of that canvas for hours, and never noticed the small "bd" in pencil, almost faded, in the left-hand corner. Lermolieff had seen it, of course, and nearly warned Holmes that he had chosen a forgery. But perhaps Holmes knew. Perhaps that was *why* he had chosen it. "She copied Vincent's paintings, too?"

"Every one of them. She was mad about the man. She thought he was a gypsy, or a pirate. She followed him everywhere about the town. One time she set up her easel next to his and tried to copy him as he painted. He chased her away. It would have been a scandal if there'd been any family to speak of. But she was no one."

I found my breath quickening. "Does she still live here, in the village?"

"Oh, no. She ran away soon after Vincent died. She wrote a few letters. Then she died herself."

There was a life in summary. I looked around, wondering. "Are any of these hers? Do you have any—?"

She only shook her head in answer.

"But then," I asked carefully, "what became of all those copies?"

Her eyes became sly. "Ask my brother."

But of course her brother wasn't there. Did he live there, I asked?

*He comes and goes.* Did she know where to find him? *Here and there.*
She was evasive at first, then she became mulishly silent.

There was nothing left to say. I thanked her for her hospitality,
scant as it had been. I wrapped up the painting again. I felt no compunction to leave it with her; nor did she ask me to. I found my way to
the door. I had all my answers at last.

"Would you like to see her?" the old woman asked.

One last surprise. At first, I had no idea what she meant. I wondered for just a moment if Mademoiselle Derousse were buried in the
garden among the bees. The old woman led me upstairs this time, all
the way to the attic. There were no curtains here. The easels of forty
years ago still stood sentry among the cobwebs.

She stood among the wildflowers and the wheat, a dark girl in a
white dress and summer hat, her eyes a million miles away. I remembered her dancing—no, Lermolieff had spoken of her, the girl in white,
lilting, a basket on her arm, gathering wildflowers behind Vincent's
hearse. Had Vincent discovered her role in the forgery ring and threatened to expose her? Or was she a woman scorned, taking revenge on her
lover, or her imagined lover? If only the canvas could speak.

My earlier vision returned, the young girl standing before her
lover as he painted, but this time she was a dark girl in a straw hat,
with no place in the world, but with her own talents, her own ambitions, and her lover standing between her and the sun. The explosion,
the startled flock of crows. Did she run then, fearing capture, or did
she step over the unconscious man, pick up his brush, and finish the
painting?

"Is this an original?" I asked.

The question seemed to have no meaning for Marguerite Gachet.

I walked back to the station under the blue sky of Île de France,
my heart hollow as a drum. I wanted nothing more than the grey skies
of London, my own fire, my own pipe, my own ghosts. Mademoiselle
Gachet's were too great a crowd.

I have no desire to be called as witness in the Wacker trial, or
in any other actions that may arise out of the tangled times when

Sherlock Holmes and I were young and willing to follow Père Tireau-clair into the lion's jaws.

The Lermolieff manuscript, together with my own addenda, shall remain under lock and key, at least until my death. Perhaps until the deaths of every actor in this tale, down to the infant child Johanna van Gogh held in her arms. How old would he be today? Older than we were then. How recklessly the trains seem to eat up the miles these days! The suburbs of London were already gathering in force against the horizon.

I asked Lermolieff once how he would answer if he were asked— who was Sherlock Holmes? The reply he sent me may have been nothing more than elaborate evasion, but I think it was his sincere assessment of the man.

He related to me something his brother had said to him when he was in high spirits, not long before his death. Theo and his little family had come up to Auvers for the day, and Vincent was swinging the little one in his arms, he and the child both laughing, though it probably made Johanna a bit nervous. Vincent told him that he wished he could abandon realism, to make of his art a sort of tonal music, but with color. Then the baby started crying, as babies will do, and Johanna snatched him away. He sat and sighed, as though he had come back down to earth, and waved the dream away. The truth was too dear to him, he said. He must be content to be a cobbler at his last, never a musician."

"Well, then?" I asked, puzzled.

"I believe Monsieur Vernet would have been a musician as well, but loved the truth too much."

Theo van Gogh was content to let his brother speak for himself. Lermolieff was content to let Vincent speak for Sherlock Holmes. I must be content to let my own portraits speak for themselves. Even when they are colorless and muddy, they are as true as I can make them. I can say this: Sherlock Holmes was a much-loved man.

Where would I hang the painting? There was a place on the wall in my waiting room, across from the portrait of Holmes by Sidney Paget. It might provide a nice counterbalance.

But no. The forgery could never hang where the public might see it. Too many questions.

And yet, the story will have to be told.

# Acknowledgments

After the plague year, I have to first thank my fearless editor, Dan Mayer, and the entire staff at Seventh Street, particularly Marianna Vertullo and Jennifer Do, as well as copy-editor Marianne Fox. Also thanks to Samantha Lien and everyone at Kaye Publicity for their hard work. Again a nod to goes to Laura Roach Dragon and Betsy Hannas Morris, my intrepid readers, who keep me honest and keep me thinking. And also to Nancy Bilyeau and Patricia "Pooks" Burroughs, who continue to guide my steps through the jungle of the publishing world. I'd also like to thank my fellow Seventh Street authors, a marvelously talented bunch who are also a great resource for information and constant source of encouragement.

I must also thank my entire family for having my back, nephews (Sean, Shaun, and Shawn), nieces, great nephews and nieces, and great-greats down to the newest, Atticus Jude. Without you I'd be nothing.

I looted too many volumes of information for this book to list them all here, but I must single out Carlo Ginzburg's essay "Morelli, Freud, and Sherlock Holmes: Clues and Scientific Method." When I read this, all the pieces fell in place. Also of great help were Aviva

Briefel's *The Deceivers* and Eric Hebhorn's *The Art Forger's Handbook*.

Finally, a huge thanks to Robert Brady, my Stamford, who introduced me to Sherlock Holmes all those years ago.